THE
TRAIL

Tragedy and Love during
the Cherokee Relocation

RANDY BISHOP

authorHOUSE®

AuthorHouse™
1663 Liberty Drive
Bloomington, IN 47403
www.authorhouse.com
Phone: 1 (800) 839-8640

Published by AuthorHouse 07/27/2017

ISBN: 978-1-5462-0196-0 (sc)
ISBN: 978-1-5462-0195-3 (e)

Library of Congress Control Number: 2017911760

Print information available on the last page.

Any people depicted in stock imagery provided by Thinkstock are models, and such images are being used for illustrative purposes only. Certain stock imagery © Thinkstock.

This book is printed on acid-free paper.

Because of the dynamic nature of the Internet, any web addresses or links contained in this book may have changed since publication and may no longer be valid. The views expressed in this work are solely those of the author and do not necessarily reflect the views of the publisher, and the publisher hereby disclaims any responsibility for them.

To my Fall 2012 dual-enrollment U. S. History students, for their inquisitive nature regarding the Trail of Tears and their encouragement for me to write this manuscript.

Introduction

January 10, 1806

Bitterly frigid winds cut into the huddled crowd gathered in Washington, D.C. The faces of the white members of the crowd were largely reddened and wind-burned. Those fair-skinned individuals had come from near and far to hear a pertinent message from the third President of the United States. With his high-pitched, somewhat squeaky voice, President Thomas Jefferson primarily directed his dispatch to a group of Cherokee chiefs, having earlier met with the group's representatives regarding their willingness to become more fully acclimated into American society.

President Jefferson's words, well-thought-out and kind in nature, were also delivered to the non-Cherokee observers who braved the bone-chilling temperatures of the day. Jefferson's verbiage was to prove ironic in the ensuing decades. The vast majority of the members of the crowd appeared intent upon hearing every word of the President's speech, one which was apparently memorized.

President Jefferson began his monologue with the hauntingly familiar and oft-used introductory words, "My friends." Specifically, and in a manner appearing rehearsed, Jefferson addressed the many Cherokee who were in attendance. With glances of approval and a slight nodding of his head, the President appeared to have made eye contact with every member of the various Cherokee villages represented in the cold and sleeting afternoon Washington weather.

Jefferson continued, "I cannot take leave of you without expressing the satisfaction I have received from your visit. I see with my own eyes that the endeavors we have been making to encourage and lead you in the way of improving your situation have not been unsuccessful; it has been like grain sown in good ground, producing abundantly."

Those Cherokee, current and former slaves, and the throngs of whites in attendance met Jefferson's words with a multitude of responses. Members of each group appeared to smile in agreement, while others sarcastically smirked or appeared to slowly roll their eyes. One group in particular was painfully aware of the hollow promises the United States government officials were fully capable of issuing.

When able to make and undetected sarcastic comment or disgusted look, slaves who stood in the presence of their white owners also noted their disgust at the words being directed toward the crowd. Apparently realizing the hollowness of the phrases Jefferson uttered, the attending black people, free and slave, who heard the message, fully recognized the lack of sincerity in the statements directed toward the Cherokee.

Aside from the variance in skin tones, the interspersed Cherokee were largely indistinguishable from the other races in attendance. Gone were the stereotypical aspects of attire traditionally used to adorn their bodies. In many cases the clothes of the Cherokee were neater in appearance than were those of their black and white counterparts. The Native Americans who were present also spoke in English.

The prime similarity shared among the attendees was their fruitless struggle to keep warm as the frosty winds increased in strength and duration. Drizzling rain, slowly changing to sleet, fell upon their dampened heads and hats. The weather seemed to extinguish any possibility of positive feelings for the presentation.

There was evident reason for the lack of appreciation for the President's words. This was based upon Jefferson's referral to the Native Americans as "noble savages" at an earlier date in his political career. After all, the Cherokee had also been designated as one of the Five Civilized Tribes among the once seemingly infinite number of bands of the original settlers of the North American continent. With the Choctaw, Seminole, Creek, and Chickasaw, the Cherokee had spent decades involved in and practicing sincere and determined attempts to adopt the "ways of the white man" as prescribed in an effort to preserve the Cherokee people from extermination.

Briefly muffled with the sounds of resounding cheers and applause that indicated the level of approval from the few members of the crowd who appeared to believe the President's proclamation, Thomas Jefferson eventually concluded his speech. President Jefferson stated to the clustered Cherokee, "You are raising cattle and hogs for your food, and horses to assist your labors. Go on, my children, in the same way, and be assured the further you advance in it the happier and more respectable you will be."

With the completion of his statements, President Thomas Jefferson stepped from his lectern and offered a labored wave to the members of the crowd. Having walked from the safety of a covering, Jefferson drew little response with his quick series of arm movements. Whether in agreement with his words, elated over their ability to move from the outdoors, or perhaps ecstatic over the conclusion of the Commander-in-Chief's speech, members of the audience offered widespread applause that President Jefferson perceived as being given in apparent agreement with the contents of his speech.

President Jefferson smiled and continued to wave to no one in particular, simultaneously signaling a gesture of friendship to every section of the crowd. The earlier displays of disparity with Jefferson's comments gave way to an apparent overwhelming act of cohesion and optimism regarding the positive aspects of the recently concluded speech.

Sadly, Thomas Jefferson would not live to see the proposed outcome of the relationship between the Cherokee and the government of the United States. Throughout the ensuing years, the issue of African American slavery would take the forefront of most political discussions and elections. Meanwhile, the "Indian problem," as some termed it, came to hold the position of a second-rate issue that was regularly used as an excuse to relieve the Native Americans of land that white settlers or others, such as the United States government, strongly desired as their own.

By the time the full fragmentation of Jefferson's words occurred, the United States would reach its fiftieth year of existence as a nation. The growing country also experienced the complete or partial terms of four additional Presidents. These Chief Executives led with varying degrees of success and caused mixed levels of controversy over a myriad of incidents.

One of the most controversial acts of the ensuing era came from Andrew Jackson, an individual who was said to have raised a Native American child as his own. Jackson, a Tennessean, served as the seventh Commander-in-Chief and pushed for the passage of the Indian Removal Act in 1830. That piece of legislation, according to President Jackson's mindset, was deemed necessary for the preservation and safety of the Native American people who provided unwilling obstacles to the advancement of white settlement. Without their removal Jackson feared that large numbers of the Native Americans would become victims to the inevitable encroachment.

By the time of Jackson's decree, the Cherokee's ability to produce ample foodstuffs, a point emphasized near the conclusion of Jefferson's speech, held little significance in the eyes of officials of the United States government. Various livestock which the Cherokee raised,, from chickens to cattle, would be viewed as inferior to what other farmers, notably those of a lighter-colored skin, produced.

The livestock of the Cherokee, in turn, were regularly seen or designated as best if eliminated. In turn, as preparations were made to enact the Indian Removal Act of 1830, the sustenance the Cherokee livestock could provide was simply brushed aside in favor of the acquisition of "higher quality," locally-raised sources of meat. The doors for corruption were clearly opened in such a set of racially-motivated circumstances.

The situations surrounding the ensuing events would prove the shallowness or lack of support of Thomas Jefferson's words. Neither Presidents Jefferson, Jackson, nor the national leaders who came between them could be singled out for the blame of the destruction of the Native American way of life. However, it was during the Jackson and Martin Van Buren terms of office that the past century and a half of animosity toward the race regularly referred to as Indians reached one of the most, if not the supreme, inhumane periods and acts of the history of the early inhabitants of the North American continent.

The removal of the Native Americans, or at least the manner in which it was conducted, drew protests that began almost immediately. The act would continue to cause disagreements over a century and a half later. Deceit, murder, hunger, ignorance, sympathy, empathy, compassion, and love were but a sampling of emotions that were to be exercised during the enactment of the Indian Removal Act and the resulting Trail of Tears.

Chapter 1

August 1838— Cherokee Council Grounds and Capital; Red Clay, Tennessee; located a short distance from the settlement of Cleveland, Tennessee:

A great deal had changed in the passing of more than three decades since President Jefferson's speech to the Cherokee in Washington, D. C. The content of Jefferson's discourse had centered upon the mutual respect between the citizens and government of the United States and those similar entities of the Native Americans. Aside from the continued population growth of the United States and a correlating increase in sectional tensions, the Native Americans, as a group and in individual nations, had failed to achieve the respect or prominence Jefferson had so confidently predicted on that cold 1806 morning.

As indications of the changing political environment in the United States, the developing nation had engaged in a second war against England. With a U.S. victory, the country completed its bid to reaffirm American independence from the centuries old European power. The subsequent defeat of Great Britain had eventually enabled land-hungry American settlers to move into areas where various nations or groups of Native Americans resided. In a succession of incidents, the Native Americans' struggles to maintain their lands and homes were regularly met with U. S. military intervention. The result was the ensuing expulsion of the "noble savages," as Jefferson once called them, from their property.

The word "noble," which Jefferson had once used to describe the different Native American groups, was no longer prevalently used. Most white citizens of the United States more commonly called or considered the once regarded "noble savages" as "Indians." As a result, "noble" had been dropped, or certainly continuously ignored, from the designation given to the members of the numerous Native American tribes. The term "savage" soon became more widely used in reference to Cherokee, Choctaw, and other Native American nations.

Shawnee, Creek, and other groups of the original settlers of the North American continent had suffered incomprehensible levels of subjugation and ridicule. In addition, dozens of the once-praised Cherokee now stood like corralled cattle in quickly erected grimy holding pens located in a relocation camp in southern Tennessee.

In the chaos of the bright-sunned day at the council grounds of the relatively new capital, babies wailed. Those children old enough to speak called for their mothers. In turn, the moms cried for their children and lamented for the sick and dying of their group. Men, initially endeavoring to hide their emotions, began to argue on a more regular basis. Small numbers of the males fought over issues that would have gone unmentioned in less-stressful situations.

Soldiers, struggling to sustain strong military images, stood erect at the edges of the makeshift prisons. It was uncommon to see a soldier who initially encountered the scenes before him and managed to do so without either becoming sick or overcome with a sense of heartfelt sentiment for the incarcerated Cherokee.

The utter filth to which the captive Cherokee were inhumanely subjected was almost beyond description. Going days at a time without a legitimate type of bathing presented an obvious and profound aroma. A lack of facilities for properly disposing waste added to the odor and offensiveness of the situation. Any previous knowledge or contact with the Cherokee before this demeaning scene would have torn at the heart of a current observer, as the once-proud people were relegated to living in animalistic states. In addition, the lack of human decency for the prisoners, combined with the emanating scents, resulted in U. S. military personnel gagging on a frequent basis. A handkerchief wrapped around the lower portion of a person's face and covering the nostrils provided a small sense of relief for the sentinels who were ordered to closely observe the Cherokee detainees.

It seemed difficult, if not impossible, to imagine any semblance of splendor in the midst of such a deplorable scene. However, not only a well-trained guard but also a casual observer had little difficulty discerning an individual who managed to provide relief for the degradation that abounded. Her presence provided a stark contrast to the otherwise uninviting situation.

One Cherokee lady, eighteen years old and possessing characteristics that clearly denoted and perfectly exemplified beauty, quietly occupied a small elevated space in the middle of one of the holding pens. From that position she carefully noted the undertakings at the chaotic camp, an establishment which was actually a base for the United States Indian Agency.

The Cherokee maiden, her olive skin slightly blemished from the effects of the sun-induced chapping and stinging sweat, took mental notes of as much of the bedlam as possible. She observed the scene with distant, dark brown eyes. Her long hair was pulled back from her face and was pulled into a loosely-tied ponytail, arranged in such a manner for the sake of practicality, rather than in attempt to become a stronger proponent of the onetime "civilized tribe" designation. Her hair color was silky black, the perfect complement to her tanned and prominent cheekbones that bordered smooth skin and led to a somewhat square jaw.

Slender in structure and possessing a shapely figure, the young lady was pleasing to the eyes of any observer. The appearance of the youthful Native American woman was the era's epitome of the commonly-held white mindset of a female Cherokee. As such, she regularly garnered a great deal of attention from those serving as guards for the captives.

The damsel's rather long dark legs enabled her to stand taller than any other Cherokee females standing nearby. Her height also exceeded that of an overwhelming number of the remaining members of the Cherokee women in the additional holding pens. Muscles in her legs indicated that the young lady had spent a great deal of her time in bouts of physical activity and work prior to being placed into captivity. With that significant aspect of her physique and standing atop a slight rise in the ground, she could clearly see over most the other people in the area and easily observe the wide-spread hysteria with relative ease.

While noticeably proud and well-kempt in such an atypical situation, the Cherokee girl's subjection to weeks of dry, hot weather had also taken a visible toll on her feet and hands. Her hair and clothing appeared heavily soiled. Dust also covered her feet and matted dirt lay thick underneath the nails on her toes and her fingernails. Despite these distractions, her beauty was evident to anyone who encountered her.

The young Cherokee looked toward her feet as her toes gently moved dust from the vicinity of the soles of her feet. She appeared to be meditating deeply, momentarily unaware of the movement of her feet or the tumultuous scene surrounding her.

Known as White Crow among her people, the Cherokee teenager captured the images and aspects of the ongoing events that surrounded her and attempted to maintain and rationalize them in her young mind. The English speaking people near her childhood home had more commonly known White Crow as Naomi Richardson, a name her family believed was more indicative of their attempts to assimilate more effectively into the society her tribal elders had sought for the Cherokee people.

The Cherokee's effort to become more respected members of U. S. society had taken a significant turn three years earlier when the group relocated from Georgia to Red Clay, Tennessee. White Crow called to mind the 1835 movement that Cherokee Chief John Ross had initiated in compliance with the controversial Indian Removal Act of 1830. That legislation would forever prove to be a dark chapter in the administration of the nation's seventh Chief Executive, President Andrew Jackson of Tennessee.

The five ensuing years between the passage of the act and the Cherokee movement to Red Clay had witnessed the beginning of the transfer of various members of the Five Civilized Tribes westward to Indian Territory. From 1835 to 1838, moving Native Americans had continued in more extreme and larger numbers, with all nations except the Cherokee suffering the relocation process enacted with the 1830 legislation.

White Crow thought about her father, as he was once actively involved in telling her about hearing President Thomas Jefferson's words while witnessing the 1806 speech. She also recalled how her father told her that Jefferson has prophesied that the Cherokee people were to become members of a great nation through their adherence to the white man's advice. Aside from that memory of her father's words, White Crow's thoughts were transformed to more violent and recent memories.

White Crow then began to recall the literal herding of her people. The forceful gathering had been carried out in a manner similar to those that a host of races had conducted upon animals prior to the Cherokee being placed into the Red Clay relocation camp. That day, perhaps more-so than during the present, was firmly etched into her mind as a catastrophic event in the history of the otherwise noble Cherokee people. Sadly, White Crow was unaware that the insensitive roundup, as well as the current state of affairs evolving around her in the camp, would both pale in comparison to the set of circumstances that lay in the immediate future.

White Crow was temporarily able to mentally escape the present situation once again and called to mind the day, only a few months in the past, when the beginnings of the relocation of the Cherokee people took place. During White Crow's mental foray, sordid memories mixed with tears of hatred and disgust over the current events her fellow Cherokee and she faced.

Allowing her thoughts to wander, and White Crow remembered the tranquility of her village as she played out the scene that had taken place a few months earlier, in May 1838. Those memories centered upon events that forever changed the manner in which her people prevailed.

Chapter 2

May 1838; the Cherokee village near the Red Clay settlement:

White Crow and her fellow present Cherokee were struck in the mid-morning hours as their ears were filled with the sounds of horses running toward their village. Horses' hooves beat quickly and furiously against the hardened ground that surrounded the well-kempt Cherokee homesteads. The resulting noise created as the animals splashed into and through the shallow waters of the nearby creeks only added to the horrific situation that was rapidly unfolding.

In contrast to the confusion arising in the village, the bright morning sun rose in the beautiful and peaceful blue eastern sky. The sun's rays seemed to pierce the green leaves of the surrounding trees and provided nature's peace to the horrid situation in the settlement. At least in the early stages of what was to become an invasion of the Cherokee homes, some matters of life temporarily bore evidence of what life had been like in the past.

A group of Cherokee teenaged boys were engaged in a game of Anejodi. Three youthful Cherokee mothers, each carrying her infant on a cradleboard, were returning from a grove of oak trees where recent winds had felled limbs from the treetops. The ladies were the first to notice the arrival of the troops.

Dropping their gathered firewood and beginning to run from the approaching soldiers, the three matrons yelled toward the village, unable to be certain that their words of warning would be heard or understood. The youngest of the three gave her child to the oldest member of her group and began running ahead of the others and shouting that soldiers were approaching.

The screams from the trio of ladies interrupted the group of teenaged Cherokee who were playing a game of Anejodi. Resembling lacrosse, Anejodi was popular among the young adults of the village and provided both exercise and distractions from the chores that served as daily tasks for the teens. The youngsters quickly abandoned their recreational activity and made haste toward their homes.

Four grieving Cherokee ladies in a nearby home were preparing the lifeless body of an eight-year-old Cherokee lad for burial. The carefree youngster had been playing with friends in a nearby field two weeks earlier, and a snake suddenly bit him an inch above the boy's right ankle.

Having suffered through a recent bout of fever and the onset of pneumonia, the youth's body was weakened to the point that there was little ability for him to fight the damaging effects of the snake's poison. Enduring a situation that a typical healthy child may have been able to survive, the youngster succumbed to the effects of the venom, breathing issues, and fever.

The young boy's corpse lay atop a bear skin rug as the burial preparations, a significant part of the Cherokee tradition and ritual utilized in preparation for the deceased individual entering the afterlife, were interrupted. One member of the quartet stepped to the door of the hut and became fully aware of what the previously indistinguishable cries and screams had indicated.

Approximately seven thousand troopers and militia working under orders from General Winfield Scott were arriving in the Cherokee village, seemingly from all directions. The soldiers were acting under the direction of President Martin Van Buren, Andrew Jackson's hand-picked successor. In addition, the elderly and portly General Winfield Scott served as the military official who issued the directive for removal of the Cherokee. On May 17, the soldiers had struck the Cherokee at New Echota and now, ten days later, they were striking the Tennessee Cherokee camp with the full intent of capturing the shocked and stunned Native Americans.

President Van Buren had been led to believe that the progression of the Cherokee assimilation was too slow to be in accordance with the treaties invoked in recent years. Due to his evaluation, the eighth President of the United States saw the completion of that situation, along with the implementation of Jackson's Indian Removal Act, as long overdue. As such, events ranging from the preparation of the boy's body for burial to more routine and mundane tasks were disturbed in forceful and unapologetic manners.

As a case in point, the ladies who were preparing the young boy's body for burial were forced from the structure where the ceremonial act was being performed. Screaming soldiers, using the points of bayonets, led the tearful women from the home. One of the ladies, aged and apparently too slow in her exiting of the building, was struck across the back of her head with the butt of a soldier's long gun.

As one of her comrades attempted to assist the now-addled mistress, she too was hit. The latter attack though came from a bayonet that was poked into the small of her back. The expulsion of blood from the lady's back, though minimal compared to a typical bayonet wound, was proof of the tenacity of the soldiers' intentions and a clear indication of things to come.

Two Cherokee boys, previously involved in throwing darts through a moving hoop, were startled when they realized the soldiers were arriving for an attack. One left the game and began running toward the home where his parents and two sisters lived. The second young man stood in defiance and lifted his arm in order to throw a dart at an approaching horseman.

The hurled dart struck the white soldier on the shoulder, but the projectile failed to deeply penetrate his skin. The jacket that adorned the horse soldier evidently eliminated any possible puncture. The reaction of the soldier atop a horse was to use his sword to strike the Cherokee's skull, killing the brave youngster immediately.

"I'll show you how to attack someone" were the words the soldier yelled at the boy as the sword smashed against the youth's head. The horrendous act sadly drew little attention, largely because the ensuing chaos of the day seemed to overshadow any remorse on the part of the soldier or feelings of sympathy from those who witnessed the initial carnage.

White Crow recalled the soldiers riding into the village, not as peaceful enforcers of the Removal Act, but as vengeful warriors who were determined to carry out their mission of relocating the village's residents as quickly as possible. She remembered the progression of the attack occurred in what the soldiers viewed as the most proficient and violent manners possible.

White Crow, standing in front of another home some fifty yards from the hut where the dead lad's body lay unattended, witnessed a soldier who appeared to be near her age and yielding a torch. The inexperienced soldier proudly carried the incinerate and proceeded to set the hut on fire. To White Crow's knowledge, the child's corpse, along with all materials inside the house, was consumed in the inferno that soon engulfed the structure. White Crow's theory about the abandonment of the child was later confirmed through a conversation she held with one of the ladies who had been actively involved in preparing the body for burial.

White Crow also noted that a group of soldiers, numbering no more than a dozen, began hoarding items of value. The soldiers also appeared more interested in improving their financial situations than fully following their military orders. While the Cherokee men were forced to leave their horses, mules and plows in the fields, the small group of soldiers was presented with time sufficient enough to literally rob the homes of the natives who were being forcefully led from the village. Hatchets, pottery, and precious metals were even dug from the graves of those whose deaths, perhaps to their good fortune, prevented them from being witness to the acts of cruelty.

Cherokee maidens were being forcefully placed into wagons while smiling soldiers, contemplating a myriad of evil thoughts and actions, commented about the appearance and beauty of the females, some just entering their adolescent years. Most of the Cherokee clearly understood English, but the words of their resistance and instructions to one another were spoken in Cherokee, hiding their intentions from their captors, but infuriating them as well.

"This one here's prettier than anythin' I done seen afore. Bet she'd look real good with a bath and a purty white dress, maybe a nice bow in that thick black hair." The words from an illiterate and unkempt soldier did little to mask his wicked intentions.

Another soldier smirked and placed his right hand upon the left cheek of a bound girl, some 15 years of age. In doing so, the soldier attempted to appear as a gentleman rather than a lustful individual. The girl pulled away as much as her hand and leg restraints allowed, but the soldier moved his hand behind her head and began to pull her face toward his.

While a kiss was to be the initial contact, the soldier's facial expressions and harsh command of, "Come here girl" indicated that a far more sinister activity was his goal. Two soldiers near him uttered that he was evidently seeking a bride among the Cherokee.

"He can't get a white woman to pay him any attention. Looks like he'll have to settle for one of these girls." The comments from one of the two nearby soldiers were almost as cruel as the physical abuse many of the Cherokee women were experiencing.

Another soldier harassed any of the ladies who appeared to be within listening range of his evil intentions. "Y'all ain't gonna talk where I can't understand yuns. I'll cut your tongue out if you don't shut those traps; come over here if you think I'm not for real."

The crimes were prevented when a lieutenant from General Scott's detachment ordered the soldiers, intent on committing an unspeakable act, to disperse and assist others in destroying the homes of the village.

"Let those people be! You'll have time in town to find a woman. We need to get these savages headed from here so they can be moved out of the way for people wanting this land. Conduct yourself as soldiers!" The officer was likely supposed to keep his revelation to himself, but the intensity of the moment proved too much for him to handle.

The soldiers who stood near the young man who had grabbed the young girl's head laughed as the appearance of guilt spread across the culprit's face. "He'll get what's coming to him," compiled the utterance from the soldier's lips as he looked in the direction of the officer who had ended his evil quest.

"You'll have to catch him when he's asleep." A trooper made this proclamation as he cut his eyes in the direction of the lieutenant and looked at the officer who had ended, or at least postponed, the degradation of the maiden.

"Lieutenant's rough. That's one tough man in a fight, and I sho ain't gonna help you", replied another bystander.

Still another solider added, "Either way, we've got work to do. Let's get to it."

This was one of the few acts of salvation for the Cherokee, as the day was to bear witness to additional acts of theft, abuse, and destruction. The lieutenant's noble intervention occurred while additional acts of varying degrees of maliciousness evolved all around the location that was quickly becoming a scene of sacrilege.

For example, Cherokee ladies who had earlier busied themselves milking cows or working in the fields were driven from their duties without the benefit of changing into clean clothing. Two Cherokee women who were involved in spinning were taken from their wheels; one suffered the demeaning act of being dragged by her hair toward the assembling line of Cherokee who were hastily being prepared to make their march from the village.

In some cases, children who had been playing were kept from the presence of their parents. Dolls were stripped from young girls' arms, despite their best efforts to retain them for sources of comfort. Though many of the young Cherokee would be reconciled with their parents when the group reached Red Clay, the effects of the situation were certain to have had severe impacts upon the young minds as well as with those of their parents.

White Crow witnessed a large number of the elderly and feeble Cherokee falling prey to abusive soldiers. The Native Americans were regularly prodded like animals as they were accused of disobeying the shouts of men who spoke rapidly and with a variety of strange-sounding accents. Seemingly unaware of, or perhaps indifferent to, the language barrier that existed between them and many of the old and young Cherokee, the soldiers often lost control of their own emotions and became deadly in their acts of coercion.

A village chieftain, suffering from an injury incurred weeks earlier during a deer hunting foray, was bedridden by the time General Scott's troops arrived. The Cherokee official was the only fluent English-speaking member of his home, although his family members were attempting to learn the language that dominated the area of their new home. The family was rounded up and orders were given for eight soldiers to shoot all five of the members of the household.

One soldier, obviously conducting a mental battle over orders to carry out the meaningless massacre of the family, reluctantly joined in the melee. As the shots fired from the soldiers' weapons pierced the bodies of the chief, his wife, and their three children, the stalling soldier was the last to aim and shoot his gun. Heartfelt tears flowed down his cheeks at the conclusion of the incident as other acts of violence, similar in nature, erupted.

The sound of intermittent weapons fire joined the shrieks of people being robbed of the bulk of their worldly possessions. Items that the soldiers regularly deemed valuable oftentimes had far less significance for their Cherokee counterparts. On the other hand, family heirlooms, some approaching a century or more in age, were typically cast aside or destroyed in the fires being set in the hold of locations within the village confines.

It became common for the soldiers to shoot into the air in order to add haste to the steps of the captured Cherokee. Sadly, many shots were more deadly. An increasing number of soldiers veered from firing their weapons toward the sky and began to aim more carefully into groups of huddled and frightened Cherokee.

With many of the shots, Cherokee were killed, yet their loved ones were not permitted to attempt to assist the wounded or dying. Likewise, there was no allowance for the living to take time to bury the dead. A trio of soldiers fired in the direction of five Cherokee, and two of the younger males fell to the ground without uttering a word. The other three were quickly rounded up and forced to move toward the group that was gathering for the movement from the area.

One soldier who shot in the direction of a group of some eight children did so in an effort to disperse the assemblage. The young soldier had failed to take proper notice of his surroundings and, in turn, the bullet struck a rock and ricocheted into the head of one of the children, killing the young girl where she stood.

As the other children began crying and offered intense looks toward the soldier, the latter individual attempted to apologize. The soldier's effort to right his wrong yielded little comfort for the children or him; the soldier threw his weapon to the ground and began sobbing into his hands.

The girl's mother and father ran toward the stricken child. As if overcome with a propitiation to kill again, the soldier ceased his mourning as quickly as it had begun. The reaction of the soldier who had unwittingly killed the girl was to pick up his weapon, reload, and fire his gun at the distraught father. The soldier was reinforced with two other soldiers who joined in the melee, sending bullets toward the parents, killing both of them with a quick combination of five carefully aimed shots.

Shouts erupted from locations throughout the village. "Tlahv" filled the air as the non-English speaking members of the village begged for the safety of their families and themselves.

The infrequent but nonetheless existent language barrier led to frustration for individuals on both sides of the struggle. "Tlahv" was the Cherokee word for "no," but the pleading manner in which it was uttered did little to deter the tenacity of the U. S. soldiers bent on following their orders and fulfilling their selfish desires.

The grisly task given to some twenty soldiers was to remain behind and gather the dead and dying. Those who had succumbed to the onslaught and those who appeared to be beyond the chance of recovering were placed upon a hastily-established funeral pyre. Clearly, some of the bodies burned in the endeavor were near death, but not fully deceased. The screams of those who were able to emit sounds and screams resonated throughout the camp. While some were only able to produce incomprehensible moans, others cried for help and pleaded for death to come quickly. The cremation area at Red Clay would serve as a symbol of early Nineteenth Century ethnic cleansing in the Southern United States.

In an effort to minimize the ability of the Cherokee to bond gather for some type of coordinated mass resistance, the soldiers quickly forced the imprisoned individuals from the confines of the village at Red Clay. The initial phase of the trip would lead the Cherokee to an area located a few miles from the settlement where rapidly-erected stockades served as the temporary homes for the displaced people.

The ensuing exodus from the camp had a strong impact upon White Crow, and she thought of the last view she had of her once-peaceful village. As cattle and horses were rounded up for personal gain for the soldiers, other animals, such as the dogs and weaning-aged pigs, were shot or forced from the presence of their panicking Cherokee owners.

White Crow neared a high point on the road leading from her village, and she slowed her pace momentarily. She swung her upper body around, attempting to observe the scene. The movement of White Crow proved to be a difficult task to perform as her torso was tied to those of the people on either side. However, White Crow managed to see the pile of dead and mortally wounded Cherokee being set afire as additional bodies were being carried to the location and placed into the growing flames. The sight itself, as well as the odor emanating from the inferno, caused several of the Cherokee near her to fight to suppress gagging reflexes that erupted amid screams and calls for loved ones.

White Crow also successfully fought the tendency to gag and managed to look in the direction of her home once last time. In doing so, she captured a glimpse of her home and those of her neighbors as flames engulfed the settlement that had been the location of tranquility less than an hour before. She became convinced that this view of the village, and not her previous glance, would be the last image she would hold of her home.

She lowered her head and saw the dust that the captives' feet stirred up. The airborne dirt encircled her lower body and began coating her sweaty feet and legs. At that point White Crow remembered another phrase her father had told her that he witnessed President Jefferson utter during the cold morning speech of 1806.

Thomas Jefferson's ironic words were, "You will find your want to be mills to grind your corn, which by relieving your women from the loss of time in beating it to meal, will enable them to spin and weave more…He will wish when he dies that these things shall go to his wife and children."

During their imprisonment near Red Clay, the Cherokee were to learn that generations-old farms that were forcefully abandoned were used as fodder for a lottery-type dispersal. A group of soldiers assigned to ensure the final destruction of buildings in the village were noted to have gambled for farms, livestock, and other possessions in the area as soon as the Cherokee were moved out of sight from the devastation of their homes and sources of life.

By sunset on that fateful day in May 1838, the Cherokee had been moved outside Red Clay and placed into the nearby holding pens. While some Cherokee, determined to be more cooperative, were allowed to enter the stockades in family units, the vast majority of the Cherokee people spent the initial days of their stay in segregated pods. Women occupied a series of enclosures, while men were placed into similar structures located a couple of hundred yards to the east. An unintentional act of mercy on the part of the soldiers was that the children, separated by gender, claimed the series of holding pens in the middle of the temporary prison.

A small number of trees lined the border of the compound, but the shade they provided was to primarily benefit the soldiers assigned to the area. The soldiers' tents were situated as far as possible from the stockades and had access to an unlimited supply of fresh running water from the small stream that meandered through the edge of the woods.

The insensitivity of the area's white citizens became apparent almost immediately after the movement of the Cherokee began. Residents of nearby towns, growing more fully conscious of the plight of the Native Americans, gathered within a matter of hours to purchase, pilfer, or plunder a wide range of the items left behind.

Chapter 3

Holding pens near Red Clay, Tennessee; late summer 1838:

In the days following her imprisonment, White Crow joined other members of her group in attempting to gain details regarding another group of Cherokee. The members of the second contingency were being moved westward along a combination of rivers and land trails. There had been escapees from the movement, and the inability of soldiers to recapture them had enabled word of the forced relocation to spread among various protected communication networks the Cherokee had established over generations.

However, the presence of a severe drought ended all speculation that White Crow and her fellow detainees would soon follow their forerunners in a similar manner. While it made a great deal of military and humane logic to move the Cherokee from the poorly-provisioned and open holding pens at Red Clay, the situation in neighboring towns proved no better.

Within a week of the group settling in the outskirts of Red Clay, drinking water became scarce. Talk quickly circulated that the situation was just as bleak as had been those with the earlier westward movement. The Cherokee, as well as the soldiers who served as their guards, began to suffer the effects of the drought as the stream that had once provided a source of drinkable water for the soldiers seemed to dry up in less than a day, leaving only a trickle of liquid flowing in its wake. The soldiers who were guarding the Cherokee had never before spent more than a couple of days in any type of situation that resembled the one they were currently facing.

As the first month of the Cherokee detainment elapsed, the inevitable arrival of disease and death came to pass. The month of June 1838 signaled the beginning of a period that came to be known as the "sickly time" throughout the ranks of the captive Cherokee. Conservative estimates were that as many as 1,500 of the 13,000 Cherokee being held in the series of stockades eventually succumbed to the lack of water, hot temperatures, and the relentless abundance of diseases.

A variety of diseases affected the Native Americans of all ages, resulting in makeshift funerals and mass burials. Daily totals of deaths and serious illnesses were staggering. It became commonplace for dozens of memorials to be held within the early morning hours when temperatures were the coolest. Additionally, the morning sunlight enabled the immediate loved ones of the deceased to properly observe the associated ceremony without suffering from the certain daily increases of temperature and humidity that tended to squeeze the breath from one's lungs. Afternoon temperatures left animals and people in lethargic states that seemed to lessen only with the far more tolerable nights.

Deep coughs were widespread among the Cherokee and the soldiers. The expulsions seemed to convulse the bodies of those exposed to the dusty areas that became more heavily polluted with human and animal waste on a daily basis. Regular maneuvers of soldiers exercising and patrolling on horseback added to the airborne contaminants that stifled many of those who in. The inhaled oxygen appeared intoxicating as it unwittingly filled the lungs of the Cherokee and soldiers with particles of impurities. As people tried to obtain needed sleep, the night air was filled with remnants of the particles stirred up during the earlier hours of each day.

As if the problems were not numerous enough, the presence of mosquitoes and flies robbed many of much needed rest. Partaking in a meal without the almost constant appearance of flies was a rarity as well. Few maladies seemed to be absent in the midst of those struggling to survive an extremely trying situation.

Eventually, the possibility and freedom of the Cherokee to attend improvised funeral services was abolished. While the actions of the guards often overshadowed the compassionate hearts in many of them, the excuse of using the shared God-fearing faith was used as a rationale for the soldiers' cruel actions. That same mindset was also used earlier as a means of justifying the removal of the Cherokee from their homes. In response to these situations, the frequency of the deaths among the Cherokee, as well the increasing tension between the Cherokee and the United States government, it became necessary for the soldiers to enforce the cessation of the Native American funerals.

During one of the final funeral observances held in mid-June, the soldiers overseeing the extradition process reached a consensus that a Cherokee family was devoting too much time to their funeral rite. A young mother from the family had passed away during the night, and the bereaved survivors were having a great deal of difficulty gathering their thoughts and bidding farewell to the recently-deceased lady.

The soldiers' attempts to bring the ceremony to a close resulted in an exchange of heated words and an eventual pair of deaths. The situation reached a highly stressful point when weary soldiers took it upon themselves to break up the gathering.

"Let's move on. She's in the ground now, get walking." The harsh and insensitive words of a nervous soldier serving on guard detail drew little initial reaction from the eight distraught Cherokee standing near a female's shallow grave.

One of the mourning Cherokee men glanced toward the soldiers and offered a heartfelt explanation. He explained, "She is my sister. Her husband and her sons will join me in a prayer for her as she moves into the afterlife."

"Drag this out any longer, and you'll be there with her. Lots of us have lost folks before and we don't need to start listening to somebody like you trying to make us feel guilty." As the blue-clad soldier appeared to revel in his words of cruelty, two men standing on either side of him smirked in agreement.

One member of the snarling trio of soldiers apparently held the opinion that the time had arrived for more aggressive action. He shouted, "Shoot 'em. Shoot all of 'em now." With that order issued, the angered soldier saw his two compatriots join him in an event intended to lessen the amount of Cherokee disparity.

The three trigger-happy and vengeful soldiers fired into the resistant mourners, and the shots immediately killed one of the group. Another Cherokee soon died from a combination of blood loss and a lack of sufficient medical care due to the nature of the "rebellious death" he suffered in retaliation for his defiance of the order to disperse.

The tragedy of the grieving Cherokee added to the growing tensions that had developed between the soldiers and the captives. In an attempt to lessen the adversity, Lieutenant Edward Deas had written General Winfield Scott, seeking permission to consolidate some of the captives.

General Scott denied the request to allow groups of families to be held in the pens. Scott felt that doing so would encourage the Cherokee to more effectively formulate and carry out plans of resistance or escape. The United States general did concede to the request that mothers be allowed to share a portion of each pen with their children. At times, this apparent act of kindness proved to present issues that would have otherwise been avoided.

For example, the ever-present aspects of disease and death continued to wreak havoc upon the captives. The care the mothers provided for their sickly children was unequaled in dedication and compassion. Those same aspects also led to an increased level of resistance on the part of a Cherokee mother whose daughter had passed away.

With increasing frequency the removal of children who had only lately passed from this world led to more negative reactions from disbelieving and grieving matriarchs. While few of the incidents led to serious injuries for soldiers, it was common for mothers of the dead children to be kicked, slapped, or otherwise physically restrained from giving one last loving embrace or a kiss upon the cheek of their recently-deceased loved one.

White Crow witnessed the exchange of animosity when a Cherokee mother proved possessive and protective of the corpse of her toddler-aged daughter. A soldier attempted to take the deceased child from the Cherokee mother and offer a token form of burial. The mother initially turned her back, shielding her dead child from his grasp. As the number of soldiers increased to six, the sobbing mom, by then accompanied with a small detachment of her own people, began kicking and hitting the soldiers in an effort to maintain a strong hold on the lifeless child.

"Shoot her, get her. Use your gun now or give it to me! If she wants to be with the child so much, I can make it possible." The words the soldier screamed were too much for the emotions of a young corporal standing on the outsider perimeter of the holding pen.

The corporal fired a shot into the air, temporarily deescalating the situation. Although the mother had a limited command of English, the corporal was able to convince her that she would be allowed to take the child's body to the makeshift cemetery where dozens of other Cherokee had been interred. While the compromise defused a situation that could easily have become explosive, the precedent it established proved difficult for parties involved in similar situations in the near future.

White Crow, becoming more discouraged with the filthy conditions and deplorable treatment of her people, bore witness to one particularly evil encounter. The bodies of two mothers who had passed away during the night were taken from their children amid the children's screams of painstaking loss. One of the ladies had left two children behind; the second mother's death resulted in one orphan. As the two children became extremely vocal about their loss, shouts from their father, who only moments before had become aware of the passing of his wife of ten years, garnered the attention of all but a few of the Cherokee.

The climax of the events centered around one of the children being held back as his mother's corpse was taken from his sight. The nine year-old sister of the young man, exceeding her brother's age by three years, was struck across the head with a soldier's sword still encased in its scabbard. The girl fell to the ground as blood poured from the gash the violent swing of the weapon had created. Large drops of blood dropped into the dust, while the girl's efforts to move her head along the ground speedily resulted in dirt becoming lodged in the deep cut.

Another Cherokee lady who had been held captive in the holding pen pushed the soldier who had used his sword to hit the young girl across her head. The matron then attempted to provide aid to the stricken lass, but the effort was about to cease in a most violent manner. Two soldiers, reportedly working without orders to do so, hurriedly approached the

Native American mother. The soldiers stood with one either side of the attempted avenger, and bayoneted the woman several times.

Before anyone from the crowd of shocked onlookers situated nearby could intervene, the Cherokee lady fell from the impact and deadly effects of the bayonets. Apparently mortally wounded with the initial, or perhaps the second strike from the soldiers, the female victim said nothing. However, the dying woman somehow managed to look toward the young girl, forced a small smile, and made eye contact with her before passing away.

This tragic event occurred while shocked Cherokee ladies and children helplessly watched it unfold. In an act of defiance toward the attempt at civility on the part of the injured child, a third soldier bayonetted the severely wounded child, killing her before one of his superior officers made a weak attempt to entice him to stop the deadly barrage of bayonet strikes.

Chief John Ross was appalled at the series of events and sought immediate relief for his people. Ross appealed to General Scott for the ability to state the objections the Cherokee held about the conditions they now faced. In response, Scott arranged for Ross to be transported to Washington, D. C. where the Cherokee leader would hopefully secure a meeting with President Van Buren. Three Cherokee males accompanied Ross on the trip in an effort to provide the other Cherokee with proof and recollections of Ross's dealings with Van Buren. Ross's wife and the Cherokee's principal religious leaders stayed at Red Clay in order to provide leadership and sources of stability for what was likely to become a lengthy stay at the detention facility.

Chapter 4

In July 1838 Cherokee Chief John Ross received an appointment as the superintendent of his people's removal. This was an unsought and undesired promotion on the part of Ross, yet it was also one that was met with the overwhelming approval of the Cherokee people present at Red Clay. The latter aspect was due largely to the fact that Ross was both a well-spoken and an extremely moral man. Fortunately, for those who had become the subjects of Ross's superintendent post, Chief John Ross quickly began to use the status of his new position as a means of securing foodstuffs for the famished and suffering captives.

During the first week of August 1838 a supply train arrived at Red Clay. The wagons that composed the train were laden with hams, eggs, flour, and corn meal for the benefit and use of the imprisoned Native Americans. The wheels of the vessels seemed to the witnesses of the arrival to creak under the strain of the weight of the vast amount of supplies. However, the enthusiasm the imprisoned Cherokee held regarding the arrival of the materials was to soon be lessened, though through no action of theirs. It was, as had taken place and would many times in the future, an empty gesture on the part of the United States government.

Sadly, corruption almost immediately reared its head at the arrival of the supplies. Ben Dixon, a captain who was assigned with overseeing the disbursement of the goods, had contacted area residents to purchase large portions of the materials. In order to save some level of credibility, Dixon usually designated approximately twenty-five percent of each shipment to pass in the direction of Red Clay. Careful to hide his ploy,

Dixon regularly ordered that the diminished amount of the food and other items be evenly divided among the remaining wagons. The farce remained hidden from the Cherokee, although they often questioned why so many wagons were used for the movement of such a seemingly small amount of supplies.

Captain Ben Dixon met with dozens of area subsistent farmers on a regular basis and allowed them to purchase their choices of supplies for pennies on the dollar. The selling price of the goods hardly paid for the cost of purchasing and shipping them to Red Clay, but Captain Dixon viewed the transactions as no-loss situations. After all, every item sold constituted pure profit for Dixon.

On one such occasion, Captain Dixon found a larger crowd than usual serving as his greeters. In his seemingly diplomatic, yet highly self-centered way, Dixon managed to resolve the issues surrounding the situation.

"In a few days I'll have more. There's no need to worry about this. Give me until next Tuesday and I assure you there will be plenty of food for you at a price you will find unmatched. Trust me." The irony of Dixon's words was prevalent, but hidden from those to whom he spoke.

By the time Captain Dixon's ploy was made known to his superiors he had become a rather wealthy man, all at the expense of the lives of hundreds of Cherokee people. One of his subordinates, feeling that the hush-money Dixon offered him was an insufficient amount, had written a letter to an Army official, offering full disclosure of the embezzlement in exchange for immunity from prosecution.

With the late-July disclosure of Captain Ben Dixon's scam and the hasty trial that followed, Dixon was sentenced to a year in military prison and dishonorably discharged from the United States Army. Dixon had pocketed an estimated $200,000 in tax-free money, an amount equal to several lifetimes of legitimate pay. While it stood to reason that the ill-gotten funds should be returned, Captain Dixon had carefully planned his swindling act.

Ben Dixon had taken extreme measures to hide the monies well and, as a result, the capital was never discovered, despite an intensive detective endeavor to do just that. Upon his release from prison, accomplished through a legal technicality, Dixon moved to Germany, having served only three months of his original ten-year sentence. Dixon lived throughout an estimated five European residences in basic anonymity until his death some forty years later. Dixon never held a viable vocation, and evidently lived off the funds he had stolen.

Meanwhile, the lack of supplies and food obviously hampered the very existence of the Cherokee people. Chief John Ross was able to secure a minimal amount of wagons filled with foodstuffs that were a lower quality than what had earlier arrived at the location. The initial effect of the charges brought against Dixon seemed to be positive for the Cherokee as the new supplies dwindled uninhibited into the Red Clay area. A literal case of too little too late could be applied to the situation of the time.

Attempts to grow mid-summer crops proved futile as sources of irrigation were largely unavailable. The extreme summer temperatures seemed to smother the flow of fresh air, yet they worked with the humidity to bake and crack the skin of the unsheltered Cherokee. The limited amounts of dug wells hardly provided enough drinking water for the healthy members of the displaced Cherokee to say alive. Access to streams and creeks, many located a great distance from the stockade, was more widespread for the soldiers as they were able to leave the confines of the prison environment.

In addition, those Cherokee weakened from want of water and food became famished to the point that dozens more succumbed. Small quantities of supplies continued to trickle into area, and parents quickly designated each family's share of food and supplies to the well-being of the children. Chief Ross was unaware of the fact that, by early September, locals were regularly robbing wagons filled with supplies. The robbers had become accustomed to the easy and low-cost access of the items which Captain Dixon's corruption had once provided to them. It now seemed similar items were becoming available in ever-increasing amounts.

As for drinking water, morning dew provided the only legitimate, yet minute, source of respite from the shortage. However, it failed to arrive in sufficient quantities to maintain a level of nourishment the beleaguered Cherokee needed in order to maintain a semblance of life.

Hardship upon hardship contributed to the tremendous increase in the death toll as the Cherokee continued to pass away in the unbearable heat and deplorable conditions. Their access to fresh water continued to be highly limited and correlated to the sporadic consumption of tainted water. The latter aspect of existence for the Cherokee led to the onset of diseases that had, to that point, been absent from the group.

The "sickly season" reigned supreme throughout July and August. White Crow and the surviving Cherokee approached the point at which all hope was lost, yet they continued to dream and pray for some type of relief. The lack of suitable water left dozens of Cherokee ill, while a comparable number passed away from the deficiency.

Mother Nature mercifully dealt the beleaguered Cherokee a much-needed respite from the appalling conditions they had endured during the recent summer months. In September the heavens opened and a series of rains began to settle the dust. The cooling temperatures also seemed to extinguish the high death rate that had devastated the spirits, as well as the lives, of hundreds of Cherokee.

Shortly after the time that the September rains arrived and began to replenish the area bodies of water, a major round of long overdue supplies and foodstuffs finally made their way to the Cherokee camp at Red Clay. The three dozen wagons were filled with every conceivable type of fare and provisions of the era and were intended to serve as a major component of the upcoming and long-delayed Cherokee removal.

Having become fully aware of Captain Dixon's corruption and the area residents' theft from earlier supply trains, President Martin Van Buren had ordered that a heavy guard detail be provided for the most recent set of wagons. An additional accompaniment of troops also served as relief for soldiers whose exposure to the lack of appropriate nourishment, as well as to the stressful circumstances Red Clay had provided, warranted their replacement.

Those extra soldiers had already proven their value during the approach to Red Clay as the rains ironically delayed the arrival of the desperately needed supplies by three days. The timeframe would have likely been much greater had the strong and healthy soldiers assigned to the sentry detail not been with a group of teamsters. The muscles of the strong men, many in the prime of life, were capable of providing the strength necessary to dislodge the heavy wagons from the muddied roads along the route.

The soldiers' skills with the use of firearms also aided in the disbursement of goods to the Cherokee. In addition to occasionally firing at ravenous wildlife along the roadside, the soldiers found themselves battling determined but inferiorly-armed citizens and bands of thieves who desired to obtain the contents of the loaded wagons for their own use.

The skirmishes had cost the lives of a half-dozen soldiers from the group designated as the Van Buren Guard, yet the number of deaths and wounds they inflicted upon the raiders was certainly many times more than the six they suffered. In addition, the number of lives their arrival and baggage saved was an undetermined positive number. Aside from the deaths of the six young members of the United States Army, there were no casualties suffered on the part of the youthful guard detail.

Chapter 5

With the appearance of the supply wagons, White Crow attempted to suppress her thoughts of recent events. Like others, she had welcomed the rains and the renewal of the earth they seemed to bring, yet the hilltop holding pen which she and some one hundred other women and children occupied quickly returned to the dusty surface it had maintained for most of the dry and hot summer. White Crow stood tall as the wagons approached and, acting as she had been taught through the customs of her people, performed a quick check of her appearance.

Aside from the dirt that stained her clothing, White Crow felt that only her soiled hands and feet would provide the rationale that she lacked self-confidence and pride in her appearance. There was no clear indication that the arrival of the wagons and, more specifically, one member of the detachment of guards, would have a major impact upon her life.

The muddied and tired members of the wagon troupe shook hands with their comrades, soldiers who had served as the long-standing guards of the detained Cherokee. Muffled talking and gestures dominated the majority of the few exchanges which White Crow was able to discern. Upon the conclusion of brief small-talk, the soldiers became engaged in moving the wagons nearer to each of the holding pens while keeping some in a line as if preparing to continue their journey.

Working efficiently and in a manner the Cherokee had failed to witness from white men prior to this moment the soldiers quickly unloaded the wagons. They then began an immediate distribution of a variety of supplies to the jailed Native Americans. Within two hours the operation had been completed, and the topic of making a westward movement took over any of the soldiers' conversations White Crow was able to hear.

Throughout the day the majority of Cherokee heartily indulged in the consumption of large quantities of food. With the area streams now filled to a more suitable level, small guarded groups of the captives were taken to bodies of water for brief baths and to fill containers with water. While this had been done on a more irregular basis during the summer, the ability to wash themselves in deeper pools was a welcomed relief for the Cherokee as well as the soldiers.

Although the ability to eat more substantial food and bathe properly served as much-anticipated and deeply-appreciated acts, the deep grief of the Cherokee continued. Sickness and death persisted. Listless children lay in their mothers' arms while elderly adults of both genders, though fewer in number than their child counterparts, were unable to make the short walks to and from the bathing locations.

No less than twenty Cherokee were able to slip away from the guards during the bathing processes that regularly continued into the late afternoon hours. The renewed growth of vegetation surrounding the water-rich streams provided adequate cover for a determined soul to make his or her way into the surrounding tree line and begin a journey to freedom. The exact number of those who escaped on the last night at Red Clay was never determined and is only based upon the legends that have been passed to the current day.

Sadly, the quickly rising streams also brought about the more vibrant movements of snakes; more specifically, water moccasins. During the latter stages of the bathing process for the women and children, a young boy and his mother apparently stepped into a bedding nest of the venomous snakes, and both were bitten several times. While the child died within seconds of the attack, his mother suffered into the night before she became the last adult to die at Red Clay.

Tensions between the Cherokee and a significant number of soldiers steadily increased during the early hours of that evening. Though the primary method of communicating with the incarcerated Cherokee was conducted through announcements, interpreters, including White Crow, were also utilized. Through such a combination of informative means, each holding pen was educated of the need to prepare for the next day and the planned movement associated with it. Few of the soldiers or Native Americans were fully aware of the trip's eventual goal: to reach Indian Territory.

The mass exodus was scheduled to begin soon after sunrise the next morning, with family units being allowed to progress together along the planned route. While the hatred for the confinement near Red Clay was widespread among the captive Native Americans, the location had previously served as the Cherokee Capital and Council Grounds for some time. Thus, the thoughts of the long-awaited but imminent move to a strange land caused the Cherokee males, now temporarily relieved of the pains of empty stomachs, to reach the point of rebellion.

Men confined to one of the pens within sight of White Crow's location began to throw items such as rocks and nails from the cells toward the guards. The rocks had been retrieved from the stream bed during the last day's bathing period, while the nails had been procured from the crates of various items placed into the holding pens. Loud voices and exchanges of insults between the Cherokee captives and the guards filled the air, and the soldiers were reinforced with additional armed sentries. The situation seemed to White Crow and those around her to be steadily approaching the point of bloodshed as some fifteen soldiers surrounded the pen and lowered their loaded weapons.

At the moment when it appeared that shots were about to be fired, the long-awaited return of Chief John Ross quelled the rebellion. Ross, as previously noted, had left the post months earlier in order to negotiate for more supplies and improved living conditions: ple. The sights and sounds Ross encountered upon his arrival at the holding pens did little to create a mindset that the trip had been worth the time a:

Among those welcoming the return of Chief Ross was his wife Quati. The royal Cherokee had chosen to stay with her people rather than being held in far more comfortable quarters as President Van Buren had ordered. Her decision had led to several bouts with illness, but

White Crow's determination and caregiving had now largely restored Quati's health.

After a brief conversation with his wife, Chief Ross made his way to each of the holding pens and conversed with the detainees. He assured them that on the following morning their homes at Red Clay would be abandoned forever. The amount of tears shed in response to the news were virtually immeasurable. Ross equated the finality of the revelation to that of a loved one passing away after suffering from a horrible disease or debilitating condition. The movement had been certain to come, but the awareness of its close proximity really hit the hearts of the nervous and reluctant Cherokee.

The venture to the area which the United States government had designated as Indian Territory would take a great deal of time and determination. Chief Ross assured his people that he would be with them each step of the way and that God would lead them through the trek together. Chief Ross, the Cherokee people, and soldiers appeared to realize the adventure would not take place in the absence of hardship and degradation. Sadly, none knew how true that realization would prove to be.

The tragic events the Cherokee had endured in being moved from their nearby homes to the holding facilities at their council grounds could only mildly prepare them for the events of the ensuing months.

Chief Ross's words of encouragement and affirmation provided his people with a boost of confidence that nothing had achieved in recent weeks. His ability to restore faith and quell the spread of riotous inclinations was as great as any leader ever possessed. The basic content of his speeches to each of the holding pens was sincere and straightforward: the westward movement was set to begin early the next morning, and Chief Ross would lead the way.

In an attempt to hasten the process of implementing the Cherokees' early morning departure from the Red Clay holding pens, members of the U.S. Army's provost units who arrived the previous day were asked to ensure the placement of the Native Americans into family units. A major exception to this policy which caused discontent on the part of many Cherokee families, was that, while collecting the family units together, the military party was to also seek the separation of sickened children from their parents.

The ill children were to be kept away from their families and be placed into hospital wagons. The goal of this endeavor was allegedly to provide peace of mind for the Cherokee parents by assuring them that the trip could be conducted under the provision of proper care for the children. Another intention of the separation of the healthy from the ill would be to limit the spread of disease along the journey that lay ahead.

The well-intended plan went awry from the onset. The lack of confidence the Cherokee held for their captors, regardless of the meaning of their efforts, was evident. The sick Cherokee children, as has been the case throughout generations, tended to require more attention than did their healthy counterparts. In turn, the removal of the incapacitated youngsters resulted in the onset of confusion, anger, tears, and physical violence.

White Crow lamented for the mothers who began to cry as their sick children were removed from their presence for the "sake of the effort." While watching the process, White Crow's attention was drawn to the soldier who appeared to be in charge of the effort to detach the Cherokee mothers from their unhealthy children. This chance encounter, though far from pleasant in its origin, would soon change the lives of the two people who played the principle parts in the scenario.

The young man leading the group in the severance of the children was a corporal named Jake Savage. Corporal Savage had seen action against the Native Americans earlier in his career, though most of the encounters had been in skirmishes that had resulted in minimal casualties for the combatants of either side. However, the tenacity of the most recent struggle had brought about the death of one of Savage's childhood friends.

Two months earlier, Corporal Savage's company had been ambushed when they entered a trap that a group of Creek and Choctaw warriors had set. The intertribal sect had gone against many of the customs of their ancestors and combined their battle efforts. The purpose was an attempt to thwart any significant buildup of soldiers who would present obstacles to the Native American guerilla activities in the small mountains and hills in the areas of northern Alabama.

An estimated two hundred experienced and well-armed tribesmen, most of whom were escapees from the United States government's earlier phases of eliminating the "red nemesis" from the southeastern section of the country, were equipped with percussion rifles and more than prepared for a fight against Jake Savage and his fellow soldiers.

In the ensuing exchanges of weapon discharges, the two groups inflicted a significant number of casualties upon their foes. Over forty Native Americans were killed during the two-hour struggle, while twenty members of Jake Savage's company, many of whom Savage had known for the entire length of his career, breathed their last that day. The loss of his company sergeant, as well as the corporal, had led to Savage's swift, but well-deserved promotion from the rank of a private to that of corporal.

Jake Savage's conduct during the ambush had earned him not only a promotion that many of his compatriots viewed as long overdue, but also the praises of those closest to him. No less than five of the warriors who were killed that day fell to shots ejected from Corporal Savage's weapon. A Choctaw warrior who had managed to penetrate the defensive perimeter that the soldiers established also fell victim to Jake's knife during a brief but intense hand-to-hand struggle.

The sight of blood he had directly shed had temporarily caused Jake Savage to enter a state of withdrawal from the events surrounding him. He grasped at the nearby blades of grass and tree leaves in an effort to remove the blood from his hands. Only the forceful and panicked words of a fellow soldier resulted in Savage's mental return to the scene.

"Savage! Jake Savage! You okay? Come on, son! We've gotta get outta here before some more of them get here and try to avenge their brothers. You with me?" The soldier, only a couple of years older than Savage, offered what he had come to perceive as a heartfelt boost to soldiers who were newcomers to the act of killing a fellow human.

Savage's timid reply, after a short nodding of his head from side to side, was simply, "Yeah, I'm okay. That's the first time I ever killed somebody." While the sight and smell of human blood affected many of his comrades, Savage was the only one who fought back the instinct to vomit.

Immediately after his elevation to the rank of corporal, Jake Savage had received additional positive comments when an article about the incident appeared in local papers. The notoriety resulted in good-natured ribbing from the same people who most admired Savage. Those men would grow to depend upon Savage's quickly increasing level of wisdom, although they would question his actions from time to time in the months that were soon to follow. Corporal Savage had become one of the pillars of his company.

Only twenty years old, Jacob David Savage was regularly regarded as a prime catch for any female desiring to establish a lasting relationship. Standing over six feet tall, Corporal Savage had light brown, curly hair. His piercing blue eyes added appeal to the muscular frame that the suntanned, clean-shaven, and well-groomed soldier possessed. A cut appeared under his right eye, the result of a knife wound he received in the action associated with the recent ambush.

A second-generation soldier, Corporal Savage's attitude toward the forced movement of the Native Americans was far from positive. While his Scottish father had had encounters with the people he called Indians, among other, far more racist terms, Jake Savage had come to deeply respect the culture and lifestyle of the Native Americans. This appreciation was especially true in relation to the members of the Cherokee nation. Additionally, Savage felt a great admiration for the respect the Cherokee people held for their leaders and for the manner in which that was reciprocated.

By contrast, Corporal Savage possessed a high level of animosity toward former President Andrew Jackson, as well as Martin Van Buren, his nation's current Commander-in-Chief. Savage's rationale for the disdain he held for the seventh and eighth Presidents was based upon the principle of the relocation of various Native American groups in recent years. Jake Savage felt a more realistic approach would be peaceful coexistence, but that was a mindset that an increasingly smaller number of his comrades and citizens seemed to possess.

The rumors of the savagery and bloodshed initiated in the relocation of other member nations of the Five Civilized Tribes had caused Corporal Savage to not only question the leadership of the United States, but also those in command of various branches of the military and his membership in the same. This contempt on Jake Savage's part was destined to increase with his participation in the largest such movement to date.

Chapter 6

As a point of his mixed perceptions regarding the treatment of the Cherokee and his personal role in this controversial act, Corporal Jake Savage had earlier attempted to comply with his most recent orders. However, he was coy in carrying out the commands he had received for the most recent day. The directive given to Corporal Savage and the group of eight soldiers directly under his command called for the completion of the removal of sick or lifeless children from their mothers prior to the onset of the march.

The determination was for the process to be completed as quickly as possible in order for the lengthy movement to quickly begin. However, when the assignment began at the earliest sign of sunlight, the resistance of the Cherokee people became more vocal, as did their reluctance to comply with the perplexing act. While Jake Savage halfheartedly attempted to carry out his phase of the movement, those who were to be the objects of the forced movement were far less secretive in their perceptions and performance in the event.

White Crow questioned the young Corporal Savage as to the rationale for his actions. White Crow asked, "Why do you take the children from their mothers? They have done nothing wrong to you or anyone. We are a people of peace. Let them keep their young."

Corporal Jake Savage, clearly nervous and uncomfortable from the situation and the tone of the atmosphere, responded in a somewhat agitated state. Although he appeared perplexed with the exchange, Savage shouted at the victimized Cherokee lady not much younger than he.

"I'm doing my job. You don't exactly seem peaceful, carrying on with all of the screamin' and hittin' and sayin' all kinds of stuff nobody understands."

White Crow replied, "Do you think you would stand by and let one of us take a child from one of your people? Does it give you power to do this and follow the orders of a man who will not do it himself?"

For a brief time, Corporal Savage and White Crow glared at one another, seemingly oblivious to the chaos erupting around them. Her stare was filled with anger and an obvious dislike for the young soldier, while Jake Savage's eyes exhibited fear and resentment. However, the surrounding events soon warranted more attention than did the increasing animosity between White Crow and Savage, momentarily ending the glaring between the young lady and the youthful soldier.

The tormented screams of the mothers who had recently lost possession of their children continued to fill the air. Meanwhile, the troops in Corporal Savage's detachment became somewhat fixated with the scene in which Jake Savage and White Crow appeared to be the unwilling primary players.

The tormented young soldier was unable to answer White Crow in a manner he felt was required. Jake Savage's stare disappeared, and he briefly stood in awe at the young maiden's question. During the ensuing seconds he appeared to be on the verge of fainting. Perhaps Corporal Savage had temporarily envisioned the Cherokee as representative of the warriors he had encountered two months earlier. Maybe his failure to distinguish between the tenacity of the recent ambush he experienced and the fulfillment of his latest orders overtook Jake Savage's sense of compassion for the Cherokee people.

Nevertheless, Jake Savage somehow managed to regain his composure while shaking his head in a quick manner indicative of "no," a gesture he had made a short time earlier. He then resumed his quest to separate the Cherokee matriarchs from their unhealthy children.

Commanding the eight troops and strongly desiring to become more focused on his orders, Corporal Savage exclaimed that three additional, seemingly lifeless infants located nearby should be taken from their mothers' arms. All the while he appeared to be retreating from the scene and backing toward the heavily-guarded lone door of the holding pen. Mixed emotions clashed within his mind and heart as Savage made one last valiant effort to see his orders through to the end.

Savage uttered, "You know the orders. Proceed and finish the job."

The young corporal briefly appeared to have forgotten the recent arguments White Crow had directed toward him. The mental presence of an inclination to carry out his orders was short-lived. Jake Savage's request to dislodge a fourth child from the arms of the toddler's mother was abandoned when he noticed White Crow comforting a mother whose child had been taken from her only minutes earlier.

The distraught mother screamed toward the heavens and then directed angered and heartfelt words toward Corporal Savage and his comrades. While Jake Savage, as he proclaimed minutes earlier, understood none of the woman's vocalizations made in her native tongue, the manner in which the Cherokee lady looked at him and the tone of voice she used in projecting the statements completely confirmed the validity of his reluctance to fulfill the commands.

White Crow joined the dismayed mother in expressing disgust and animosity toward Corporal Savage and his eight attendants. The actions of the two females created a cessation of the activities and led to Savage ordering his fellow soldiers to temporarily abandon the efforts of extrication. He appeared to have regained his strong sense of admiration for the Cherokee people as he engaged in another exchange of words with White Crow.

"Leave us alone! We want you to leave us alone," White Crow yelled at Savage.

"You need to be sick and dying instead of these babies. I hate you!" A third Cherokee female interjected. Corporal Jake Savage felt an intensity of hatred that seemed to exceed what he had experienced in combat. He looked toward the ground and forcefully swallowed as apprehension overwhelmed all other emotions and feelings.

Meanwhile, the distraught mother of the fourth child continued to scream in Jake Savage's direction. "I hate you. I hope you die. You are evil." While the mother spoke in a sporadic combination of English and Cherokee, Corporal Savage's lack of knowledge regarding the Cherokee language presented little problem with him understanding that the verbiage sent in his direction were filled with strong animosity and a high level of disgust toward him and those who were attired in the issued clothing of the United States Army.

The words and actions of White Crow, the mother, and the third lady cut deeply into Jake Savage's heart. While Corporal Savage had largely proven to be a pillar of strength and emotional stability in an otherwise chaotic combat scene in the ambush, the recent events related to the angered and melancholy Cherokee mother had taken a sudden and heavy toll upon him.

"The orders will be carried out more fully at a later time. It's time to begin the march. Let them gather themselves while we do the same." Corporal Savage concluded his agonized statement by physically exiting the holding pen. He wiped his eyes, giving the appearance of removing sweat from the side of his face. A closer examination of the action revealed that the young corporal was wiping tears from the outside corner of his right eye.

Corporal Jake Savage had undergone a nearly-complete transformation in a matter of minutes. Emotionally, or at least from the point of fully supporting what he conceived to be the mission he was to oversee, his exodus had taken place quite some time earlier.

Chapter 7

Corporal Jake Savage's difficult decision to forego the administration of his orders, as well as his display of the emergence of his admiration for the Cherokee mother, had served to gain him a small amount of esteem in the eyes of White Crow. She had noticed and mentally recorded the entire series of events, and her significant participation in the situation had caused her to realize that Jake Savage was not like the majority of soldiers she had encountered in her recent months of confinement.

At almost the same moment that Jake Savage retreated from the assignment of separating the mothers from the sick or lifeless children, Chief John Ross called for a gathering of the Cherokee people. Permission was granted to Ross to do so in order for him to conduct an early-morning prayer service before the onset of the westward trek. Chief Ross's words were simple and straightforward as he spoke to his faithful but saddened Cherokee followers who had gathered on the foggy and unusually cool summer morning.

Chief Ross began his speech in a tone of voice far from the calmness he typically displayed. In the midst of frequent pauses, some of which enabled him to regain his composure, Ross was recorded to have said, in part, "Today we leave this place. We do so with mixed feelings. The deep sadness this place has caused us in the days soon passed overshadows the great joy we once felt for the area. Our future is in the strong hands of the white soldiers in uniforms, but our God watches over us to protect us from the unknown."

Jake Savage listened closely to the words Chief Ross imparted to the saddened Cherokee. By contrast, a small number of soldiers appeared indifferent, if not inattentive to the speech Ross made. Corporal Savage's attention was evidently strengthened with the realization that the God of which Ross spoke was the same God Savage prayed to daily in his youth and continued to pursue through his recent military activities.

Jake Savage reached inside the collar of his shirt and removed the homemade cross that hung discretely from a sinew necklace positioned on his neck. Carved from the antler of a deer Jake's father had killed years earlier, the cross immediately provided peace for the beleaguered young soldier. Sadly, the tranquility the trinket gave to Jake was missing from the minds and hearts of many Cherokee who lamented throughout Ross's discourse.

Chief Ross continued, "There is a long journey ahead of us, and we go to an unknown destination. We must support one another and show our love for God and our fellow Cherokee. We are strong; let us show it by obeying the soldiers. I ask that the days that are ahead will not be filled with hatred to our captors or with questions or signs of distrust to each other. Our new homes lie at the end of this journey. May God in Heaven be here for us and during our trek as we begin the new phase of our people's history and our lives together. I ask that the soldiers treat us kindly, and that we will respond to them in the same way."

While several of the Cherokee stood resilient as Chief Ross delivered his final statement near their homes at the Cherokee Red Clay base, the number who broke into heavy sobbing was substantial as well. A large representation of the crowd was also characterized by men, women and children whose bewildered expressions seemed to signify the overwhelming emotions and uncertain thoughts that prevailed. Ross himself wiped tears from his eyes and embraced his sobbing and ailing wife as he epitomized the perspective of a burdened husband torn between his need to appear strong and the urge to cry.

With the conclusion of the Cherokee worship service, Jake Savage took an even more sympathetic view of the displaced people. The words Chief Ross had uttered were filled with the foresight and wisdom of a man who had only the safety and best interests of his followers in mind. The comments also burned into Jake Savage's heart and mind as he pondered how he would react if he were placed into the same set of circumstances.

Comparing the leadership of the Cherokee people to those of his own superior officers and government officials, Corporal Jake Savage privately questioned whether or not his country's leaders held the same interest of their constituents at heart. The brief contemplation gave way to an overwhelming desire to state his feelings to someone.

Corporal Savage turned to one of the men in his company and solemnly expressed this concern. "I just wish I could say something that heartfelt and meaningful to you and the others. It would mean a lot if someone would offer some reassurance to us before we force these folks from their land."

A brief pause and a glimpse at the ground enabled Jake to comment further, "That Indian knows what he's doing. I had never really realized their God is my God too."

As if realizing his comments might later result in negative repercussions for himself, Jake again shook his head side to side and added, "I really hope he doesn't cause us trouble during the trip. It'd just be great if somebody in charge of this operation could explain our purpose in such a convincing and reassuring way." The soldier who had listened to Jake hailed from the low-rolling hills of West Tennessee and was largely neutral on the idea of the treatment of Indians.

The young soldier looked at the perplexed Jake Savage and replied, "I guess we're about to find out. If we want to or not, it's gonna be clear pretty soon if what them people want in Washington's right or wrong. Don't really matter what you or me's contemplatin'. It's gonna happen if we help carry it out or not. Somebody's gotta do it, and I ain't ready to end up shot or on the end of a rope for not follering what we's told to do."

Bugle sounds signaled the onset of the event that had been apparently awaiting the Cherokee for several months. The supervising soldiers had performed their tasks at hand with determination and obvious steadfast resolve. By contrast, the careworn Cherokee, from the youngest child to the tribal elders, had strolled into their places in line in a trance-like state.

With the sun now fully visible and the early morning fog quickly and completely dissipated, the soldiers and the Cherokee, in their respective positions, completed lining up and awaited the onset of the march. The sun glistened on the quickly drying dew as well as through the overhanging leaves and provided a peaceful image that contrasted with the confusion that began as the initial steps of the march were made.

Wagons, horses, and hundreds of Cherokee on foot joined the soldiers in turning their backs toward the holding pens and other structures at Red Clay. Hospital wagons held sick and tearful youngsters, while saddened faces dominated the majority of the Cherokee people.

Any witness to the event would have been totally oblivious to the scene had they failed to sense the glances of those undergoing the exodus. It was easy to notice the large amount of Cherokee, equal numbers of both genders and indifferent to age, turning their heads toward the rear of the train in order to catch what they were certain would be a final glimpse of Red Clay, Tennessee.

The soldiers were largely aware of the quick looks being undertaken. Corporal Savage, sitting atop his horse, took notice of the turning heads of the Cherokee. In witnessing the glances and often hearing the related sobs, Savage felt a deep sense of guilt. He ducked his head toward the neck of his horse and caught a vision of White Crow to his right. With a glimpse in her direction he offered a tight lipped expression and his regular practice of a quick shake of his head in sign of disbelief and disgust.

"Get on now. No need in lollygagging 'round here no more. Ya'll get on and head out or more of you'll die here and it won't be from no sickness." The harsh words of an older soldier, a veteran of years of fighting and ill relations with Native Americans, cut a sharp comparison to the stance of Jake Savage and the small contingency of those of like mind.

Some of the other soldiers were also far less sympathetic than Corporal Savage. These individuals displayed their lack of compassion with the expulsion of angered shouts and emphatic gestures.

One of the more cold-hearted soldiers, a man known throughout the regiment as Aniston, shouted, "It's time to get on, you heathens. My gun's sorta heavy and I don't mind emptying it on you if you don't speed it up."

No less than three soldiers placed their hands near the faces of male and female Cherokee who they determined were too slow in making progress. Another member of the military entourage, a former cavalryman, appeared to snap his gloved fingers toward a lady and placed his boot into the middle of her back. Only the backward movement of the soldier's resistant horse kept the soldier's action from knocking the dazed female to the ground.

The compassion Jake Savage and like-minded soldiers and cavalrymen held far outweighed the volume of the shouts and exaggerated flailing of arms. Nonetheless, the veteran military personnel, as well as those recently inducted, began their burdensome duty of moving the Cherokee contingency from their base and toward an unfamiliar land to the west. None of the group, Native American or soldier, could have envisioned either the mixed array of emotional extremes or challenges to physical endurance that lay ahead.

Chapter 8

The general direction the troupe followed in the early stages of the forced march was toward the Hiwassee River, located northwest of the small settlement of Cleveland, Tennessee. The military personnel were expected to closely watch the Cherokee and to prevent straggling or attempting to escape.

Despite the best efforts of the soldiers to carry out their duties during the primary hours of the relocation, Corporal Jake Savage found it extremely difficult to fully concentrate on the adventure. The earlier incidents involving White Crow, the group of saddened mothers distressed about the loss of their children, and the sight of the neglect of innocent children burned at Savage's heart for the next two days.

Meanwhile, the group of soldiers and Cherokee managed to travel several miles during the first day of the westward movement. This was not an alarming fact, considering the determination of most of the well-rested soldiers and the recent acts of compliance the Cherokee had exhibited throughout the various stages of their incarceration. No incidents of note occurred during the first two days of the journey, yet at least four of the younger males in the group of Cherokee managed to hastily slip away from the wagon train in undetected quests for freedom.

Failing to clearly identify a Cherokee escaping, Corporal Jake Savage actually thought he caught a vision of a moving shadow. In the haze created through the mixture of the early morning sun and the dust from the trail, Savage totally missed the flight of the first three Cherokee. With the level of heat quickly entering into the scenario, Savage had taken a moment to wipe the saturating sweat from his brow. In doing so, he was unsuccessful in realizing that the shadow was, in fact, one of the four escaping Cherokee.

The fleeing of the four Cherokee men occurred as the portion of the group Jake Savage was responsible for guarding was rounding a curve in a wooded section of a narrow road. Unaware of the successful escape, but attempting to negate the possibility, Corporal Savage continued to think of the incidents of the morning and attempted to befriend some of the Cherokee in his charge.

As the steadily advancing train of humans, wagons, and animals reached that curved point of the road, Jake Savage's attention was diverted from daydreaming and personal grooming. The digression was caused by what appeared to be someone running into the trees that thickly lined the right side of the road. Rationalizing the blurred object, Corporal Savage dismissed the vision as a possible mental trick, the result of insufficient drink in the overwhelming sun that was infrequently blocked by sparse overhead foliage.

A headcount of the Cherokee was conducted the next morning, and the act confirmed Corporal Savage's dismissed observance. Each soldier in charge of a detachment of Cherokee was also responsible for an accurate count of his respective party. Jake Savage's count was not the only one to reveal a decrease from the previous day's total. However, he was unaware of the commonality of the count and chose to mentally justify the associated tally as being the result of an inaccurate count conducted at the onset of the march.

In doing so, Corporal Savage's number of people in his group would remain the same, at least on paper. When he was informed of the shortages among other groups, Savage momentarily pondered revealing his vision of the previous day and to attempt to justify what would be disclosed as an inaccurate count that had resulted from inexperience. Fearing a reprisal, or perhaps more fully accepting the act of escape as justifiable, Jake Savage kept the incident to himself for the time being.

"Looks like some of 'em ran away," remarked one of Savage's comrades.

Savage, attempting to remove any foreknowledge of the matter, was quick to reply. "Imagine that. They better not try that when I'm around. I guess we'll have to shoot 'em if we see one of the men trying to run away. I gotta tell all the boys to be especially mindful of any weird movements or actions. Keep your guns loaded."

The early stages of the entourage's movements along the trail also included the group crossing the Tennessee River at a location known as Ross's Landing, a frequently used ford and the site of a trading post. A small amount of provisions for the group were obtained at the landing. While the foodstuffs had been neatly packed into wagons, the realization of the shortage of the needed materials, as well as the substandard quality of what was actually obtained, was not at first recognized.

The site of Ross's Landing would eventually be renamed Chattanooga, and the location later played an integral part in the struggle to control Tennessee during the American Civil War. In addition, the town also became a major iron center in the state of Tennessee. Sadly, an incident at Ross's Landing would lead the location to become a point of sadness and sacrifice in the early days of the relocation process.

As the wagon train progressed through the watery crossing, ruts were created in the riverbed. The heavy-laden wagons struggled to negotiate the crossing, but the vessels were able to overcome the obstacles to some degree, largely through the efforts of trained teamsters.

The intensity of the wagons' weight and the force of the water moving across the wheels required intermittent carriages to be abandoned in an effort to lessen the burden. The speed and strength of the water led the passengers who had exited the wagons to hold to the sides of the wagons in efforts to ensure their personal safety. However, the ability of strong and healthy adults to perform this task was not met with similar success when younger or lighter weight passengers were involved.

A wagon filled with unhealthy children approached the crossing. Many of those aboard the wagon were sleeping as the vessel entered the water. Unfortunately, no one had thought or managed to unload a single passenger prior to the carriage entering the stream. The results of this shenanigan would prove devastating in a matter of a few short minutes.

Some of the children, ranging in age from three to six, were swept from the wagon when a wheel broke. Quickly, yet seeming to take forever in a type of slow motion, the toddlers fell into the swollen river's waters. The heartbroken and panicked mother of two of the children escaped from the nearby guards and attempted to save her children who were among those who had fallen into the rapidly moving waters.

Unfortunately, the mother was also caught in the current, and her body disappeared a short distance from where she entered the water. The driver of the wagon was a young soldier who was among the most respected members of the unit, and he attempted to guide the heavily-laden wagon toward safety. Doing so caused him to jump from the seat at the wagon's front, and he entered the strong currents of the water.

The young soldier became frightened in the chaos and struck the team of horses in a frantic manner as he leaped from his roost. He began yelling at the top of his lungs and attempting to simultaneously gain assistance from anyone within hearing range.

"Here, here! Come on girls, pull us on. Get up now!" His words to the team of animals proved futile as the horses, one by one, lost their footing. The team of four animals also apparently became unnerved and neighed as loudly as the teamster yelled; the children aboard the disintegrating wagon screamed in expressions of panic and fear.

"Help us, boys!" The young man's words were unable to speed up the steps and swimming strokes of those attempting to reach the scene.

The driver pleaded, "Come here and help me, we ain't gonna let these children drown!"

With those words the teamster sprang from his seat and jumped to the left front of the wagon, the site of the recently dismounted wheel. The current pushed the wagon violently in his direction, breaking both of his legs and ripping his left arm from his body. His screams of agony only added panic to the frantic scene, as the eight children on the wagon, now breaking apart in the crashing waves, blood-colored water, and pools of debris, appeared to be consumed by the vessel that was seemingly acting upon the will of a demon.

The mother of one of the screaming children managed to reach the remnants of the ravaged wagon just as her child grasped her hand. As if planned, the mother grabbed the child and the two took a deep breath a split second before disappearing under the churning Tennessee River waters. The remaining children shrieked for help, but they were swept away with the current, destined to meet similar fates.

The scene caused bedlam, but it also created a brief respite from the duality of the groups of people participating in the removal of the Cherokee. Case in point: a desperate situation had resulted in the Cherokee working in conjunction with the military personnel in an effort to save the group of children. At least for a brief moment, the degree of compassion and admiration the soldiers and Native Americans shared were at a high level.

In an effort to restore some semblance of order, the group of people resumed their westward drive. While the wagon train progressed in its movement across the river, a detachment of a dozen soldiers and six Cherokee men went in search of the children. Only one of the children's bodies was found, and it was decapitated, apparently the result of the wagon falling on the child's body. The other children, the two mothers, and the wagon were evidently taken miles away. As far as any members of the party knew, no reports of the discovery or recovery of the additional dead or the carriage were ever known to be made.

A family of Cherokee took advantage of the confusion of the situation and managed to escape the movement at that time. Yielding to their own desire to escape what was viewed as an inevitable fate similar in nature to that of the wagon-load of children, the group seized the advantage of the moment's mayhem and fled. Ironically, Marcus Aniston, the soldier who had yelled at the Cherokee during the early stages of the journey was near the family and unsuccessfully attempted to end the escape attempt.

"Hey! Where do you think you're goin'? Ya' bunch a heathens. Git on back here." Aniston's words continued clearly exhibit both his hatred for the Cherokee as well as his lack of education.

Driving his horse toward the riverbank where the Cherokee family had disappeared into the brush, Aniston seemed to also be enveloped by the vegetation. Jake Savage saw Aniston dismount his horse, yet Corporal Savage believed the act to have been from falling or being pulled from his mount. Another soldier entered the underbrush a few seconds after Aniston, only to find Aniston's dead body.

Marcus Aniston had earned a solid reputation as a violent soldier; ironically, he was found with his skull crushed. A rock covered with blood and hair lay on the river bank near his body. His horse, presumed to have been used in the escape of the Cherokee family, was nowhere to be found.

With some stroke of luck the family of five Cherokee managed to safety in a nearby cave. In order to account for the loss of these and the children, it was stated that the river must have claimed them all. For this or some other reason, the hunt for the missing family was never undertaken. The majority of soldiers, discussed in hushed tones, held the belief that Marcus Aniston's death was the catalyst involved in an immediate neglect of searching for the escapees.

A soldier who had closely witnessed all but Aniston's actual death was heard to exclaim, "Murder is murder, and somebody must answer."

While these words were uttered to Corporal Savage and a soldier nearby, it was a widespread feeling that the soldier whose skull was crushed was much more deserving of his fate than had been the teamster who died soon after his broken body had been pulled from the water and placed on the bank that was on the opposite side of the river.

The soldier who had given his life in a futile attempt to rescue the Cherokee children in his care was buried next to the lone recovered corpse of the Cherokee child. Mourners from both groups shared in the short service that was held that afternoon at the location where the wagon train stopped to camp.

By contrast, the soldier whose head was crushed had been buried at the top of the river bank where he was killed, only a short distance from where the family of five Cherokee successfully sought refuge. Unknown to the burial party was the fact that the hiding family heard the comments of the group's members as they hastily dug the grave and buried the body.

When the soldiers returned to the location of Marcus Aniston's internment months later, they discovered the grave of the murdered soldier in a state of disrepair. His body had been removed from the site. The corpse had been dismembered, not from the bites of ravenous animals, but cut apart with sharpened instruments used in an act of disrespect. There the bones lay unburied, as none of the discoverers of the bones held remorse or enough respect to conduct a funeral service during their quest to return to their respective homes.

Chapter 9

Corporal Jake Savage and White Crow were among approximately seven hundred original members of the Bell Group. That contingency was comprised of a collection of Cherokee men, women and children, as well as soldiers in the United States Army. The varied crowd of people had initially begun their westward migration with approximately three hundred twenty horses, in addition to those used to pull the fifty-six wagons. With supplies being aboard some of the wagons, the initial days of the relocation had allowed for proper food consumption and plentiful foraging for the animals.

The amount of provisions the assemblage possessed at the time of its departure, coupled with a small amount of consumable foodstuffs from the predominantly unsuitable items received in the early stages of the journey, initially allowed a majority of the members of the Bell Group to maintain their proper level of nourishment. That bright spot in an otherwise dark situation soon became clouded when the composition of the group was altered.

A number of other smaller parties eventually mingled into the detachment, creating both more camaraderie and strength in numbers for the Cherokee. However, the consolidation also brought about an unfortunate strain and drain on the available resources. While the supply of food and other supplies were sufficient for the number of participants in the original troupe, the same proved to be far below what was required for the steadily increasing immigrants.

Plans had not adequately provided for the massive numbers of human and animal foragers moving through various points of the trail.

As such, Corporal Jake Savage's personal doubts about the inefficient leadership of the U. S. military, points he had earlier pondered and clearly expressed, seemed to also become more apparent to the individuals participating in the forced march.

Likewise, the sudden abandonment of their homes had not provided the Cherokee with ample time in which they could gather proper clothing or sufficient numbers of blankets. In addition, numerous issues involving the infrequent distribution of proper food had hampered the captives since their placement into the holding pens. As an overall result, a notable number of people among the Cherokee lacked a suitable level of nourishment and corresponding amount of health required for undertaking, not to mention survive, the lengthy march they faced.

The lack of adequate forage soon began to cause horses in the drawing teams to fall victim to malnourishment. Another aspect of the increasing death rate for these animals was undoubtedly related to the fact that the privation of foodstuffs had not resulted in lessening the loads of provisions and/or human cargo the horses were expected to pull along the primitive roads that served as the group's planned course.

"There's not even enough food for the teams," one of the soldiers stated in a grumbling manner. "All of this crowd and we gotta go hungry 'cause ain't no more to eat. Who's gonna die next, us or them Indians?"

The soldier's harsh statements were laced with an unfortunate air of foreboding. There was, in fact, a challenging situation in regard to members of which faction, the Cherokee or the soldiers, would become the next to fall victim to the situation. In addition, there was the regularly-noted fact that there was an inefficient amount of food for both groups. There was also, though not part of the soldier's proclamation, an increasing level of tension on a daily basis.

The positive aspect of the fact that proper forage was in short supply was that the train's animals were beginning to succumb to starvation. The result was that the carcasses of the horses came to provide suitable, though not strongly-desired sources of meat for the famished travelers. While the meat from some of the horses was aged and, in turn, far less than easily-consumed, it did prove to be a temporary relief from the insufficient diet available at the time.

"I guess I've had worse," a comrade of Corporal Savage's stated. "We've gotta put up with them filthy people all day long and listen to 'em gripe. Then we eat the same mess they do, stuff like I never ate at home or while I've been wearing this uniform. It's ridiculous!"

"Bet it's better than anything you've ever cooked," was Jake Savage's reply. "Lookin' at you, I'd say you ain't missed too many meals in the last year. I don't like eating horse meat any more than you, or probably than those folks do. We can hope that these people help us track some animals along the way. Otherwise, there's gonna be some dying going on."

"Won't bother me. Less of them Indians to look after will make it a lot easier on us. Ain't got as many to take care of and yell at all the time. Besides, that'll mean more food for us too." The soldier obviously held little admiration for the Cherokee captives.

Jake Savage expressed his disgust with the soldier's statement in saying, "You keep thinking and talking like that. Those Cherokee don't take too long to figure out where a man stands with them. Before you know it, we'll have a fight on our hands. Some of them will grow even more upset at us and begin running away. They may decide to take you, me, or someone else before they leave. They'll kill somebody. Remember Marcus Aniston?" Savage's words bore a sense of warning to the soldier.

Not to be outdone, the soldier tersely replied, "You likely know about 'em runnin. From what I hear, some of your guard ran away before we got very far out. Word of that reaches the officers, and you'll be done for. Maybe you need to eat more horse meat and watch 'em closer. Don't worry about me saying nothing; I've lost a few myself. Wouldn't bother me none if some more of 'em drowned or ran off. When we get back home, I'm leaving this detail and findin' me another way to make money. Life's too short to be dealin' with this kind of work."

The rest of the day largely passed peacefully, with no sense of tension exhibited among the soldiers. The same could not be said for the relationship between the soldiers and the Cherokee. The lack of proper food apparently added to the growing animosity the two major groups involved in the relocation process held for one another.

Private Stephen Willis, a young soldier on horseback, managed to pull a portion of jerky from his saddlebag during the final miles of the day's route. A group of almost twenty Cherokee located nearby passed resentful looks toward the soldier. Willis witnessed the glances and heard Cherokee making comments that were undoubtedly related to their disgust.

An act of kindness temporarily lessened the tension when Private Willis pulled his horse to the rear of a wagon and passed the remaining contents of his saddlebag to the Cherokee children riding aboard the craft. The young man may have offered the meat as an act of pure kindness, but the rationale was just as likely to have been that he perceived a need for self-preservation from the hungered children who greatly outnumbered him.

Prior to making the offer of food to the children, Private Willis had performed a quick scan of the advancing Cherokee onlookers and evaluated the situation with an open mind. The looks he had received from the Native Americans were a mixture of strong animosity and utter hunger. Passing out the pieces of meat served as the epitome of a good-will effort and likely saved the young soldier's life. At least for the time being, the action also allowed him to avoid serious bodily injury.

The Cherokee men who had been inching toward Private Stephen Willis halted their steps when one of the men in the group held his hands outward in an apparent sign to hold their ground. The immediate outcome caused the group to not encroach upon Willis or the Cherokee children.

"Y'all look like you might enjoy this. Come on and try some; it'll help you make it through the day." Looking for approval from any adult within range, the reluctant children yielded to the soldier's request when one of the wagon's older children, a boy who appeared to be about nine or ten years old, took a portion of one of the pieces of jerky from the soldier.

"There you go. See, we can all get along. I don't want to hurt any of you. Sure don't want to see a kid hungry." Private Willis's cautious actions and continuous glances toward the Cherokee adults clearly indicated that he was as uncomfortable with the gesture as were the hungry children. News of his conversation and the related actions of Private Willis quickly spread throughout the ranks of the Cherokee.

The camaraderie the generous soldier managed to invoke with the wagon load of Cherokee children appeared to be conveyed to the other soldiers as well. At least for a short time during the early hours of the night, the tension between the members of the U.S. military and the Cherokee captives appeared to be lessened.

The soldiers who gathered around their campfire that night seemed to enjoy the renewed fellowship that the horsemeat and subsequent distribution of the same had somehow managed to create. Just as the laughter and relaxation appeared to be the norm, orders came for Corporal Savage and a number of those around him to relieve soldiers guarding some of the Cherokee.

"Corporal Savage, it's your turn. They seem a little rambunctious tonight. Better tell your boys to keep their powder dry. Remember, sharp eyes tonight." Those words from another corporal seemed filled with tension and indicated a sense of alarm, if not foreboding, for Jake Savage and his group who would fill the need for the night's guard detail.

"All right boys, looks like it's time to earn this horsemeat supper. Let's get to it. Be vigilant tonight. From what he said," Jake paused and nodded toward the other soldier, "we may have some issues tonight."

"Sounds like one of those great times to be a soldier. Tired but full. I think I may have trouble staying awake." With those words Wade Heatherton, one of the soldiers in Corporal Savage's guard detail, laughed as he stood up and retrieved his musket from its place of rest.

A rather obese man, Heatherton was known for his great sense of humor and astounding appetite. While he was full of leadership potential, Heatherton made it apparent that he was a soldier who was only interested in seeing different parts of the country and in leading others into situations or locations where they would not likely want to go. The admiration Heatherton held among most of the men, combined with his physical size and excessive strength, caused anyone holding an authoritative position to be desirous of remaining on his positive side.

Corporal Jake Savage, apparently more moved by the other corporal's warning than were those around him, took exception to the nonchalant perspective Heatherton and those laughing at his comments possessed. Literally biting his lip, Savage carefully pondered his words as he issued a warning that was undeniably fused with an order.

"That's enough men! We have to be sharp. The time to be serious is now. Those people may try something tonight. It may be running away. It may be killing one of us." Jake Savage's words rang true in the ears of those standing to join him for guard duty.

"It could be you." Jake Savage had never uttered sterner words, nor certainly any more direct prose than he did at that time. His pointed comments, filled with frequent glances toward Wade Heatherton, motivated the remaining members of his detachment to pick up their weapons and make their way toward their posts for the evening.

Fortunately, the remainder of the night passed without the occurrence of a single negative incident. Aside from the distribution of the less than desirable meat to the wagonload of children, another reason for this may have been the mood Savage set for the guard detail. Full stomachs and alert guard details combined to make a difficult situation far more bearable.

In addition, the march of recent days had left the soldiers and Cherokee extremely tired. The vast majority of the Cherokee huddled in family units and took advantage of what was the best night's sleep of the journey to this point. A member of Corporal Savage's guard detail offered the statement that he felt more comfortable that night than he had during any dealings he had had with the Cherokee. The peace and quiet present that night would seldom be obtained throughout the remainder of the relocation process.

A notable incident took place during the night. That particular occasion initiated a series of events and significantly affected the lives of two people, each one from an opposite side of the forced march. While heavily guarded groups of Cherokee, never numbering more than five, made their way toward a nearby stream in order to wash or relieve themselves, White Crow and Jake Savage briefly conversed.

"You seem more peaceful than the last time we spoke." Jake's words appeared to be more of a concerned nature than those of a soldier charged with guarding a captive. His words initially rendered no response. However, Jake Savage's obvious interest in the young Cherokee female invoked another statement.

Jake Savage continued his inquiry, "Did you get enough to eat? I understand that some supply wagons are coming here from a fort that's not too far away. They are supposed to arrive in the next couple of days. If they do, that should give us enough food for a while, some good food at that. We'll also be meeting another group of wagons later; or at least that's what I'm hearing. Just, just let me know if there's something you or any of your people need. I don't want any of you to suffer any more than you already have."

White Crow ceased her movement toward the stream and stared angrily into Jake Savage's eyes. "Suffer. Your people took all of us, my people, from our homes. We are strong. I am fine, and my people will be fine. You even watch us as we bathe or make waste."

Jake Savage responded, "I think you know that I am not to blame. You have to understand this is a job I have to do. Please let me help you. We can get through this somehow and maybe even become friends. I don't want to hurt you or any of your people. I hope that you'll realize that. I am a man of my word. It's not good for us to talk too much, but I want to make the best of this for you, me, and our people."

White Crow managed a brief but sincere smile and said, "I believe you, I think. I have watched you. You are not like so many of your soldier brothers. You are still one of them though. Thank you for your words and for trying to help us. I will remember your words. Now please, leave me alone. My people don't want to be any closer to you. Like you said, it is not good for us to talk too much. I think we have already spoken too many words, ones that mean little unless you act on them. Words can be said and nothing done. Is that what you offer?"

While a brief respite from the ordeal of hunger had been provided through the events of the day, not all aspects of the recent hours were positive. An obvious negative point was focused on the elderly, the invalids, and a host of small children. Many of them were among those who were originally passengers in the some of the wagons which had deceased pull teams. The animals were gone, and the aforementioned individuals were now being forced to walk. As a result, injuries became more frequent and ranged from turned ankles to more serious snake bites and sunstrokes.

The possibility of long-term foraging was negated, as there was nowhere to store additional foodstuffs. Empty wagons had been routinely abandoned along the trail in recent days. Horses, at least those not becoming sources of food for the hungered soldiers and Cherokee, originally used to pull the vessels, had been left on the trial's wayside.

Residents who maintained home sites along the trail eventually claimed the wagons and any supplies that were left behind. At times, these actions were done almost immediately upon their abandonment. Corporal Jake Savage and others in the group, Cherokee and soldiers alike, often witnessed local citizens waiting beside the trail, apparently grasping any opportunity to gain possession of a wagon or its contents. More often than not, the vessels left behind contained a sufficient enough amount of a variety of supplies that the new owners could sell or consume.

One of the soldiers who became the most disgusted at the abandonment of the wagons and of the combined presence of his personal hunger was Stephen Willis, the soldier who had fed strips of meat from his personal allotment to hungry Cherokee children riding in a wagon.

"I ain't gonna kill a child, but I'm not gonna kill myself by not eatin'. These Indians ain't no better than me. All they been doin' to me is beggin' for food since I first shared some with 'em. I'm finished trying to help 'em out." Willis's words intrigued Jake Savage who took it upon himself to question Willis's drastic and seemingly sudden change of attitude.

"What happened? Didn't it make you feel better when you helped out those kids?"

"I got a little brother and sister back home. My drunk pappy probably lets 'em go hungry while he's at the tavern. When we wrap up this foray I'm heading home, getting them young 'uns and making it better for 'em. Not gonna give up my stuff anymore to take care of these stinkin' animals. That's what they are, animals. Our goats in our yard smell better than those little ones do. I say it's take care of your own, and these Indians don't mean nothing to me."

Jake Savage replied, "You can't mean that; they're people. We've all gotta give to make sure they make it to where we're headed."

"We're all headed to a grave if we don't eat. You need to get that through your head and forget about that little squaw you've been chasin." With that, Stephen Willis pulled his horse's reigns to the left, kicked his mount, and rode away.

Corporal Jake Savage looked to his right and saw White Crow. The beautiful maiden, recently walking as closely as possible to Savage's steed, had witnessed the brief but heated exchange between Jake Savage and Stephen Willis. White Crow was steadily growing more appreciative of Savage, primarily for his display of compassion toward the Cherokee. She looked into Savage's eyes and offered a wide smile.

"Better be careful, Jake Savage. She'll grin at you and cut your throat at the same time. Don't let her pretty smile and that nice little dress fool you. Willis may be right. It's either them or us. She's a killer, a savage. Your name and her instincts. They're the same." The words came from a soldier who admired Jake Savage, but also feared for the safety of all of those engaged in the responsibility of moving the Cherokee westward.

Chapter 10

Corporal Jake Savage's earlier conversation with White Crow had regarded the arrival of supply wagons. Sadly, the soldier's prophecy had failed to be readily fulfilled, as days passed without additional relief from the shortage of food and other needed supplies. The result of this fact, not relegated to the interpersonal relationship between Jake and White Crow, was the increase in animosity. Likewise, hunger and sickness also became more prevalent among the members of both the soldiers and the Cherokee.

As the days passed and the troupe made its way further west, the frequency of clashes within the ranks of the military personnel increased. Jake Savage had heated words with no less than three other soldiers who questioned Savage's obvious feelings toward White Crow or made accusations regarding his lack of compliance with orders from his superiors. While the Cherokee seemed totally committed to maintaining supportive relationships within their race, the soldiers, reportedly far more civilized than their captives, regularly broke into heated arguments or rude exchanges with one or more of their comrades. The strain of maintaining his more passive position toward the Cherokee crept into Jake Savage's conduct toward White Crow as well.

The primary sources of animosity lay on the part of the bulk of the soldiers toward the Cherokee. Although most of the Cherokee spoke clear English and many of them possessed the ability to write it as well or better than members of the guard detail, the frequent use of a "foreign language" to communicate within the Cherokee ranks deeply aggravated a large number of the soldiers. Those members of the army tended to resort to violent means of discipline directed toward the captive Native Americans. Hateful words and actions seemed to multiply as the soldiers' levels of disgust increased almost as rapidly as the amount of control they held over the Cherokee decreased.

Irregular meals and the various maladies associated with being confined to a saddle for hours upon end caused an increasing number of the soldiers to become aggressive toward the Cherokee. As had taken place in the early stages of the trail and would take place in an almost innumerable amount of days in the remainder of the journey, horses would be used as battering rams against the Cherokee. That type of aggressiveness occurred as the captives marched too slowly to satisfy their captors, entered what soldiers perceived as safe distances from the Cherokee, or failed to maintain what was seen as coherent grouping.

When the hot summer weather began to give way to cooler nights, the necessity of proper covering added to the level of discomfort for the weary travelers. Stern requests for blankets were issued on behalf of the group. Many of the hard-hearted of the soldiers often gave their blankets to the Cherokee children rather than seeing or hearing the youngsters suffer on the increasingly cold nights. The inability of some of the troopers to comprehend spur-of-the-moment acts of kindness among their peers added more tension within the ranks of the soldiers.

A sad aspect of the journey lay in the fact that blankets from a Tennessee smallpox hospital were issued to the Cherokee. The act was two-fold. While providing a clear means of disposal for the otherwise unwanted blankets, it also gave a means by which the "less desirable" or "savages" would be infected with smallpox and ultimately meet an untimely demise. As had been noted during the earlier history of the American nation, this was not an effective means of warfare; the smallpox virus was not regularly transmitted through such a means.

However, when knowledge of the disbursement of the blankets was circulated in period newspapers and through word of mouth, most towns, villages, and hamlets along the trail refused to allow the Cherokee to pass through or near the area where the objectors lived. After all, the Cherokee, a group already regularly deemed as subhuman in many locations across the Southeastern U. S., now faced the added weight of possibly being carriers of a deadly disease.

In addition, the members of the military lacked a great deal of admiration among many residents along the trail. There were rumors of theft, physical abuse, and a lack of respect for any personal property. Assuredly, some soldiers took advantage of free-roaming domestic animals in the area and likely made fair game of other property. However, the vast majority of men, such as Jake Savage, were simply attempting to carry out their duties efficiently and in a timely manner.

As a result of the disbursement of the blankets and the widespread accusations of misconduct on the part of the military personnel, the band of displaced travelers had to regularly take long routes around settlements that lay in the path of the intended trial. This was allegedly done in order to allow the Cherokee and their guards to avoid the agitated and possibly evil-minded white citizens of each area.

The rationale stood upon the issue of the local homesteaders possibly encountering a source of smallpox and likely causing an epidemic. In turn, homeowners at various points along the trail continued to act as snipers in order to lower the numbers of the "less desirable" travelers. Those targeting the troupe reportedly aimed their weapons toward the Cherokee. Nonetheless, it was not uncommon for a soldier or his horse to be struck with a projectile fired from the gun of an unseen civilian marksman.

At least from a long-range perspective, such conduct would also persuade any of the soldiers from establishing a permanent residence in the area after his time of service had reached its conclusion. The hypocrisy, as well as the distrust of the government, was widespread among the people who lived in the areas that were traversed in the opening months of the trail.

A small number of the people who took shots at the Cherokee and succeeded with their marksmanship also attempted to sue the United States government. The lawsuits called for a payment of thirty five dollars for each murdered member of the beleaguered individuals. The fee was estimated to be needed in order to properly bury each of the butchered Indians. One such case of corruption involved a Tennessean named Jason Turner.

Turner was known in the area where he resided as a hardhearted individual whose animosity toward anyone other than his family, and sometimes in their direction as well, was evident. The would-be assassin presented a rather imposing sight, standing 6 feet and 3 inches tall with a muscular frame and knife-scared face. A middle-aged farmer, Jason Turner spent most of three separate afternoons firing intermittent shots into the entourage as it proceeded along the road that bordered the northern edge of his Middle Tennessee farm.

Jason Turner's patient and accurate aim proved fatal to no less than fifteen Cherokee men and at least three each of the banished children and women. The actual number may have been higher, but at least two of his victims fell into a river running along the trail and their bodies were swept away. This fact angered the high-strung Turner, resulting in him taking aim at another Cherokee who was mourning one of the most recent fatalities. The cold-hearted Turner ceased his rampage only upon running out of projectiles for his weapon. His bill of seven hundred thirty-five dollars was sent through a local official and was paid to Turner within a month of the deadly endeavor.

During the last afternoon of Turner's indiscriminate murderous escapade, a group of seven Cherokee men, none older than twenty years of age, managed to take advantage of the hysteria the carnage had evoked. The result was that the young men planned and implemented an escape from the trail and into the surrounding countryside.

Soldiers intermittently fired shots in the direction of the fleeing Cherokee, but none of the four combatants shooting at them managed to hit their marks. The inability to strike their targets would eventually lead others to question the true intentions of the soldiers who apparently felt no guilt at the fact they were unable to cause the escaping men to slow or end their determined flights toward freedom.

"Let 'em run. They'll die out there before long," were the words of Stephen Willis.

"This is how it's done." With those words, Willis, atop his horse, took aim with his rifle and struck one of the escapees in the right hand.

The seemingly lucky shot removed the index and middle fingers from the left hand of a male Cherokee child.

"You could have done that if you'd tried. You must be growing soft on them. It ain't worth it; all they'll do is bother you like a pack of wild dogs. I'll see that you're written up for allowin' them to leave. That little buck I shot will bleed to death out there like the animal he is." Willis had become obsessed with his disdain for the Cherokee and was more determined than ever to eliminate any individual who failed to agree with his new-found stance. His attitude was present in some who served with him, but others held a far more compassionate attitude toward the Cherokee, especially as the journey endured.

Chapter 11

The military's policy of the time did not allow any of the Native Americans to slow the march or otherwise attempt to assist an injured or sick Cherokee. That same guiding principle, despite the intentions of some of the soldiers, was irregularly enforced. The general mood of the respective day seemed to dictate the level of the soldiers' compassion exhibited toward the Cherokee and the directly correlated amount of miles to be covered on any given day. Earlier episodes, most notably the one involving Jason Turner, had caused Corporal Jake Savage and most of the other soldiers to attempt to force the continued flow of the Cherokee along the trail.

A teenaged Cherokee girl stated that she felt the man who was shooting the Cherokee was one of the soldiers, as not a single shot approached the vicinity of a member of the guard detail. Such indiscrete proclamations, as well as the inconsistencies regarding assistance toward the sick and injured Cherokee, gradually led to the return of a lack of trust and increased tension between the Cherokee and the soldiers assigned to guard and protect them.

As the days passed and the group made its westward passage along the trail, the growth of the tense coexistence between the soldiers and the Cherokee reached a seemingly insurmountable level. The major catalyst that came to provide the relocation journey with its heart-wrenching name that lives in history actually took place due to the lack of proper food and nourishment the Cherokee people received.

When a particular Cherokee mother on the trail lost her malnourished infant to a slow and painful death, Jake Savage was ordered to keep the grieving mother marching. Included in the command Corporal Savage received was that he was to avoid allowing the grieved matriarch to bury her deceased infant or even briefly pause to offer a prayer on the child's behalf.

The anguish of the past weeks' incidents, coupled with the near animalistic manner in which the Cherokee had been herded and hurried along the trail, caused Corporal Savage to reevaluate his assigned tasks and performance of orders. Jake Savage managed to hide his inner turmoil until his superior commanders had all passed the scene of the distraught mother lamenting the loss of her child.

Corporal Jake Savage, in an act that defied his orders, initially instructed the saddened mother to quickly bury her child. She was also asked to immediately rejoin the march upon the completion of the interment. However, the soldier was overcome with sympathy as he witnessed the Cherokee lady attempting to dig a suitable grave in the soil of a small ravine some ten feet from the edge of the trail. Accompanied by another soldier and two male Cherokee teens, Jake Savage began assisting in the digging.

Corporal Savage expressed his sympathy to the saddened mistress who clearly sensed the sincerity of the young soldier's comments. As the ordeal progressed, the vast majority of Cherokee slowly continued to pass the scene under the close supervision of Jake Savage's subordinates, although none of the Native Americans failed to seize an opportunity to acknowledge the situation.

Shouts of "Uwedolisdi," the Cherokee word for sympathy, were regularly heard as the caravan of saddened individuals passed the scene of the grief-stricken mother burying her child. "Adadolisdi," a word that meant "sympathize" to the Cherokee people, also resounded when the various mourners reached the location.

White Crow was among the handful of exceptions to those forced to continue the march. She joined approximately five other Cherokee of a wide age range, as well as another soldier, in joining the final preparations of the quickly dug grave and assisting in the subsequent burial of the recently deceased toddler.

As one soldier held the reigns of Corporal Jake Savage's horse, the guard regularly turned his head to maintain visual contact with the nearby small contingency of Cherokee. A third soldier continued to assist the visibly-shaken corporal as Savage joined the effort in the burial of the child.

"I'm so sorry for what has happened. Nobody, especially a child, deserves this kind of death. It ain't a great burial, but I'll try to help you make it that way." Corporal Savage's words were filled with sincerity. Jake's voice broke as the emotion of the moment overwhelmed him.

"You are a good man," the lady stated as she wiped tears from her face. "My people know you are not like so many of your friends. You will see no harm from my people."

This exchange of conversation was a matter White Crow witnessed, and it caused her to smile at Savage. As Jake Savage, the second soldier, and the small group of Cherokee accompanied the bereaved mother back onto the trail, they heard approaching horses.

In the company of six soldiers, Colonel Mark Tetleton, Savage's commander, neared the burial party and the distraught mother. Tetleton was obviously angered and began shouting in the direction of Jake Savage, yet the steps of the horses rendered Colonel Tetleton's words inaudible.

"Did I not make myself clear?" were the first of Colonel Tetleton's words that Savage and the others understood as they were questioned. "I hope there's a reasonable explanation about why you have disobeyed my orders. There are to be no stragglers on this trip. Why, Corporal Savage, have you and these people lagged behind?"

"Sir, there's been an accident. I've rounded up these people who were assisting this lady who had fallen into the ravine and appeared trapped in the undergrowth." Jake Savage impressed those Cherokee around him with his obvious but convincing lie.

"This ravine?" questioned Colonel Mark Tetleton as he pointed to the tearful mother of the deceased child. "Your conduct of late has been questionable Savage. I'll see for myself where this alleged entrapment occurred."

Colonel Tetleton and four of his accompanying soldiers took Jake Savage, the two additional soldiers, the mother in mourning, and White Crow and walked to the edge of the steep-banked ravine. When the location of the grave was reached, Corporal Savage managed to falsify the location as that where the mother had become entangled in the brush.

While the grave had been covered with vines and branches from nearby sources, the area did in fact hold the appearance of a spot from which the emotional and grieving mother had struggled to free herself.

Corporal Savage quickly took charge of the personally-threatening situation in stating, "This is where she was found. We heard her screams for help and I forced these Cherokee to come with me and these two soldiers. I wanted to be sure she wasn't faking some kind of injury and trying to escape. If she'd really been hurt we would have shot her or knocked her senseless. No need in one of them slowing the progress. I wanted to make sure she was sincere."

Colonel Tetleton looked at the other two soldiers with an inquisitive glance. The men, despite the fear of retribution, confirmed Corporal Savage's words by nodding their heads to the affirmative. Having witnessed the positive outcome of Savage's ploy, the two privates felt compelled to preserve the mother's secret. At least in this respect, deceit was the apparent victor.

"Very well, Corporal Savage. You have apparently provided a true statement in relation to the situation. Let's rejoin the main body immediately. Perhaps there will be no more falling into ravines or inhibiting the speed of the march." Although his sarcasm was evident, Colonel Tetleton appeared satisfied with the statements, as did those who had been with Jake Savage. The child's burial site as well as the burial itself remained well-kept and heavily-guarded secrets.

The impromptu charade managed to convince Colonel Mark Tetleton that Corporal Savage had fulfilled the request made of him. In addition, Colonel Tetleton was certain that Jake Savage had managed to keep the lady, whose true identity as a bereaved mother remained undiscerned, on the trail and moving westward.

Corporal Jake Savage's cohorts in the misguided tale, two privates surnamed Howell and Perry, glanced at Savage upon the conclusion of the conversation with Colonel Tetleton. The three soldiers nodded toward one another, making a silent pact among themselves to stand firm to the adherence to Jake Savage's words which he had proposed to Tetleton.

More pleasing to Jake Savage was the look he received from White Crow. The lovely maiden looked deeply into Savage's eyes and appeared to praise him in saying, "You are good."

Those words from White Crow inspired Jake Savage to forever maintain his secrecy regarding the burial of the Cherokee child. Jake also made a determined decision to do everything within his power to shield White Crow from any type of harm. The plan to keep the burial of the child a secret would be a far easier task to accomplish than the latter, keeping White Crow safe, would prove to be.

Chapter 12

Lieutenant George Brantley, Corporal Jake Savage's regimental commander, was assigned the task of being in charge of the relocation of the Bell Group, one of over a dozen clusters of Cherokee who were being forcefully pushed westward. The number of people comprising the Cherokee and soldiers within these groups continued to vary. In turn, so did the amount of available supplies and provisions within each.

In relation to the Bell Group, there would be two additional crossings of the Tennessee River in the future. Each of these endeavors yielded far less tragic results than the first, that being when a wheel fell off a wagon and several people met untimely deaths near what became the city of Chattanooga.

The Tennessee River crossing near Savannah, Tennessee enabled another small group of Cherokee to escape. The slowness of the first groups to actually progress to the opposite side of the body of water resulted in a massive bottleneck at the location. Those Cherokee who brought up the rear facilitated the captives near the back of the line to make an uninterrupted trek for nearby woods. Soldiers in the rear guard were largely occupied with another matter at the time and their inattentiveness led to the quick dispersal of escapees.

Perhaps intended as a decoy, a Cherokee mother and her child fell from the rear of a wagon as the vessel entered the swiftly moving waters near the center of the river. Apparently in extreme danger of drowning, the duo began screaming and flailing their arms in a state of panic. Two sympathetic soldiers who attempted to provide assistance to the mother and child were pulled from their horses. The first was able to make his way to the safety of calmer waters, and he soon reached the banks of the river. The second soldier, unable to swim, joined the mother and child in screaming for help.

The incident drew the attention of the majority of people on either bank, where those who had completed the crossing gathered on the western bank. Others awaiting entry into the waters seemed bewildered at the situation unfolding a short distance from where they stood. Avoiding their training to maintain vigilance, all of the soldiers' attention focused upon the struggling group in the river. Seizing the opportunity, five males and two females quickly crossed the open field that joined the river bank where the majority of the Bell Group stood. It took little time for the determined individuals to traverse the field of approximately one hundred yards in length.

No shots were fired at the escaping Cherokee. This was largely due to the fact that the shouts of men, women, and children on both sides of the river shielded the screams of soldiers who were attempting to alert their comrades of the getaway. Those same soldiers who had the angle of view that enabled them to witness the escape were located too far from the fleeing Native Americans to effectively fire at them. By the time a soldier was able to cross the river and gain the attention of a distracted officer, the escaping Cherokee were well on their way to safety.

A group of four soldiers, later sent to retrieve the group of Cherokee escapees, was unsuccessful in the attempt to capture the Native Americans. In fact, one of the soldiers, an immigrant named Vincent Martini, was killed when he slipped off a small cliff only a short distance from the point where the escape occurred. Martini was a corporal and was leading three privates on the quest to locate the seven Cherokee.

Corporal Martini had become separated from the three soldiers and called out, "I have one of them. It's a young girl."

At that moment one of the three remaining soldiers heard what he described as a thud preceding the unmistakable sound of small tree branches breaking. The sounds of scampering feet and the continual cracking of limbs continued to fill the air. Running toward the sounds, the three soldiers who had made the movement with Corporal Martini found the body of Martini, with his skull burst open, lying at the base of a fifteen-foot drop off.

Questions existed as to whether Corporal Martini fell or if he had been pushed from the eminence when he approached the girlfriend of one of the escaping Cherokee males. The quick examination of Martini's corpse yielded little information in relation to the cause of his death. It did provide a confirmation of what Lieutenant Brantley proposed, that either the fall upon rocks at the cliff's base, or Martini's head being hit with a rock had provided fatal wound. A bloody rock found near Corporal Martini's body only added credence to the argument that Martini was likely the victim of an enraged Cherokee male.

Another aspect of the Corporal Martini incident took place with the mother and son who fell from a wagon. When a soldier reached the duo and attempted to assist them, the matriarch produced a knife and stabbed the man in his heart. The mother and her child, a boy about seven years old, managed to get on his horse. With no one else in range of the couple, the mother and her son were able to move from the water and ride to safety. The body of the murdered soldier, as well as that of the soldier who was unable to swim, was retrieved in a short time.

Jake Savage, White Crow, and the hundreds of forgotten individuals involved in one or another aspect of the Trail of Tears knew little of the details of the Martini incident and continued their trek. The westward movement involved the group traversing the terrain of southern Middle Tennessee, climbing Monteagle Mountain on the Cumberland Plateau and moving through a number of Tennessee towns such as Winchester and Fayetteville.

The descent along the southwestern side of Monteagle Mountain enabled Jake Savage and White Crow to briefly make contact in a positive manner. The steep trail on which the Bell Group was traveling had become slick with the rains of the past two days. People and animals alike found the footing insufficient to properly progress along the trail, and the number of falls and related scrapes and similar injuries mounted quickly.

Jake Savage pulled his horse beside White Crow as she traveled on foot and assisted an elderly lady who was having great difficulty staying afoot. The seemingly inevitable exchange of conversation lent itself into a compassionate direction. Corporal Savage led his horse to the side of the trail where White Crow continued to struggle in her efforts to help the elderly lady move along the mountain trail.

"Hold on to the saddle. That'll help both of you." Jake Savage's words were quickly adhered to and apparently welcomed on the part of White Crow. There appeared to be no insurmountable language barrier as White Crow quickly intervened.

White Crow turned to the older lady and stated something in Cherokee, a language Jake Savage was unable to fully understand. Corporal Savage had an extremely brief time to see the reaction of the elderly woman. A broad smile came across her wrinkled face as she shook her head in a positive manner and waited for White Crow to walk to the opposite side of the horse.

Jake Savage readily responded by asking the elderly Cherokee lady to take his place atop the horse he had been riding. A quick translation and explanation from White Crow led to the aged woman's acceptance of Jake Savage's offer. At that point, Jake Savage and White Crow worked together to assist the tearful matriarch in taking her place in Savage's saddle.

Several times during the descent of Monteagle Mountain, White Crow and the elderly lady, who Jake Savage learned was called Wise Leaf, engaged in conversation. Twice, White Crow's response to Wise Leaf's comments was to look at Jake Savage and bow her head in apparent embarrassment, resembling the look of a teenage girl who had been staring at her subject of a crush. The level of affection that was quickly developing between White Crow and Jake Savage was becoming more clearly apparent by the day.

The conversation and time of matchmaking in which White Crow and Jake Savage had participated under the watchful eyes of Wise Leaf provided a strong contrast to the resentment the same three individuals and those with them had felt and were to eventually experience.

Aside from the occasional ridicule from citizens along the route no noteworthy acts occurred in any of these towns. There would be name calling directed toward the soldiers and the Cherokee, providing justification for avoiding so many of the other settlements along the way.

Near the Tennessee towns of Winchester and Fayetteville, residents yelled at the soldiers, warning the blue-clad troopers to heighten the pace of the Cherokee march and to move from the area immediately. At least three Cherokee were hit when white children from the Pulaski area, at the encouragement of older siblings and adults, hurled rocks in the direction of the weary Cherokee. Among those hit was White Crow, when a five-inch rock struck her right shin and caused an extremely painful break in her skin.

"I got one of 'em!", yelled one of the boys. "It hit her in the head and I see some blood." Jake Savage's instinct was to yell at the group of boys, but his movement toward them was impeded.

"Hey, Savage! Don't do it. They're kids, and they don't know no better. Your time in the army, maybe your life, and some of theirs could be at risk." The man speaking to Jake Savage was a captain named Eric Campbell.

Captain Campbell managed to prevent what would have likely become a riot. Aside from this interaction, Campbell and Jake Savage would have a limited amount of contact in the ensuing days. The next time they were to engage in any measureable amount of conversation would be a time that Jake Savage would remember for the rest of his life.

Meanwhile, the group continued its westward progress. Within a short time the Bell Group moved toward what they perceived to be a more peaceful setting. In doing so, they camped at Agnew Creek, near Pulaski, Tennessee.

An estimated twenty Cherokee escaped from the Agnew Creek bivouac. The mixture of an almost equal number of males and females had managed to slip away from an unguarded section of the camp. An unusually dark night provided the necessary cover for the individuals to make their way into the cover of woods.

Unfortunately for those seeking freedom from the forced movement, they had unknowingly moved toward a settlement of a religious faction that held, among its numerous misguided beliefs, the attitude that all Native Americans were demonic. As a result, when the fleeing Cherokee attempted to navigate their passage through groupings of cabins and surrounding fields of the settlement, the noise and attention they unwittingly created and drew proved detrimental to several members of the group.

The next morning, four of the escapees were returned to the caravan, with the captors demanding an immediate monetary reward for providing the service of capturing and returning some of the missing Cherokee. The ensuing conversation was filled with a series of words that fully exhibited the animosity the pious organization held for the Cherokee.

When Lieutenant George Brantley informed the self-appointed jailers, men who were under the leadership of an individual named Russell Brown, that they would have to write military authorities in Washington, there was a great deal of objection on the part of those who had retrieved the missing Cherokee. Lieutenant Brantley notified the group that he would gladly sign any letter that could be written and given to him by the time the rear guard left Pulaski, but stronger objections erupted.

Russell Brown argued, "None of us standing here can read or write. We just want to get our money. We heard you pay folks for burying them; we brought them back alive." The stance of Brown and the additional captors certainly had substance.

Lieutenant Brantley replied, "Sir, I am not the individual to whom you are referring. The payments will come from elsewhere, and I can provide you with the name and address of the individuals you will need to contact. I am not at liberty to pay you today."

The obvious disenchantment with Lieutenant Brantley's comments was widespread. It was easy to notice the negative body language among members of Brown's followers as well as the close proximity the captors held their guns to their bodies.

The primary source of discourse came when Lieutenant Brantley informed Russell Brown that the four captured Cherokee would not be allowed to leave camp. Mr. Brown expressed his disgusted feelings while wielding his shotgun in a dangerous and aggressive manner.

Brown then stated in an agitated tone, "I'll take that address of the person we need to get in touch with. We got folks 'round here who can write. We won't be bringing no more live ones to you though."

Against his instincts, Lieutenant Brantley provided Brown with the name and address where requests for burial payments could be made. With the time-consuming task completed, Brown's band again left camp and made its way toward the west.

Sadly, as the soldiers in the rear guard were leaving Agnew Creek, they heard shots being fired. An estimated thirteen shots were heard, although that was the simply the best concerted guess of the guards, and the estimation lacked proof. Little imagination was needed to determine that the shots were ending the lives of the Cherokee who had escaped from the Agnew Creek camp the previous night and had been captured with the supervision of the greedy Brown.

Chapter 13

Along the trail, Private Stephen Willis, the soldier who had provided Cherokee children with strands of horse meat, had drastically changed his stance and attitude toward the once-mighty Native American group. With no clear indication as to why this altered attitude took place, Willis seemed to transform from a kind-hearted individual into a man bent on destruction of the misplaced Cherokee. Private Willis showed no preference or regard for the age or gender of the individuals who received his torment.

After intervening with a group of four Cherokee children who were taking meat from one of his saddlebags, the young soldier apparently lost his composure. Private Willis began yelling at the children to leave his possessions alone. As the children, whose fear now overshadowed their hunger, ran from the horse, other soldiers and four Cherokee men made their way toward the angered Willis.

Private Willis, a soldier who appeared to be in his early twenties, fought with three soldiers who attempted to suppress his sudden rage. The Cherokee men, each protecting a child, stared into Willis's eyes as the exchanged glances mixed hostility with perplexity.

Private Willis yelled toward the Cherokee men, all of whom were imposing in stature, "I don't want your nasty kids messing with my stuff. Ain't nothin' to me no more if they all starve. I'm tired of this caretaking; you can all die."

Pointing toward the children, Private Willis proclaimed, "You and them rats can eat grass to keep from starving. Otherwise keep away from my food. I'm not gonna die to save any of you animals from croaking. You smell like a bunch of nasty goats; eat grass like 'em." Young Stephen Willis's words were ended when one of his comrades pulled a pistol and hit him over the head, rendering Willis unconscious.

After the incident the group began moving toward a Tennessee settlement once known as Hatchie Town. Having been renamed Bolivar a little more than a decade earlier, the West Tennessee settlement was located on the banks of the Hatchie River. Residents from nearby towns such as Jackson and Middleton, located to the north and south respectively, had made day-long journeys to Bolivar for the purpose of witnessing the exodus of the Cherokee from the area.

Little children from those settlements formed an almost parade-like atmosphere as they waved toward the Cherokee children. White Crow noted the innocence of the children of both races as they expressed sincere signs of humanity toward one another. For the vast majority of the white children, the day provided the first glimpse of Cherokee people.

A lamenting father who brought his wife and three children to Bolivar from Middleton, Tennessee, located only sixteen miles to the south, sat on his wagon with two horses pulling the front. "Take a look, kids. Those are the proud Cherokee, and they're being moved away from here. I heard my daddy talk about them saving his life when he was hurt in a fight with the British years back. They don't deserve what's being done to them."

The children listened intently to their father and stared in bewilderment at the process that unfolded before them. The lesson these children learned was seldom taught to others in their age group who were able to partake in such an event.

As Jake Savage passed the family, he grasped the bill of his hat and dipped his head toward them. As if trained to do so, Corporal Savage's horse appeared to shake his head up and down while his steps staggered as if in a review parade. The young boy, obviously impressed by the gesture, waved at Savage and then turned to his father.

"Pa, why is that nice man on the horse making the Cherokee move? He don't seem like he would do that." The boy seemed to readily sense the kind heart Jake Savage possessed.

The father searched for the right words to say to his son. The father's emotions at the keen observation of his ten-year old son brought the rugged farmer to the brink of tears. After successfully attempting to gather his thoughts and sense of strength, he said, "A man has a job to do. He might not agree with it, but sometimes you have to do it. I don't like to whip you, your brother, or your sister; but there are times when things have to be done. The preacher says that he thinks the Cherokee are being moved to keep them from being killed. Men can be cruel to each other. I don't see that soldier being a killer, at least not killing someone who is doing right."

The last of the Cherokee convoy passed the family from Middleton. In turn, the dust that the Cherokee and soldiers had created began to settle, and the curious crowd disbursed from Bolivar. The small town in northern Hardeman County became like so many others along the trail, as witnesses to the event allowed other situations to supersede that of the Cherokee.

For Jake Savage, White Crow, and the other human participants of the westward movement, Bolivar faded into their memories as an anonymous town where nameless faces stared at them and offered mixed emotions. While the Bell Group's reception at Bolivar was positive in all respects, the incidents that lay ahead overshadowed those that occurred in passing through the small Tennessee town.

The Bell Group progressed from Bolivar, Tennessee and made its path toward Memphis, located approximately sixty miles to the west. With the November weather quickly becoming far colder than any the members had experienced in recent months, the effects upon the majority of participants was highly negative.

The Bell Group managed to reach the western outskirts of Memphis and the Mississippi River in mid-November. Almost immediately they were assaulted by the early onset of freezing temperatures, sleet, and snow. The ruthless precipitation caught the contingency by surprise, battering humans and animals alike.

"We're gonna freeze tonight. I'm colder than I've ever been," a soldier said to Jake Savage. Corporal Savage sought diplomacy to overcome the frigid temperatures but managed only a small smile and a slight nod of his head.

Additional blankets, as well as winter coats, would have made the situation far more manageable, but the fact of the matter was that few of either was on hand. The insufficient number of blankets, shoes, and warm clothing had been apparent, but not a top priority, for the previous couple of weeks. The pleas to send the same to the group had just recently been made, with no positive results taking place.

Requests for the needed attire and coverings were sent, but the quartermaster who was responsible for providing the items to the Bell Group had been ignoring the appeals in lieu of personal gain. The irresponsible quartermaster, Ezekiel Conrad, was engaged in selling requisitioned supplies to non-military personnel.

Ezekiel Conrad was small in stature, standing only 5 feet 4 inches tall and weighing less than 120 pounds when attired in his full uniform. While his skills as a fighting soldier were far from efficient, Conrad's organizational abilities, as well as his mathematical and communication skills, were among the best of the members of the military. This set of circumstances not only enabled Conrad to fully develop his selfish plan of gaining personal wealth at the expense of the Cherokee, but they also allowed him to accumulate a sizeable fortune for the time in history.

The subpar financial auditing utilized in the various branches of the military at the time of the Indian Relocation contributed to Ezekiel Conrad's ability to quickly acquire a sizeable fortune in a relatively short amount of time. Conrad managed to safeguard his shenanigan through the onset of complaints associated with his lack of proper performance received the attention of higher-ranking officials.

Benefiting from his own set of bribed politicians and employees in carefully selected departments in Washington, Conrad had managed to become aware of investigators' knowledge of his ploy. The planned date and time more conscientious military personnel arranged for Conrad's arrest were among the information the swindler had been able to learn. In turn, Ezekiel Conrad was well-prepared for their arrival.

The situation became a classic case of "too little too late," as Ezekiel Conrad's plan for a quick and successful escape was well developed and skillfully executed prior to the time of the arrival of his captors. As investigators issued the proper paperwork for Conrad to be processed for arrest, and hopefully, for his impending prison term, the conniving quartermaster began his exodus from the United States.

Meanwhile, the number of victims resulting from Ezekiel Conrad's money lust and deficient tactics related to product disbursement began to escalate. At frequent intervals along the trail, the bodies of innocent Cherokee children and adults began to appear in numbers that resembled battle casualties from the era's more violent confrontations.

The absence of suitable blankets for the Cherokee clearly exemplified this fact. Colder weather created a clear need for an increased number of coverings for the Cherokee. The nights were growing increasingly frigid, and a malady of afflictions, ranging from frostbite to freezing to death, were the tragic results of the extreme shortage.

During this time filled with the horrible combination of death and utter sadness, a brief glimpse of humanity and compassion appeared. All but a half dozen soldiers who were serving with Jake Savage gave their blankets to a respective amount of the Cherokee children in order to preserve the youngsters' lives.

Adult Cherokee attempted to huddle with children in order to keep the younger Cherokee warm, but the endearing efforts often proved futile. As the daily high temperatures decreased into the low-40s, the nighttime temperatures grew almost unbearable for those individuals who lacked proper clothing and bedding.

Endeavors toward gaining warmth caused individuals of all ages to fail to attain a suitable level of rest. The tired and hungered Cherokee were being placed into a situation that would only worsen when far colder weather arrived. Sickness and death, in continuously increasing frequency, became the ritual for the displaced Native Americans.

A faction of the group that had initially been overlooked, to a large degree, was the elderly members of the Native Americans. The morning after the party spent their first night in the outskirts of Memphis, Jake

Savage supervised a burial party that had the responsibility of placing three deceased members of the oldest travelers into graves.

The resulting affair greatly affected Jake Savage and led to another alteration in his concept of the Cherokee people. Minutes literally seemed like hours as Jake Savage engaged in an event that he considered the most touching and trying of his young life to that point.

One of the deceased individuals was a Cherokee woman who was over seventy years of age. The elderly lady had been recently resting near White Crow. White Crow had earlier awakened and began to rub her own shoulders in an effort to increase the blood flow through her body. White Crow then attempted to wake the aged woman approximately fifteen minutes after sunrise. White Crow's inability to revive the lady led to the realization of the first loss of the day.

White Crow then joined no less than thirty Cherokee of various ages in participating in the burial ceremony. Jake Savage and four other soldiers under the command of Colonel Mark Tetleton were responsible for ensuring the safety of the burial group as well as making certain that escape attempts were negated.

"Watch 'em close. They'll take advantage of the situation to sneak away." The tone of Tetleton's words indicated his full transformation from helping the Cherokee children gain strips of jerky to threatening to kill them.

"They're people. They want to bury their dead. There hasn't been a chance for them to do that for weeks without thinking one of us will shoot them. Let them have their ceremony and you show some respect to the dead." Jake Savage was becoming ever-increasingly empathetic to the Cherokee.

Jake Savage's words drew a look of sincere and deep appreciation from White Crow. The young lady who had once held a high level of animosity toward Corporal Savage was becoming more and more infatuated with his persona and the positive feelings he evidently held for the Cherokee people. The growing affection White Crow possessed for Jake Savage in no way applied to the additional members of the United States military or the purpose with which its members had regarding the Cherokee nation.

"You speak kind words from a gentle heart. My people say that some of your people are good. I see good in your heart, but not in the others. They try, but only you are complete in your attempts. Your nation, your President and the people in your government's camp are filled with evil and greed." Despite the general content of the conversation, particularly the words centering upon the dislike directed toward the military and the United States government, White Crow smiled as she stared deeply into Jake Savage's eyes.

Pointing to the partially-filled grave that held the body of a woman White Crow greatly admired, White Crow said, "She liked you. Once she said if the two of us, you and me, were in a different situation, we would be together."

"Together? You mean like husband and wife? I...well, I don't know what to say." Jake Savage's stuttering and confused words contrasted with his broad smile. Just as he placed his right hand on White Crow's left elbow, in an apparent attempt to display a mild level of affection, Corporal Savage was berated with more harsh words from Colonel Tetleton.

"What are you doing? Get away from that woman, Corporal Savage. She'll use a rock or something to bust your skull; if you're lucky, she'll rob you of any trinkets you have. Stay away from her and remember what your job is, or I'll have you placed into chains and subdued in a wagon. You're asking for trouble hanging around the likes of her."

Colonel Mark Tetleton was clear in his words and the volume of his discharge drew the attention of those involved in the burial party as well as others within the surrounding area. Jake Savage stared into Colonel Tetleton's eyes, but Savage knew that any verbal exchange with a commanding officer would end with Jake being arrested. Using the better sense of judgment, Savage chose to avoid such an incident and simply walked away from the possible confrontation.

In turn, Jake Savage made another effort to clearly indicate to White Crow that his feelings were similar to hers. A smile and a weak attempt at waving, with his hand raised no higher than his chest, assured White Crow that Jake Savage was interested in her well-being. However, Corporal Savage knew that any stronger indication of the same would likely end the possibility of the sustainment of not only the feelings between Savage and White Crow, but also their very lives.

After all, both White Crow and Jake Savage had seen the results of attacks from the Cherokee upon the soldiers, as well as the reverse situation. For the time being, it appeared that any violence directed toward either Corporal Savage or White Crow would most likely come from a randomly-selected soldier. An anonymous soldier who Colonel Mark Tetleton would secretly or indiscriminately order to carry out an act of violence would likely be the culprit.

For that reason, Jake Savage and White Crow determined that they must remain not only vigilant regarding their personal safety in the increasingly cold weather, but also from those who were aware of, and fully disproving what seemed to be a budding romance between members of two groups who were, for all practical purposes, at war.

Chapter 14

An estimated five thousand Cherokee, including White Crow, spent the next three weeks in an improvised camp near the Mississippi River port city of Memphis, Tennessee. The group had to remain at that location for the unplanned and rather prolonged period of time as they were unable to cross the Mississippi River due to the heavy ice flows that clogged the major waterway. While the seemingly unbearable cold winds of the season, as well as the icy conditions would negate any serious attempts at escape, there was one major incident in which such an act was pursued.

The massive chunks of ice that slowly floated along the unbearably cold waters of the river moved more rapidly than the typical pair of eyes perceived. Jagged edges on the masses of frozen river water would quickly prove injurious or even deadly to anyone who happened to fall onto them. The same held true for individuals who braved entering the congested waters of the Mississippi in an effort to flee captivity. Despite the level of apparent and hidden risks, a small group of Cherokee, seeking the freedom that the Arkansas side of the river appeared to offer, made a valiant effort to gain their freedom.

As the sun began to set one Sunday, the organized worship service, which an estimated two hundred people attended, dispersed in order that the attendees could reach their night's resting location before the complete departure of sunlight. Interestingly, soldiers who had attended the services regularly grew somewhat negligent in their administration of guarding the Cherokee. The Cherokee Christians, some of whom also participated in the makeshift worship service, were far less attentive to the circumstances unfolding around them.

A group of an estimated sixteen Cherokee made a break for the largely frozen Mississippi River, clearly planning to use the approaching darkness and lack of security to move toward the Arkansas side of the waterway. Forgetting, or perhaps overlooking, the outcome of the members of the last group of Cherokee who attempted to escape, the individuals ran toward the slick bank that served as the western-most point along the Tennessee side of the river.

Almost immediately trouble erupted for the determined escapees. While the Cherokee troupe was able to safely make their way to the river bank without any soldiers readily detecting them, the tributary's edge proved to be the escape plan's initial undoing. A middle-aged Cherokee man, clad in shoes inhibited with rather slick bottoms, swiftly slipped and tumbled down the icy river bank head first. The man's body slammed to the ground with a sufficient enough force that his left leg and right arm were broken.

Screaming in agony, the injured Cherokee man brought unwanted attention to the group. A large number of his fellow tribesmen, largely unaware of the situation evolving along the river's edge, turned their heads in the direction of the calls of agony.

While a contingency of soldiers bravely placed themselves between the ice-capped river and the gathering crowd of angered Cherokee, another cluster of military personnel ran toward the panicked escapees. Trudging across the snow-covered ground and reaching the bluffs of the Mississippi River in a matter of seconds, the soldiers began discharging their weapons in the direction of the fleeing Cherokee.

"I can't see what I'm shooting at," were the words of one of the soldiers. "It's too dark!"

Another member of the military guard used coercion in turning to his comrades and stating, "Aim at the voices you hear out there, or at least the spots where they're coming from. They're out there; shoot 'em!"

The deadly scene at the river bank and the related shots carefully aimed in the direction of the Cherokee voices were causing an increasing level of discontent among the Cherokee who were not directly involved in the set of critical events. Many of the younger Cherokee men, muscular and approaching a state of high agitation, were slowly edging toward the river bank in hopes of discovering the truth behind the screams of the injured Cherokee man.

Jake Savage took it upon himself to gain the services of four young Cherokee men and made way toward the river. This was also undertaken in an effort to not only locate, but also rescue the injured and suffering man. Savage also determined that such an act would negate, or at least lessen, the possibility of a riot ensuing among those Cherokee pressing toward the location of their wounded fellow tribesman.

"You, as well as you and you two men; come with me. We need to find the man who's hurt." With his words and pointed finger initially creating little response, Jake Savage raised the level of his voice and implored, "Now!" The urgency of his speech, combined with Jake Savage's growing positive reputation among the Cherokee on the trail, apparently appealed to the four reluctant draftees. In response, the four selected Cherokee adhered to Jake's earnest plea and followed him toward the sounds of the screaming man.

Jake Savage and his four Cherokee attendants then made their way toward the river. By that point, someone had managed to take a torch to the scene, and Savage took it upon himself to utilize it for the safety of his new quartet of searchers as well as himself.

Meanwhile, the scene at the river, a close distance from Jake Savage's vantage point, was becoming deadly for the escapees. It appeared that at least two shots fired in the direction of the bolting Cherokee had hit their intended marks. Military participants in the event, as well as Cherokee witnesses to the travesty, heard the painstaking cries of two distinct and weakening voices.

"Sounds to me like we may have got a couple. Don't know how many are left, but there's shore a couple less now." The heartless words of a soldier served as witness to only two other soldiers, both of whom found the humor, amid near deafening gunfire, a reason for erupting in callous and maniacal laughter.

The light from the moon, visible in the clear early evening sky, revealed a portion of the effectiveness of the event's dastardly deeds. Two seriously wounded Cherokee men were lying on frozen areas of the river. The order was given for them to be intentionally left to suffer on the ice where they would eventually die from their horrid wounds. However, as if nature held more mercy for the duo than did the soldiers who determined to abandon the suffering Cherokee, the icy waters of the muddy Mississippi River soon swallowed the increasingly lifeless forms and swept them from the area of the seemingly needless bloodshed.

Approximately four other Cherokee huddled behind an ice boulder in an attempt to avoid the incessant gunfire. The additional weight of the three men and one lady, all in their early twenties, proved too substantial for the ice upon which they were hiding.

The young lady began to scream as she heard the ice cracking, a noise she initially and incorrectly discerned as being the sounds the soldiers' muzzleloaders emitted. Her panicked words and the screams for help were audible above the gunfire, and it seemed that every soldier had begun to reload their weapons at the same moment. Cries from a Cherokee couple on the bank, obviously recognizing the frightened voice as that of their teenage daughter, resulted in additional heartache for the captives.

The four fleeing Cherokee rapidly encountered their deaths as flowing blocks of ice impeded their only possible path of escape. Adding to the situation's sadness was the fact that no one clearly witnessed the incident or was able to determine if the four had somehow managed to reach the Arkansas side of the Mississippi. Conjecture forever served as the major mindset in relation to the specifics of the tragedy.

The remaining eleven escapees sadly met a variety of fates. Five were known to have been able to make it to the freedom of the Arkansas side of the river, and their shouts of defiance cut through the still night and resounded in the ears of their cohorts along the Tennessee banks of the Mississippi. Unfortunately, the outcome of four additional escapees was never clearly determined. Two more of the fleeing individuals, both boys in their mid-teens, fell into the river's waters and were last seen as they were swept away in the frozen quagmire.

The exact number of those making their escape from the Memphis camp that night was never stated, but rumored estimates placed the figure between sixteen and twenty-five. For that reason, the number who died on that dark and cold night, as well as the figure for those who attained freedom from the trail, was largely left to speculation.

Chapter 15

Residents of the Memphis area began to perform the same grisly tasks as had some of their Middle Tennessee fellow statesmen earlier in the relocation process. Visits from locals, most of whom were little more than self-appointed vigilantes, were usually filled with the comments of hatred toward the Cherokee and a strong desperate desire for the group of soldiers and Cherokee to move from the area.

Even the local constable made it a point to grace the camp with his presence. On one of the coldest mornings of the three-week period in which the group was based in Memphis, the law official, known throughout the area as Michael Kline, entered the camp. Kline requested to speak with the leader of the soldiers, as well as with the man who was "responsible for them Indians who've come here uninvited."

"I've got word about your group causing some issues around here. It would probably be best to keep these folks who live in these parts happier than what you've been able to do so far." The words from Mr. Kline were directed toward Colonel Tetleton and quickly drew a heated response.

Colonel Tetleton rapidly recanted, "I am Colonel Mark Tetleton, and I assume I am the man you're seeking. I think someone's been lying to you and your townsfolk about these people. These Indians haven't been a problem to anyone except our guards, and that's only when some of them were trying to get to the other side of the river. That wouldn't have my prisoners going in the direction of your folks or even bothering them. Would you prefer we make them invisible?"

The agitated Kline replied in a like manner, "Mr. Colonel, if the folks around see your captives, they're gonna shoot at 'em. I know for a fact, they're all pretty good shots. Maybe if you could just move these Redskins away from here, things would settle down and I would get some rest at night."

"Rest!" Colonel Tetleton's reaction was terse. "How can you talk about not getting rest? Come out here and sleep on the ice and snow without cover. Most of those Indians have had little to eat in weeks. My own men are faring little better. Listen to these children dying from the cold. Think about that when you're home in your bed or eating a full meal."

Kline, the disconcerted lawman, concluded the conversation in issuing a stern warning, "I'm tellin' you one last time, if the people around here grown tired of these Indians, and I think they are, you'll soon be burying even more than you have been. It's your call, Mr. Colonel Army Man. Anything that happens to 'em is your fault. Their blood's not on my hands!"

"Reminiscent of Pontius Pilate. No guilt on you, nicely done." Colonel Tetleton's words were no less filled with animosity than were those of Kline.

With that said, the lawman who introduced himself as Michael Kline turned his back toward Colonel Tetleton and took his first steps in the direction of his point of origin. The time that elapsed before additional words were expelled was short in duration.

As Michael Kline began walking from the meeting, Colonel Tetleton shouted words that he was uncertain the constable heard. "You'll have to answer for any killings that go on around here. There'll be blood on your hands, Mr. Kline. You are to blame for anyone who your townspeople kill."

In an effort to safeguard the Cherokee forcefully placed under his care, Colonel Tetleton placed extra guards on the perimeter of the Memphis-based camp. This effort, while temporary in nature, brought the documented number of escapees to the lowest levels of the journey. Not a single person, as far as records indicated, escaped from the area in the three days after Colonel Tetleton's confrontation with the lawman known as Michael Kline.

Sadly, there was a significant increase in the numbers of deaths for both the Cherokee and Colonel Tetleton's soldiers. The variety of diseases that had emerged in recent weeks rose to a major level. No less than forty-five Cherokee passed away in the week following Tetleton's heated meeting with Kline. In turn, half a dozen soldiers fell victim to a smallpox outbreak.

A trio of soldiers who had been actively involved in the process of guarding the Cherokee recovered from an onset of measles, but had each had subsequently developed dysentery. The three young men were diagnosed as being too weak to be of any level of valuable service, and they were placed into a wagon to be returned to Red Clay. Two of the most recent recruits were used as escorts for the recovered soldiers who lacked a sufficient level of strength in order to be able to effectively drive the team of horses pulling the wagon.

Adding to the desperation of the situation for those who intended to continue the westward trek was the fact that the Cherokee, as well as the soldiers guarding them, were temporarily prohibited from starting fires in the nights immediately following the Kline and Tetleton confrontation. The purpose of this negation was to prevent local residents from correctly determining the exact location and disbursement of the troupe and possibly rob or otherwise assault them. The effort was also believed to limit the ability of Memphis residents to more accurately aim shots, should they become so inclined. The absence of heat and light proved disastrous for both groups, and the ban on campfires was hurriedly lifted.

Also increasing the level of misery present in the nights was the fact that members of both the Cherokee and the soldiers had to sleep on the frigid ground without the benefit of proper bedding. In order to keep from literally freezing to death, the Cherokee regularly lay in groups beneath as many of the wagons they were allowed to approach.

The typical gathering of the Cherokee featured children of varying ages crowded on the ground directly under a wagon. Ladies enveloped the children, often laying with their outside shoulder against, or aligned with, the wheels of the side of the wagon under which they rested. The husbands, or groups of otherwise significant males responsible for the care of corresponding females, encircled the wagon. With supplies low, or oftentimes totally absent from the wagons, it became a common practice during the Memphis stopover for individuals to crowd into the wagons in an effort to procure some amount of rest. The down side of that endeavor was the point that any possible heat emitted from the ground, once the snow was removed, failed to reach the people inside the wagons.

After a period of two days and nights in which the campfires were barred, the position was altered. Colonel Tetleton came to fully realize, after the elapsing of a sufficient time in which he calmed down and developed a new mindset toward the situation, that the pleas from his subordinates were filled with purely good intentions.

Jake Savage was among those soldiers who approached Colonel Tetleton and asked for permission to reinstitute the policy of allowing campfires. Corporal Savage avoided using White Crow's name, and he took it upon himself to steer clear of implying that he had any interest other than that of cooking his own food while his tent mates and he used the stoked fires to get warm during the cool night air.

Jake Savage's formal request was presented in a manner that sounded memorized and highly respectful. "The boys and I have had a couple of pretty rough nights, Colonel Tetleton. With no activity reported around our camp in that same period, I request permission to tell those in my company, as well as the Cherokee, that small fires will be allowed during the night. If the fires are to be used only for cooking and keeping warm, I see no harm in stoking those during daylight as well. We are losing prisoners and guards with the policy, and there doesn't appear to be a noticeable number of belligerents in Memphis peering toward us."

Savage's words appeared as sincere as they actually were, and Colonel Tetleton yielded to the heartfelt and seemingly honest request.

"Very well, Savage. Your desire for a change in my tactics and orders are likely made in the best interests of everyone here. Let's try it tonight and tomorrow to see how it goes. If that Mr. Kline and his band begins to make trouble, we may have to defend our camp like a secure post. We'll put extra guards in addition to what we've been having. I may even use a few of the more docile Indians to help with the guard detail."

With that point in mind, the condition of the entourage, at least in relation to the level of comfort regarding warmth, greatly improved for the remaining duration stay in Memphis. For a brief period of time the cooperation between the soldiers and Cherokee greatly improved as unarmed Cherokee men were placed in tandem with soldiers to reinforce the guard.

Corporal Jake Savage served with one of two Cherokee males for two twelve-hour shifts during the final days at Memphis. The first Cherokee to work with Jake Savage was named Strong Buck, and he seemed to hold a great deal of respect toward the young soldier. Corporal Savage learned that Strong Buck, twenty-one years old, was a longtime friend of White Crow's family. The bold Strong Buck faced Jake and stated that White Crow had developed really strong feelings for Savage.

Strong Buck explained, "White Crow knows that you are a good man. Many of our people speak about you and your kind ways. She needs someone like you. You are not like so many of the soldiers who guard us and make us walk when our feet are tired. What will happen to White Crow, you, and the rest of my people when we arrive at the place you are taking us?"

Jake Savage attempted to assure Strong Buck that he, like the Native Americans, was not totally sure of the destination. "I have heard talk that we're headed to a reservation in Indian Territory. If that's true, we only have to cross this river and then walk across Arkansas. It was made a state just a couple of years ago, and I don't know a lot about it or the people in it. I promise you that I don't know what will happen when we finish the march. It's out of my hands, but I will try everything I can to keep as many of you alive.

"And White Crow. Will you take her with you, Jake Savage? If you try, they will punish you and kill her. Some of our people, those who do not want to know you, think your people should stay away from us and let us alone. While I do not want to leave our homes, I think you and White Crow have a bright future together. One of our wiser mothers has said so. If that is to be, I am to be your friend. I have known White Crow since we were children. I do not remember not knowing her."

When their shift of guard duty came to an end, Jake and Strong

Buck shook hands and assured one another that their friendship would continue throughout the journey. Their gestures toward one another, as well as portions of their conversations, served as sources of comfort for White Crow and those Cherokee who spent time with her.

Two nights later, Corporal Savage worked with another Cherokee who appeared to be the approximate age of Strong Buck. However, the man refused to speak with Savage during the entirety of the duo's guard assignment. Jake was unable to learn the man's name and spent the time in which the two were together daydreaming about the comments Strong Buck had made.

"You got a name?" were the words Jake Savage uttered to the man at least a half dozen times in their first hour together.

Aside from finally nodding his head in a slow up and down motion, the man never offered additional efforts to communicate with Jake Savage. Jake reasoned that this man held a level of contempt for him due to Savage's position in the military, or it could have been based upon the fact that the feelings White Crow held for Corporal Savage were becoming commonly discussed among many of the Cherokee people.

Chapter 16

Occasional smiles and intermittent waves were the primary means of communication between Jake Savage and White Crow during the latter portion of the stay in Memphis. Although Jake had readily accepted the relationship's growing intimacy, he was well aware that few people in either camp could be trusted with a firm knowledge of the same. As such, Jake managed to keep his own increasing admiration for White Crow to himself.

By and large, the soldiers were friendlier to the Cherokee during their time in Memphis than they were during any time prior to or after the bivouac along the Mississippi River. There were no documented attempts at fighting, no recorded cases of physical abuse, and no openly-uttered cruel words exchanged between the captives and captors. Jake Savage rationalized that this was due to the need to watch for and be mindful of a common enemy in the people who Michael Kline spoke of a few days earlier.

The five days after Kline's visit were as peaceful as could be expected. Despite the continued shortage of food, there were no grumblings or threats regarding hunger or the need to abolish it. Late on the fifth afternoon following Kline's visit, just as the sun was beginning to set on the horizon that was fronted with the icy waters of the Mississippi, two soldiers on patrol witnessed a group approaching the camp.

"Colonel Tetleton, there's a long string of torches headed this way. We might ought to get everyone ready for an attack. Them folks 'pear to be 'proachin' and they're moving fairly fast. Looks like some of 'em got somethin' in their arms."

Colonel Tetleton wasted no time in ordering his troops into position. "Bugler, round up the troops. Corporal Savage, use your company to guard the Cherokee, all others troops move to your previously assigned positions."

Jake Savage quickly and efficiently moved the Cherokee from their bedding locations into as compact a group as could be formed. Jake took it upon himself to send one half of his company to assist in guarding either flank. The remainder of Colonel Tetleton's men was aligned behind rudimentary barricades and awaited the assault from the men of whom Kline had spoken.

As Corporal Jake Savage watched the approaching torches, White Crow quietly made her way to stand at his side. Both of them were concerned with the appearance of the situation and, in turn, felt as helpless about the possibility of an impending battle as did the Cherokee children. At one point White Crow's right hand gently touched Jake Savage's left hand. Without stopping to think about the possible ramifications of doing so, Jake took the opportunity to reply in a like manner. He held White Crow's hand for a matter of seconds and then squeezed it gently before struggling to gain his battle-ready composure.

"They look like they brought a lot with 'em tonight. I bet," Jake continued, "there's at least a hundred of 'em. You'll need to get back there with most of your folks to keep safe. I don't want anything to happen to you. Please, go back there."

White Crow tenderly responded, "I will do what you ask, although I do not want to. You must also be careful. They may hurt you, Jake. Please be careful. I do not want you to be harmed. I really want you to be safe."

As White Crow's words left her mouth, she turned and briskly walked from Jake. She also placed her hand over her mouth, though it was unclear if she was attempting to hide her embarrassment over the near expression of her feelings, or if she was on the brink of crying.

Jake Savage also began moving from his assigned position and headed toward the approaching lights that came from the uplifted torches of the crowd. Corporal Savage noticed that by that brief interlude in time, the bulk of the lights were flickering in the cool breeze of the night, yet they were not directly moving toward the Cherokee camp.

Another facet of the apparent standoff was that Colonel Tetleton had taken three soldiers with him to participate in an apparent meeting with a group of seven shadowy figures advancing from the large halted group of torch-bearing marauders. Corporal Jake Savage attempted to discern what was taking place, but the darkness made his desired detection an impossible task. The disclosure of the process didn't take long in becoming apparent.

Ben Swanson, one of the soldiers who had joined Colonel Tetleton in the advance toward the torches, hurriedly returned to the Cherokee camp. He ran to the area where Jake Savage stood, and Swanson appeared to be struggling to gain his composure in the wintry air. Before he could complete his imparting of information and provide an update to the soldiers who stayed behind, Swanson was distracted. Members of the group to whom Swanson was speaking began to point behind him, specifically in the direction from which he had recently returned.

"It's like it's a miracle. What's going on will make things so much better. I just…" At that point the soldier's words were interrupted when more soldiers and dozens of Cherokee began pointing toward the moving torches. The thoughts running through Jake Savage's head centered on carefully aiming and firing into the advancing lights.

Private Swanson resumed his speech to those who were within hearing range, "They're from a local church, and they've got food for us. Seems they don't think we're all the trouble that that Mr. Kline made us out to be. The preacher, a man named William Thatcher, is going to help us feed our group and move to a safer place." The short but simple explanation was concluded without interruption.

William Thatcher, the preacher of the group that numbered some ninety-four souls, led his group into the camp and made a speech explaining his intent. Imposing in size, Preacher Thatcher also possessed a booming voice that seemed to accentuate his body's frame of six feet three-inches and almost three hundred pounds. He stood on a snow-covered stump in order to deliver a speech. The words were presented prior to what most of the participants along the trail had determined to be a highly pivotal event during the months of marching.

Thatcher proclaimed, "It's my pleasure to bring some food to help you all get through the next few days. I know that your limited resources have kept you from hunting game in the area, and I'm aware that the deer and other animals have fled from the area around your camp. So, we have brought you some of what we have killed. However, my visit tonight comes with mixed news. At this moment a group of opposite-minded individuals, murderers if you will, is making its way toward this very spot. My parishioners and I will lead you to safety and take you to a crossing that lies only two miles upriver from where we now stand. The ice is currently solid all the way across the river at that spot; if we leave soon we can get all of you across the muddy waters by sunup. I ask you to trust my church members and me. Much more delay could prove deadly to a large number of you."

Thatcher's words were forceful and to the point. There was no doubt among those who heard the delivery that the time for the entourage to leave the area was at hand. Within thirty minutes from the end of Thatcher's speech, the wagons were loaded with children and the supplies the church folks had provided for the journey. Although the wagons had been parked in the mud and snow for several days, the draw teams were well-rested and able to dislodge every wagon of the train from the sunken resting spots.

The entire group of Cherokee, soldiers, and church members advanced two miles along the river and began crossing the frozen waters of the Mississippi just as the evil-minded Michael Kline's intended thieves and murderers approached the location that had served as the Cherokee campsite for weeks. A most difficult task lay in determining which set of travelers was more emotional. Was it the participants in the relocation striving to complete a successful trek to the river crossing, or did the prize go to the cruel-hearted members of Kline's band who reached the Cherokee campsite only to discover an abandoned bivouac?

"Where are they? You said there would be here. You've been telling us for days to hold off on sending snipers in here to pick 'em off one by one. Now we've got a good night of weather and everyone's guns are loaded. I think someone should pay for this mistake. You let them savages stink up our town, and now they're headed off to do the same to some other settlement." The angry man who spoke directed his words to a bewildered and obviously nervous Michael Kline.

"Now hold on. They were here when I seen 'em a few days ago. Just this morning I got word from my son that they were camped and set up, waiting for an attack. They didn't even have a good line of defense; I'm telling you they can't be far off." Kline's words were given in an attempt to obtain the time needed to develop a ploy for his escape.

"No women, no horses, no wagons. You and your ideas have cost me, Mr. Kline. If your son saw 'em here then bring him here." The angered leader of the group quickly seized any remaining authority from Michael Kline, as the latter and his son became the targets of the blood-thirsty gang.

"Hang 'em both," one man yelled.

Another man, one as agitated as the first speaker, offered a different solution. "It'll be quicker and easier to shoot 'em. Unless you want to do to one of 'em what we was a gonna do to the redskins. Let me take the daddy and we'll skin him."

The riotous group had no problem with three men grabbing Michael Kline and throwing him to the ground. Kline's last words, uttered in a tearful plea seconds before his death, were, "Please men, I've got a wife. This is all a mistake. You know I ain't lying to you. Why would I protect a bunch of Indians and try to deceive you? Please, my wife needs me."

A third man replied, "No need to worry 'bout her. She'll be dead by morning too."

A shot's echoes filled the night air as Michael Kline was allowed to stand and make a run for it, but quickly fell to the ground with a bullet through his head. His son screamed out for his father before a knife sank deeply into his back, ending the life of the seventeen year-old.

At the point of death for Michael Kline's teenaged son, a scout from the group arrived from his trek upriver. "They're crossing the river and almost all of 'em are across. Looks like they're running on the ice. I wanted to shoot at 'em, but I knew that wouldn't do nothing 'cept speed 'em up. We can't catch 'em before they finish. If we start that way now, it'll be sunrise before we get there and I bet some of the ice will be melting. It's already warmer than it was a couple of hours ago. This deal is done."

The scout looked from his position atop his horse and peered downward at the bodies of Michael Kline and his son. "Good riddance. They deserved it and more. Whatever was done was done too quick. We ain't been able to find any game to kill around here 'cause that man wouldn't let us raid this camp before tonight. Now, with the Indians and the government boys gone, things might get back to normal. "

Another member of Kline's group turned to the scout and said, "We're gonna go back and kill his wife. He's the reason we didn't get here in time to round up the women and wagons."

The group made its way from the abandoned Cherokee camp and headed in the direction of Michael Kline's farm. Although no account of the murder of Kline's widow was written, it was stated in area lore that she was first tied to the bed in which she and her husband usually slept. The cabin in which she was bound was then set on fire. There was credence to the story, as smoke was seen coming from the general location of the cabin the morning after the raid. Inquisitive neighbors who witnessed the smoke made their way to the structure, only to discover a pile of rubble. The remains of Mrs. Kline were never found.

The heartless alleged act of the brutal group upon Kline's wife was not the only degradation directed toward the Kline family on the night of the unsuccessful raid on the Cherokee camp. The bodies of Kline and his son were left unburied and became food for scavenging animals. The irony of this lay in the fact that that was the original intention of Kline's foray into the Cherokee camp; he planned to rob the train of all possible items to be sold and would have allowed the bodies of the victims, Cherokee and military members alike, to rot away in the harsh elements. Poetic justice, it appears, reigned on that night of bloodshed.

In contrast, Jake Savage and White Crow were able to join the band of Cherokee and soldiers as they safely crossed the river into Arkansas. This major accomplishment would have proven difficult, if not impossible, without the assistance of William Thatcher and the members of his congregation. The genuine level of respect Thatcher felt for all people was clearly demonstrated, as the feat he masterminded could have easily led to attacks upon any member of the church he served, his family, or himself. Fortunately, that was not the case.

Jake Savage took the initiative of thanking as many members of the Thatcher congregation as he could. The foodstuffs the members of the church brought to the soldiers and the Cherokee were welcomed beyond the ability the members could express. Not only were there items to eat, but also a wide collection of Christmas presents for the Cherokee children were brought.

Thatcher admitted to Colonel Tetleton during their parting conversation that members of Michael Kline's group had informed them of the number of Cherokee children who were present in the group that was being moved westward.

"Five members of the group were planning to get rich from the sale of your wagons and horses. When they discovered how many children were in the group, they changed their minds. All five of them were baptized last week and have promised to work the rest of their lives in the service of God. While there have been some tragedies involved in your trek, I know that some good will eventually come from it as well."

With the last member of the relocation group setting foot on the Arkansas side of the river, parting words and waves of appreciation were shared among members of Thatcher's party and those of the Cherokee and soldiers. In an act of appreciation, and unaware that the Kline group had abandoned their pursuit of them, the vast majority of the Bell Group stalled their westward progression and held prayer for the safety of the members from Thatcher's God-fearing and well-intentioned congregation.

"May God be with you," was one of the numerous replies from Thatcher and his followers. The members of the extremely conservative congregation made their return across the frozen river while singing verses from church hymns.

Chords from the songs filled the air, and soldiers and Cherokee who were familiar with the songs joined in singing. White Crow managed to stand beside Jake Savage and joined in a verse of a song. As before, their hands touched, as did many of the members from both groups.

Like no other time in the journey, the tensions of the trip disappeared in a sign of group unity.

The success of the hurried Mississippi River crossing lifted the spirits of the people who had thus far managed to survive the treacherous trail. There was an abundance of gestures of compassion as well as genuine celebration of the deliverance from what many regarded as having been a literal death trap along the barren landscape on the Tennessee side of the river.

After crossing the river the Bell Group made its way along the banks toward what would have been the original point of entry into Arkansas. Jake Savage and others seized the opportunity to glimpse across the river at the Tennessee location that had served as their temporary home. At that point, the discovery of the cessation of the Kline group's pursuit of the Cherokee/soldier contingency became clearly apparent. Embers from the abandoned fires, along with the light provided from the rising sun, revealed no human presence in the abandoned camp.

The Bell Group's tragic tenure in Tennessee had officially come to an end. While the culmination of this time had been a welcomed event for the vast majority of the assemblage, it also signaled many of the Cherokee that it was the last time they would see the state that had served as the home for many of them for a lengthy period of time. Likewise, for a sizeable number of the party, the parting was a welcomed sight. That viewpoint was based upon the stance that the state where many had died would now fade into their memories as had numerous other unforgiving events of recent months.

Chapter 17

The Bell Group used the momentum gained from setting foot on Arkansas soil to progress over ten miles into the state on their first day after crossing the Mississippi River. The accomplishment marked the first time in over a month that the band had made any significant progress in their hampered and tragedy-filled westward journey.

The first night in an Arkansas camp was filled with the highest level of morale the soldiers had exhibited in weeks. In addition, the Cherokee made no attempts to escape from the site. Lieutenant Deas, along with Colonel Mark Tetleton and Lieutenant George Brantley, joked that the positive state of emotions was due to full stomachs of Cherokee and soldiers alike. Another aspect of the positive mindset laid in sanitation in that the same parties were able to move from a campsite in which the life-sustaining supplies had been depleted and in which the perimeter had served as a massive latrine.

The cheerful and rather carefree mood of the early evening hours was spent in celebration of the Christmas season. There were times of song and dance as well as an unusually large amount of food. The children in the group took time to enjoy the carved toys and other items they had received from the church members from Preacher Thatcher's congregation. The soldiers seemed to revel in the new socks and preserved fruits they had been given the previous night.

By eight o'clock that night the celebration had concluded, and all but a few guards were asleep. Little movement took place that night as Corporal Jake Savage and approximately ten other soldiers served as sentries for the first hours of darkness. One of the few interruptions of the night took place when White Crow accompanied a group of children to the edge of camp in order to relieve themselves.

"White Crow, you should be more careful. We're still a little apprehensive about the group who was chasing us last night." Jake Savage's statement to White Crow seemed to fall on deaf ears.

White Crow smiled at Jake and placed her hands in his. The young couple stared into each other's eyes; there was no need to express the growing affection they held for one another.

The brief delay ended as the beautiful maiden replied to Savage's words, "I had to see you. I think you and I are good friends, Jake Savage. There is something I need to say to you."

At that moment two girls, no more than six years of age, came running toward White Crow. Speaking in Cherokee, the girls were obviously concerned about one of their friends. When the girls finished speaking, White Crow motioned to the girls to return to their friends several feet away from where Jake and White Crow had been standing. White Crow alternated looking at the girls and Jake, and she began laughing when she focused on one of the children.

One of the girls in the group of youngsters had evidently eaten too much of the homemade candy a member of Thatcher's congregation had supplied. In turn, she had become sick, causing her friends to seek help from White Crow. The conversation between Jake and White Crow evolved into a more lighthearted topic.

"She is sick. The candy from the Christians has made her stomach hurt. Her mother told her it would happen, but she had never tried the candy before. It is funny that she would not listen, but she had to learn." White Crow managed to produce her sentences through her chuckling at the situation.

Corporal Jake Savage said, "It's like you."

White Crow looked at Jake with confusion in her eyes.

Jake Savage continued, "You know that you shouldn't be here. I know I need to tell you to leave, but just like that little girl with the candy, I want to be with you. Instead of getting sick, you and I may be arrested or even worse."

White Crow replied, "You are making me think. It would probably be better for me to go and take the children to rest. I will see you, right Jake? You will be here tomorrow, won't you? Tell me I will see you."

"I will see you tomorrow. Take the children back before they get too cold. You need to get some sleep. I am off duty in about an hour. That's when I'll go to sleep too."

White Crow and Jake Savage embraced one another. The hug in which they participated lasted approximately five seconds before another interruption took place.

The young girls returned from a point nearby in order to accompany White Crow in moving toward the main portion of the camp. The children stopped and began laughing at the couple expressing their seemingly innocent love for one another.

As White Crow began to walk away from Jake, she took one more opportunity to place her right hand in Jake's left, while she did the same with her left and his right. There was an unintelligible whisper from White Crow to Jake Savage, and one of the girls imagined that she heard what was said and felt that the time to state the obvious was at hand.

Speaking English with extreme clarity, the child uttered, "She said she loves him! I have heard my parents say that to each other. I think they will get married. Then it won't be long before White Crow has a baby!"

The children again giggled at White Crow and Jake Savage as the young couple said good night to one another. The youngsters followed White Crow as she led them in their return to camp. Corporal Savage spent the last hour of his time on guard duty talking with Strong Buck, the Cherokee man Jake had served with only a few nights earlier. This night, Jake had been assigned to work with another Cherokee man who had tended to wander toward where Strong Buck and a second soldier had been positioned. The moments not spent with Strong Buck allowed Jake Savage the opportunity to ponder the situation into which Jake and White Crow had begun to place themselves.

Speaking aloud, as if conversing with someone, yet believing that his words were only discernable to his own ears, Jake Savage evaluated his options. He realized that the budding relationship he shared with

White Crow would eventually evolve into a problem if the issue became public knowledge. In contemplating his options, Jake rationalized that he would have a major problem keeping the matter private, especially given that no less than a dozen people whom he knew were aware of the situation.

Another option Jake Savage surmised was to keep the budding bond with White Crow at the point where it currently stood. He could then wait for the voyage along the trail to come to an end before allowing the relationship to progress. At that time, Jake anticipated, the couple could speak with higher ranking military officers and hopefully obtain the official blessings required for Jake to take White Crow as his wife.

By contrast, Corporal Savage also felt that the most viable option would be to end the relationship. The general societal view of such a marriage tended to be overwhelmingly negative. The couple could proceed with their individual lives and hopefully find love with another. However, both White Crow and Jake would be unlikely to accept such a resolution. Jake had seen other soldiers talking with Cherokee females and felt doing so was not a cause for concern.

The dilemma Corporal Jake Savage faced would cause him a great deal of concern in the final minutes of his guard detail that night. It also served as a dream that interrupted his sleep during the same period. More so than the chill and snow of the night, the thoughts related to what should be done in relation to White Crow harassed Jake Savage throughout many hours of the night. Jake finally made peace with himself that he would attempt to speak with White Crow about the situation and seek a means by which the association could be preserved without becoming more public.

That would hopefully be done the next day. As Jake Savage was well aware, at least subconsciously, nothing went according to plan while the soldiers and the Cherokee were moving along the trail.

Chapter 18

Early in the morning that followed the Arkansas-based night filled with restless sleep, Corporal Jake Savage was fully awakened in his lean-to shelter that was loosely connected to the side of a wagon. A soldier who had been inducted with Jake shook him shortly after sunrise and urged him to get into his full uniform.

"Jake! Jake! We gotta get in formation. Deas, Brantley and Tetleton are ordering all of us and the Cherokee to assemble in less than ten minutes. There was a bugle call a couple of minutes ago, and Colonel Tetleton was yelling like I've never heard him. He sounds some kinda mad. I wanted to give you a couple of more minutes to sleep since you'd been movin' around all night. Something must be bothering you real bad."

Jake Savage wiped the sleep from his eyes and slowly spoke to his friend, "What's the talk, Stephen? I've never known them to do something like this unless it's been a major problem or escape."

Corporal Savage pulled his pocket watch from the coat he had used as a portion of his bedclothes. In viewing it, he exclaimed, "It's only been four hours since I went to sleep! A couple of hours before that, I was on duty. I didn't see anyone escape, just you and some others roaming around. I guess you were playing cards or something. I better get ready."

Within five minutes Jake was in full uniform and approached his fellow soldiers who were gathering in an official formation. The soldiers looked as puzzled as the Cherokee who stood attentively in the cold Arkansas early morning air. Fortunately, the distance the troops had placed between themselves and any major body of water allowed the temperature to seem far above what it had been in recent days.

"Does anyone know what's going on? I am tired." Jake Savage seemed to completely sum up the feelings of those around him, most of whom acknowledged his statement with nods to the affirmative.

Colonel Mark Tetleton moved into the center of the gathering, the soldiers to his left and Cherokee to his right. As Tetleton turned to face the latter, the mood of the typically calm and disciplined Tetleton was altered that morning with an obvious level of disgust and concern displayed upon his frowned face. His eyes appeared to glisten far more than they had on previous days that had dawned with temperatures far below what was now faced.

Colonel Mark Tetleton stood next to Lieutenant Deas, with Lieutenant Brantley to the right of Deas. The three officers scanned the gathering crowd and snapped to attention as the bugle sounded the same. Jake Savage thought he had detected all three of the men glance in the direction of the soldiers in the seconds preceding the bugle being blown.

As the enlisted men who were under the command of the three officers snapped to attention as had their leaders, the Cherokee grew quiet and awaited word as to why the assemblage had been initiated. The Cherokee generally appeared attentive, although they were not attempting to stand in any type of manner that indicated the rigidity of the soldiers' stance.

Colonel Mark Tetleton stepped forward and said, "I had hoped that within an hour from this moment we would be progressing westward toward our eventual goal. This day has taken a new perspective with the news that I received during the course of this past night. The action that is about to taken in regard to the disclosure of the information given to me leaves me troubled. I ask that God forgives me for what is about to be done. I also hope and pray that no additional action of this type will have to be imposed upon our detachment."

The Cherokee who stood within hearing range of the speaker began to look at one another and a discernable mumble arose from the crowd. There was speculation that another escape attempt had been made or perhaps even successfully carried out.

"Did someone run away, or did they catch one of 'em trying?" was a question that came from the puzzled yet largely-attentive soldiers.

Colonel Mark Tetleton looked toward the soldiers and continued his well-prepared and corrective speech. "It has come to my attention that a major military rule has been broken. Developing a relationship with the enemy, in this case the Cherokee captives, is against United States military protocol. This rule has been broken, and communication exceeding that level has taken place between a United States soldier and a female Cherokee."

Jake Savage felt that he would faint when he heard the initial sentences of Colonel Tetleton's statement. He knew that the contact he had with White Crow was far from inappropriate. The couple had displayed little more affection than holding hands. In a matter of two seconds Jake began contemplating his defense should he be placed in front of a military jury.

Corporal Jake Savage and his comrades had little time to wait for Colonel Tetleton to continue his disclosure, a feat that began as soon as the low level of comments and related looks of bewilderment drew to a close. In the moments of silence, and despite the multitude of thoughts filling his mind, Jake Savage managed to find White Crow in the crowd. The beautiful maiden was located some thirty yards to his left.

White Crow looked at Jake with the same level of concern he held for her. Standing beside her was the elderly lady whom Jake had helped during the decent of Monteagle Mountain several weeks earlier. The matriarch placed her right arm around White Crow's shoulders and her left around the front of White Crow's slim waist.

"I don't know what will happen. He can be taken from me and I may never see him again." White Crow spoke in Cherokee and began to cry.

The wise lady replied to White Crow, "Wait, my young one. We will try to work this out for you and your friend. Let us see what the army man has to say."

Strong Buck, the man who had served on guard duty with Jake and knew of the admiration White Crow and Jake Savage held for one another, looked toward Jake and then made a quick glimpse in the direction of White Crow. While the confusion and fear in Jake's eyes caused Strong Buck a great deal of concern, it was the fact White Crow was becoming noticeably upset that garnered the bulk of his attention.

Colonel Mark Tetleton continued, "I have asked Lieutenant Brantley to continue the implementation of this gathering and to supervise the administration of the penalty."

Jake Savage braced for his name to be called out, and the young soldier looked at White Crow. The object of his affection was beginning to cry strongly enough that those around her joined the elderly lady in consoling White Crow.

Lieutenant Brantley stepped forward and began to read from a prepared statement, "It is the policy of the United States that any member of its military engaging in inappropriate contact with a member of an enemy force shall be duly punished. Twenty lashes from a whip shall be inflicted upon such a member who is enlisted in the service of the United States in an effort to suspend further action on his part and deter any other member from doing the same."

As Jake Savage looked toward the ground and contemplated the punishment that was to come, his peripheral vision detected a soldier who was standing three men from him and to the right. The other soldier, a corporal named Stephen Cook, began to stagger as Brantley continued. However, Corporal Jake Savage felt that the soldier was merely overcome with emotion for him.

"Corporal Stephen Cook, please step forward." Captain Brantley issued the order as gasps were emitted from soldiers standing near Corporal Cook. A scream from a Cherokee girl standing a few feet from White Crow also filled the air with echoes.

Corporal Cook, the man who had briefly conversed with Jake the previous night, stepped forward as he wiped his eyes. Cook looked toward the object of his affection, a Cherokee girl no more than seventeen years old. As Cook issued hurried and muddled words of apology to his fellow soldiers, the young Cherokee girl continued to scream in more audible tones.

"No, no. It is my fault! Do not hurt him! He has not done anything wrong." The strong feelings the young girl held for Corporal Cook were evident, yet Captain Brantley maintained his focus upon the situation and the related punishment to be inflicted.

Before the gathering, Lieutenant Brantley had arranged for four soldiers from Cook's company to serve as a detail responsible for taking Cook to the location where his punishment would be imposed. The four men stepped forward and took control of Corporal Cook. The guilt-ridden soldier initially offered no resistance to the evolving situation. That fact changed when the Cherokee lady with whom he had broken military protocol became more vocal and animated in her evaluation of the state of affairs.

"Let him go!" were the words the Cherokee maiden screamed as she burst from the grasp of those who were attempting to keep her from assaulting her suitor's captors. Soldiers yelled for her to return to her position, but she ignored their heated commands.

At that moment Corporal Cook, held only loosely by his left arm, pulled from one his attendants and began running toward the Cherokee maiden whose name was Dancing Flower. With Cook's attempt to intervene, bayonets were pointed toward the approaching Cherokee men who were intending to stop Dancing Flower before she placed herself in harm's way.

"Stop her now!" yelled one of the four men who had lost control of Cook.

With that request, a soldier who had been only an observer to that point, grabbed the barrel of his muzzle loader and used the butt of the weapon as a club. Dancing Flower was struck across her head, immediately rendering her unconscious. Seeing this, Corporal Cook changed the direction of his advance, and he moved toward the soldier who had struck Dancing Flower.

"You'll pay for that you coward. I'll have your blood if it's the last thing I do!" Having completed his pledge, Corporal Cook was again apprehended and thrown to the ground. Before he was able to offer any resistance to his renewed captivity, Cook was bound hand and foot.

Colonel Tetleton appeared to have been overcome with the emotions that the scene invoked. In an effort to diffuse the tension of the situation, he fired his pistol into the air. Doing so caused an estimated dozen Cherokee men, moving toward the soldier who had hit Dancing Flower, to temporarily cease their advance.

"That will be all! Get those people back and prepare them for the day's march. We leave in fifteen minutes." Tetleton unscabbered his sword and pointed it toward the halted Cherokee. Captain Brantley and a half dozen enlisted soldiers flanked Colonel Tetleton, and their presence seemed to calm the situation for the time being.

Jake Savage was only able to make brief eye contact with White Crow as he was given the task of joining the majority of his company members in securing the area where Cook's punishment would be carried out. White Crow and those with her saw that the children in the group were able to gather their limited amount of belongings before being placed into a series of wagons in preparation for the continued march.

Dancing Flower soon regained partial consciousness, but she was unable to walk. Lieutenant Deas ordered a quartet of Cherokee men, under the supervision of an identical number of armed soldiers, to move Dancing Flower to a wagon. She would hopefully receive medical attention upon her placement in the wagon. The command was carried out, but the medical care Dancing Flower so desperately needed never came.

Meanwhile, Corporal Cook, saddened from the treatment of the object of his affection, offered no further opposition and was tied to the wheel of a wagon. Cook was helped to his knees, and the shirt was removed from his upper body. The tail of his shirt was left tucked inside his pants. The sides of his shirttail hung loosely as they had been pulled out during his earlier struggle to assist Dancing Flower.

Asking for a volunteer to administer the whipping, Lieutenant Brantley found no takers. The officer was obviously upset at the situation and the fact that Cook had to be penalized. Brantley looked at Jake Savage and the others who were serving as security personnel in an attempt to locate one who he felt could be ordered to inflict the lashing.

"I can't find it in myself to make one of you do this. Are there no volunteers? Are there no volunteers?" Lieutenant George Brantley, apparently emotionally overcome with the fact that one of his soldiers was about to receive a grave cycle of punishment, reached a rapid resolution to the situation.

"Then I'll do it." Lieutenant Brantley called for the whip and a soldier brought one from its storage location on a wagon. Ordering those in the area to back away from the range of his backswing, Brantley prepared to inflict the thrashing upon Corporal Cook.

The cracks of the whip from the first two lashes cut through the cold air that engulfed the scene. With the third lash, Corporal Cook yelled from the intense pain. Each subsequent strike of the whip resulted in either a scream of penetrating and increasing pain or a call for Dancing Flower. By the twelfth stroke Cook fainted from the agony and a substantial loss of blood. At the completion of the brutal punishment, Cook's limp body was removed from location and carried into a nearby wagon.

Having reluctantly finished the infliction of the prescribed punishment, Lieutenant Brantley forcefully threw the whip to the ground and began walking away. The officer, only a couple of years older than Corporal Cook and originally from the same small town, had known Cook prior to their enlistment in the military. The situation had evidently gotten the best of Brantley's typical level of composure. The incident caused Lieutenant Brantley to begin wiping tears from his cheeks. He attempted to hide that fact from the soldiers in the area, but Jake Savage and no less than three others witnessed the act. At least in the case of Corporal Savage, the deed of Brantley crying and wiping away his tears would remain a secret. The other witnesses failed to undertake the same level of respect or admiration for Brantley.

The wagon bearing Corporal Cook's mutilated and seemingly-lifeless body was positioned near the center of the train as it proceeded westward at approximately 8:00 a.m. The wagon in which Dancing Flower was riding was directly behind Cook's wagon. There was to be no contact between Cook and Dancing Flower, but the soldiers in either wagon managed to relay the condition of the passenger of one wagon to the soldiers who were in attendance with the patient in the other wagon.

A team of two soldiers, neither of whom was versed in treating wounds of the nature inflicted upon Corporal Cook, attempted to dress and treat Cook's deep cuts and related seepage. The extreme lack of sanitation inside the wagon, coupled with the dirt and other debris that entered the wounds from the horse whip used in carrying out Cook's punishment rapidly resulted in discoloration and swelling of the areas around the wounds.

Corporal Cook slowly appeared to become more aware of the people around him, but his times in states of consciousness were only in short bursts. Those signs of awareness or Cook's part grew highly infrequent. By the end of the day of Cook's whipping, he began to mumble indiscernible words and phrases. Jake Savage made a point of pulling his horse near the rear of the wagon, and the sight and associated smell of Cook's hastily infecting wounds caused Savage to gag and reel his horse away from the makeshift ambulance.

When Jake Savage pulled his wagon to the rear of Dancing Flower's wagon, he was amazed to find that White Crow was one of three Cherokee women who attended the conscious, but emotionally-depleted Dancing Flower. A soldier named Tom Baker had been given the task of guarding the four Cherokee as the wagon progressed along the trail.

"How are you, Corporal Savage?" asked the guard.

"I am doing well aside from the weather. The sight of Cook was more than I can handle. Are you okay, Baker?"

"I'd trade places with you in a heartbeat. These ladies know I had nothing to do with what happened to Cook, but they think Lieutenant Brantley is a marked man. Savage, I don't like the way things are going. I'm ready to head back to Georgia and get out of this here army. Things just ain't like I thought they was."

"I understand, Baker. I'll guard these folks if you need a break. Be careful with my horse, he's about worn out from walking in this snow the last couple of days."

Jake and Tom Baker traded places, with Baker having become overwhelmed with the situation taking place inside the converted hospital wagon. The move would have certainly been looked upon with disgust if the relationship between White Crow and Jake had been more public in nature. Little would have likely been said if it had been though, considering the general mood of the majority of the soldiers in the train. Their concern for Corporal Cook was well-founded, and the number of soldiers beginning to join Jake Savage in questioning the rationale of the entire relocation process was beginning to increase greatly.

Jake Savage managed to carry on a small amount of conversation with White Crow while the lovely damsel provided some primitive care for Dancing Flower. The primary reason for Jake making comments to White Crow, at least in the eyes of those around the wagon, was for him to provide updates on Cook. In actuality, it took little imagination to see that Jake Savage was inclined toward maintaining contact with White Crow in a more romantic manner.

Within four days Dancing Flower had overcome the majority of the physical signs of her injuries. However, she was unable to walk with other Cherokee as they traversed the snow-covered terrain. Dizziness was the regular attendant when she attempted to stand, and the affliction negated her attempts to walk.

Interestingly, a train of supply wagons that had been sent from a series of local churches located near the eastern Arkansas portion of the trail had arrived the day after Dancing Flower's injuries were inflicted. Three hundred thirty-four pairs of shoes were among the items sent for the aid of the Cherokee. Through the intervention of Jake Savage, Dancing Flower was able to obtain one pair of the shoes. They were placed beside her bedding until she was able to wear them and begin walking with her people.

The wet snow regularly caused the uncovered feet of many of the Cherokee to wrinkle and eventually crack. The cracks would inevitably bleed at regular intervals, leaving clear marks as to where the Cherokee had stepped on their westward journey. This fact upset Dancing Flower greatly, and she routinely offered to give her shoes to others who were less fortunate, but Dancing Flower's delicate condition caused all of those she offered to decline.

While Dancing Flower had made tremendous physical progress in the days since the incident, the deep emotional scars were resisting any signs of healing. She had managed to avoid the early animosity many of the Cherokee held for the soldiers. That mindset had seemingly led to her relationship with Corporal Stephen Cook. While her love for Cook was as pure and sincere as any relationship could hold, Dancing Flower refused to speak to any other member of the military aside from Cook or Jake Savage. Her comments toward Jake were confined to the topic of Stephen Cook, although she would also indicate to White Crow that the budding relationship between White Crow and Jake would lead to a similar outcome.

Dancing Flower also faced the detail that the object of her affection, based upon the regular reports she received, was enduring a slow and painful death. The guilt Dancing Flower felt because of this aspect of recent events was, needless to say, overwhelming. Those caring for Dancing Flower had literally forced her to eat, and that had seemingly been the greatest contribution to her hasty physical recovery as proper medical attention was absent.

Corporal Stephen Cook was far less fortunate than Dancing Flower. The attempts at providing care for his cavernous and abundant wounds had been admirable, but insufficient. The cold weather that usually inhibited the spread of infection had done little to prevent the foreign matter imbedded in the lacerations from becoming gangrenous. On the fifth day after the infliction of punishment upon Cook, he took a drastic turn for the worse.

The activity around Corporal Cook's wagon during the night's encampment was noticeable to everyone in the Bell Group. Soldiers who had known Cook were routinely making their way to the rear of the wagon in order to speak to Cook. Few felt that he comprehended anything that was said, until Lieutenant Brantley appeared. The ensuing comments resulted in a massive display of sadness and related tears.

Lieutenant Brantley offered a heartfelt apology to Cook for the punishment that had been imposed upon him. Corporal Cook briefly opened his eyes and seemed to nod in agreement with Brantley's proclamation. The tears Brantley shed noticeably affected dozens of people who had slowly gathered to witness the conversation.

Brantley spoke with Colonel Tetleton and Lieutenant Deas who agreed that it would be in the best interest of the morale of the remaining members and timeframe of the trail to allow Dancing Flower to enter the wagon where Cook lay. Well over a hundred people were present by the time she was allowed to leave the area of the camp to which she had been assigned earlier that evening. Using White Crow and a Cherokee lady of some sixteen years of age as supports, the emotional Dancing Flower slowly stepped to the rear of Cook's wagon.

Although his salutation drew no verbal response from Dancing Flower, Lieutenant Brantley's deep concern for the suffering Stephen Cook created a smile on her face. Upon receiving Dancing Flower at the back of Cook's wagon, Brantley said, "Dancing Flower, he wants to see you. I will leave you alone with him."

With that said, Lieutenant Brantley made his way toward a wagon that was serving as his quarters. The act would come to have serious ramifications in the coming days, but no one realized that at the time.

Corporal Cook was prostrate, lying at an angle in the wagon, with a lantern burning dimly at his feet. His feet were positioned near the wagon's center. His body was on its left side as his head lay near the wagon's back. From this position he was able to listen to the many visitors who made their way to his location. Cook occasionally responded, but the words he uttered were frequently faint and indiscernible.

Dancing Flower arrived at the wagon for her last visit with Corporal Cook around 8 o'clock. It had been five days since the infliction of the devastating punishment upon Cook; the rationale of the same was for his contact with Dancing Flower. Her words were filled with compassion and a longing for the love they would never fulfill.

"I love you. You have been so good to me. I will join you in Heaven someday, and I plan to never love another man."

Corporal Cook briefly opened his eyes and made a statement that was among the few comprehensible comments he made during his final days on earth. Cook also managed to lift his right arm as his mangled left arm, swollen and heavily discolored, lay limp at his side.

"You are the one girl I have truly loved. Everything I have suffered has been worth the weeks I spent with you. I hope that one day we will be together forever. I love you."

Cook completed his monologue, closed his eyes, and breathed his last. The smile that covered his face as he passed away reassured those around him that he was leaving the pain and agony of the recent days and entering a far more peaceful existence.

The deceased trooper's body was taken to the edge of the camp and, under the light of approximately a half dozen lanterns, placed into a shallow grave. The gently falling snow of the night covered the freshly dug earth and most signs of the existence of a grave. The only evidence of a burial having taken place was the small mound and a cross. The latter element was made from two small tree limbs bound together with Cook's belt taken from his blood-soaked trousers.

Dancing Flower's screams of mourning and distress were heard across the valley where the Bell Group was camped. Only the consoling from White Crow and two other young Cherokee women seemed to temporarily ease her agony. Jake Savage maintained his distance from the scene, although he was given the assignment of serving on the burial detail.

Corporal Savage also made a visit to Lieutenant Brantley's wagon, but a soldier standing guard informed him that Brantley had given instructions for no visitors to interrupt his privacy.

"I'd like to tell him what has happened, it's not his fault." Savage pleaded with the attendant, but to no avail.

"I have my orders and I cannot stray from them, Savage. I don't want to have the same thing happen to me that happened to Cook."

A voice from inside the wagon interrupted the conversation and made it evident that Brantley was fully aware of Savage's presence. "I ain't gonna punish anyone. Tell Corporal Savage I am aware of what has happened; I hear the screams, the cries of Cook's woman. This all has to stop 'fore we have a riot on our hands."

The message appeared to have come from Lieutenant Brantley, but his words were not presented as clearly as the young officer had ever spoken in the past. The reason for such was revealed in a matter of a few seconds, as an empty whiskey bottle was hurled from the back of the wagon with enough force that, when it crashed into a nearby tree, it shattered onto the surrounding snow.

"Now leave me be. I have work to do. Gotta write to that man's family and let them know he has died, or that I killed him. He was so young. Whole life ahead of him. Go! Go away! I don't want anyone telling me things will be alright. This is a horrible thing I've done."

News of Corporal Stephen Cook's passing had spread throughout the area quickly and seemed to rank among the most agonized deaths of those who lost their life traversing the trail. The symbol of reconciliation that the relationship Stephen Cook shared with Dancing Flower seemed to pass with his burial. Perhaps as unsettling was the knowledge that Corporal Cook's death would be far from the last to be mourned on the trail.

Chapter 19

The mood was maudlin on the morning after Corporal Stephen Cook's death and burial. The sound of the bugle call that signaled assembly seemed to crudely cut into the otherwise quiet atmosphere. Beleaguered individuals from the Cherokee and military ranks alike stood silently and awaited the orders of the day.

Colonel Mark Tetleton struggled to order respective personnel to conduct the daily count. This task was completed with no comments or conversation aside from the reports of the total numbers of Cherokee present. There appeared to have been no escapes and no Cherokee deaths during the twilight hours, a situation that was a rarity during the trek along the trail.

Wagons were hitched to their horses with little dialogue among the teamsters. Strangely, even the animals seemed less resistant to the morning ritual. The light snow that continued to fall brought about a stillness that is fully understood only with individuals who have witnessed such an event first hand. The combination of the snow and the emotional numbness prevalent among the soldiers and Cherokee did little to disturb the area's wildlife.

Three deer walked through the snow and approached the brink of the Bell Group before systematically scurrying from the area at a much slower speed than deer usually utilize. Rabbits and birds were far more numerous on that morning than they were in a typical setting. The usual clatter of preparations for hooking up wagons, shouting orders, and general banter gave way to an almost incomprehensible level of quietness.

The morning's march began in a comparable level of complacency and continued as such until the noon hour. As the mid-point of the day's sun arrived, the snow finally ceased, and the temperature approached a recent high temperature of forty degrees. The train of wagons came to a halt in order to allow a moment of rest and refreshment for the teams of animals. Brief chattering eventually erupted among small factions of the group, but that was largely relegated to soldiers instructing Cherokee children to remain in the wagons and to terminate their singing.

The somberness of the day also affected the amount of territory covered that day. Despite the best efforts of those in charge of leading the group that day, only nine miles were covered from the morning's starting point. The primary reason for that fact rested in an incident that occurred just past two o'clock in the afternoon.

The Bell Group had been crossing a relatively low hill that rested in the center of an otherwise insignificant range of similar outcroppings. The particular rise that hampered the contingency's progression included a steep portion that overlooked and bordered a drop of almost one hundred feet. At the bottom of the noted precipice, jagged rocks dominated the landscape. No less than three wagons, victims of previous trips through the location, were distinguishable at the foot of the rise. The snow did little to conceal the associated decaying bodies of horses scattered among the vessels from civilians who had earlier passed that way.

The distraught Dancing Flower had said nothing to anyone that morning. She attempted to walk at times, seemingly doing so in efforts to test the strength and resiliency of her muscles. She rode beside one of the teamsters the majority of the morning's journey. Dancing Flower slowly stepped from the perch and strolled along the trail as she neared the treacherous location. Closely following her, primarily in order to watch for her well-being, was Strong Buck. White Crow had appealed to the young Cherokee male to provide protection for Dancing Flower, should she fall prey to the vengeance of soldiers or another Cherokee who could hold the relationship with Corporal Cook against the lamenting lady. Likewise, Jake Savage led the way for the wagon directly in front of

Dancing Flower as she blindly followed her comrades walking solemnly in a westward direction.

When Dancing Flower reached the imposing overlook she was apparently overcome with the grief of Corporal Stephen Cook's death. The guilt associated with her role in the events that precipitated Cook's passing evidently weighed heavily on her mind as well. Dancing Flower strangely appeared to regain the stamina she exhibited prior to her injury. Immediately, she made a strong approach to the edge of the peak with the full intention of leaping to her death. Fortunately for the preservation of her life, Dancing Flower slipped on a sheet of ice that rested beneath two inches of snow only three feet from the brink of the trail.

Dancing Flower hit the ground with a force that cracked the ice upon which her right knee hit. She attempted to rise to her feet in order to complete her quest, but found herself unable to do so. Dancing Flower fell again and grasped her knee in agony.

At that moment, Strong Buck reached Dancing Flower in an effort to prevent the saddened lass from inflicting harm upon herself. Unfortunately, one soldier saw Strong Buck's gesture incorrectly and determined that Strong Buck was actually planning to throw Dancing Flower from the hillside.

"Help her, she is going to die!" A Cherokee lady yelled at the top of her lungs, hoping to acquire assistance for Dancing Flower.

The call for support, as well as Strong Buck's order of "Stop" issued toward Dancing Flower also caused Jake Savage to move quickly in her direction.

Ryan Winston, the soldier who reached Dancing Flower and Strong Buck prior to Jake Savage, dealt a mortal wound to Strong Buck. Corporal Savage was only able to reach forward in an attempt to halt the action that seemed to transpire in slow-motion.

Jake Savage's vain effort to thwart the soldier cut through the air as Savage yelled, "No!"

Simultaneously, Ryan Winston's bayonet plunged deeply into Strong Buck's back, penetrating the robust man's left kidney. Strong

Buck's shout of utter suffering annulled Winston's ability to hear Jake Savage's cry to terminate the action.

Winston violently exacted a quick second wound to Strong Buck. The soldier's bayonet glanced off Strong Buck's outstretched left hand and created a gash midway along the Cherokee's ribcage. Blood spurted from the first wound and began doing the same from the second as Jake Savage reached Strong Buck's location.

Two other soldiers arrived seconds after Savage, eliminating supplementary exploits of fierceness from Winston. One of the soldiers informed Winston of the situation and the young soldier was overwhelmed at his own misinterpretation of what had been taking place.

"What have I done? I thought he was trying to kill her. Forgive me, God, for what I have done and for what I am about to do." With that said, Private Ryan Winston jumped from the very bluff he misconstrued Strong Buck was using to end Dancing Flower's life.

The second soldier who had reached Winston before a third strike could be delivered attempted to keep Winston from committing suicide, but failed in his effort. Winston had knocked away the soldier's hands, but the fighter managed to gain a grip on Winston's coat. Having come unbuttoned in the fray, Winston's coat slipped from his body and remained in the attempted rescuers hands as Winston plunged to his death on the serrated rocks below.

Corporal Jake Savage saw Winston disappear from the edge of the cliff. However, Jake was so concerned with the mortally wounded Strong Buck that he neither said nor did anything related to possibly rescuing Winston.

"Jake Savage, I am dying. Please take care of White Crow. She loves you, and I know that you feel the same for her. I will see you on the other side, my friend." The volume of Strong Buck's words hurriedly diminished as he continued to speak. "Help me, God."

"Strong Buck, help is coming. Hold on to my hand. I see the doctor now. White Crow is here as well." Jake's words were sincere and full of emotion.

"I don't need a doctor, Jake Savage. I am a dead man. My mother and father await me."

While White Crow held Strong Buck's right hand, Jake Savage struggled to assist in providing his limited knowledge of medical attention to the gasping and crying warrior. The same physician who had provided the primary care for Corporal Stephen Cook arrived at the scene of Strong Buck's wounding only two minutes after the incident.

"I'm afraid I can't do anything for him. The wounds are too deep and he'll bleed to death. I'm sorry; I don't know what to say." The doctor looked toward the ground and viewed the blood easing from Strong Buck's body and spreading across the freshly-trodden snow.

Strong Buck was placed into the wagon that had earlier served as Dancing Flower's mode of transportation. Within four hours Strong Buck had breathed his last breath on earth. As with so many other men and women who had met their demise on the trail, Strong Buck's corpse was not properly buried. Despite the protests of Jake Savage and other soldiers, the Bell Group had to continue on its journey, and Strong Buck's body was given to the elements.

"We can't stop and bury every Cherokee who dies on this trip. We'd be forever in reaching our objective." Colonel Mark Tetleton was adamant in his statement.

Corporal Jake Savage recanted, "And just where is our objective? We've been walking for months and we still don't know where we're headed. You've hidden it from these people and the members of your own command."

"Corporal Savage, you're being highly insubordinate. I'll have you arrested and placed into chains if you continue this conversation. I'd think twice before making another statement on behalf of this dead Indian." Colonel Tetleton made his stance clear with his sword drawn and pointed toward Jake. Savage knew there was no need in objecting or pursuing the matter further.

Jake Savage returned to his saddle and rode his horse until sunset. His sense of duty to the United States government had been damaged beyond repair. Not only had he lost a brother in arms with the death of Corporal Stephen Cook, but Jake had also lost a friend and confidant through what he determined was the murder of Strong Buck.

Colonel Savage managed to briefly speak with White Crow at approximately nine o'clock that night. His disgust over the situation of the loss of two people for whom he held a great level of respect occupied the majority of the conversation. The two young people were also distressed over the condition of Dancing Flower, who had ceased all verbal communication with anyone, and she had refused to eat since the injury and death of Strong Buck.

Being more talkative than the night before and that they had been during the day, the remaining members of the Bell Group spent a restless night in camp. While no escape attempts had been made the previous night, the hours following Strong Buck's senseless death indicated far different results for the party.

Chapter 20

The roll call taken on the day after Strong Buck's death revealed the escape of twenty-four Native Americans from the overnight encampment of the Bell Group. The disclosure of the loss sent Lieutenants Tetleton and Deas into outbursts that were directed toward those on guard duty. Leaning against a wagon, Brantley initially said nothing and appeared to have aged tremendously since making his last appearance; that being the beating of Corporal Stephen Cook.

"I should each of you jailed for your failures. I would hate to think that any one of you would allow these people to walk away without having fired a shot at the insurgents. There is no way twenty-four people could leave a well-guarded bivouac unless blind eyes are turned their way. Someone will pay for this debacle, and it won't be me. This will be fully investigated, and I will have due and proper punishment inflicted upon the culprit or culprits and anyone who has knowledge of the ploy." Deas was almost uncontrollable in his anger.

Lieutenant Brantley took exception to the heated lecture Lieutenant Deas provided. Stepping away from the wagon that had served as his support, the officer threw an empty whiskey bottle to the ground. To those who witnessed the affair, it seemed reminiscent of Brantley hurling the whip to the side after inflicting the deadly beating upon Corporal Cook.

The rumor that Lieutenant Brantley had been drinking heavily since thrashing Cook had been circulating throughout the Bell Group from the hours that immediately followed the tragic event. Recent heartbreaks had resulted in far less time being devoted to the gossip, yet a major aspect of the blather lent credibility to the matter. Brantley had not been seen and had reportedly placed himself into a reclusive state since the incident.

Brantley had also apparently failed to bathe or administer any form of personal hygiene while in hiding. The mental stress associated with Corporal Cook's beating and death had led to Lieutenant George Brantley suffering a noticeable mental breakdown. His recent speech was either heavily slurred or completely failed to make sense. Either was a colossal regression from his usual concise presentation and professional conduct.

"All of you listen to this gentleman." The sarcasm associated with the final word of the sentence indicated that Lieutenant Brantley held little respect for his commanding officer.

"I think this is only going to be ended and solved with another beatin'. I 'member one day back in children times; I found the government was right and Indians was wrong. That's a lot like the things that happened and was like rain on my little parade. You gotta look out for…"

At that point Lieutenant Deas and Colonel Tetleton ordered three soldiers forward to restrain the ranting and emotional Brantley. The determination of Lieutenant Brantley to settle the issues he saw as detrimental to the common good of those involved was admired among many of those who witnessed the monologue. Nonetheless, Deas and Tetleton were convinced the speech should be brought to a concise conclusion.

"Place Lieutenant Brantley in his wagon and do not allow him to leave. His insubordination will not be tolerated, nor will any such conduct from him or another member of the United States Army." Colonel Tetleton showed a strong stance against the words being said regarding recent events.

"Now, ain't we talkin' tough. Take the drunk man who's done all your killin' and rule makin'; he's had all he's gonna take. You are the one, Colonel Tetleton, who needs to be jailed."

The three soldiers adhered to Colonel Tetleton's command and struggled to remove the drunken officer from the scene. The scuffle was brought to a sudden end as Brantley broke free and began running from them. The snow, although hardly covering the warming ground, combined with Brantley's drunkeness to make his efforts at running completely unsuccessful.

Lieutenant Brantley rounded the rear of a nearby wagon that had earlier been loaded with children in order to begin the day's march. An armed soldier stepped forward at the same time. Catching Brantley by surprise, the soldier noticed Brantley instinctively place his hands over his head in an act of surrender.

The soldier determined that Lieutenant Brantley was insincere in his action and ordered him to end his escapade. Brantley jumped as the soldier yelled, "Halt!"

Lieutenant Brantley was then struck over the head with a limb that the soldier had used to move the team of horses into position. The blow from the stick of wood not only knocked Brantley unconscious, but it also broke both of Brantley's thumbs and a total of three other fingers. Colonel Tetleton ordered that the incapacitated officer be picked up and placed into the wagon that had served as Brantley's place of solitude for recent days.

What originally seemed to be a minor head wound quickly grew infected, evidently a reaction to the large amount of alcohol Brantley had consumed over a period less than a week. The officer suffered throughout the day's journey and died just before midnight.

In order to avoid an outcry from Brantley's supporters, Colonel Tetleton ordered the man's body to be buried before daylight. Tetleton and Deas joined three Cherokee males, working under forced means, in burying Brantley. There were no words read or said before or after the officer was buried, an act of disrespect toward a man who Colonel Tetleton felt had become uncontrollable in his actions.

The ploy regarding Lieutenant George Brantley's internment would not be discovered for three days. Colonel Tetleton largely managed to convince the three Cherokee that they would be severely punished should either of them disclose the events of the midnight burial. Two of the men maintained silence in respect to the situation, but one member failed to do so. On the third day after Brantley's burial in an unmarked grave, the man told his wife all that had transpired.

The wife felt that making everyone aware of the incident would be beneficial to her people. If there was such a lack of respect for the life of a fellow soldier, the Cherokee lady surmised, there would be even less for the group of Cherokee captives. Such an admission would lead to a revolt and freedom for her people, or so the woman determined.

Although the discovery of the events that followed the publicly-acknowledged injury of Brantley failed to cause the planned purge of military authority, it did result in punishment. The morning after his disclosure, both the Cherokee man who told his wife, as well as the wife herself, were found beheaded. There was a great deal of speculation as to who committed the heinous crime, but suspects were never brought forward.

Jake Savage and White Crow discussed the incident and reached the conclusion that either Deas or Tetleton would have benefitted the most from the deaths of the two Cherokee. However, both men were in wagons that were surrounded with guards on the night of the murders. The guards were deemed as necessary for the preservation of the two officers' lives, yet they also provided to be sufficient and convenient alibis for both Lieutenant Deas and Colonel Tetleton. The murders of the talkative Cherokee couple would not be the last to go unsolved on the hated and tragedy-laced trail.

Chapter 21

As the Cherokee procession progressed slowly across Arkansas, additional tragedies and deaths occurred. The supplies that had been provided as the group hurriedly left Tennessee were depleted, and the acts of hunting and foraging for food began in earnest. The norm again became for Cherokee fathers and mothers to live off little or no food in order for their children to maintain a semblance of health and nourishment.

An arresting tragedy from that time frame of the trail's perusal involved Hornbeak, a malnourished mother of three. The matriarch suffered to continue the march while carrying her four-month old daughter. Her other children, approximately three and five years of age, walked to either side of her as the Bell Group made their way toward the setting sun.

Pulling away from the child on her right, the mother of three placed her hand over her chest and fell backward onto the ground. As Hornbeak succumbed to her body's extensive malnourishment, she collapsed upon one of her children, breaking the infant's neck as she slammed to the ground. The recurrent lack of proper nutrition had taken its toll. The dying Cherokee mother was no older than her mid-twenties.

Seconds after landing on the packed ground that marked the trail, the young mother violently twitched as life escaped her body. Her two remaining children stood to either side, one holding the mother's right hand with another clinging to her left. The group was forced to walk by the children without offering any acknowledgement other than literally looking in their direction for a brief moment. The evolving scene caused many Cherokee and no less than five soldiers to flinch in attempts to step toward the recent orphans. Sadly, none took more than a couple of steps in the direction of the wailing children.

There were those brave few who attempted to help the children, but the standing order of continuing the movement of the party along the trail held firm. The sight of the crying children tore into the hearts of many members of the Cherokee and soldier factions alike.

The incident proved devastating to the emotional state of Corporal Jake Savage. The tormented soldier wheeled his horse toward the tragedy-stricken family, but Jake soon realized that there would be no way he could carry the two living children with him. With tears in his eyes, he tugged at the reins of his steed and returned to the trail.

Other soldiers were less compassionate toward the lost lives. The heartless comments were tossed around like an individual would be speaking of an inanimate object rather than a living being whose demise created two mournful orphans.

"Kids will have a reason to cry now. They've cost their momma her life 'cause they ate too much and dragged her down. That's four we got rid of with that one woman dying. I take it that the little kid is gone too. Animals got food tonight. Wild party's gonna take place soon."

"How can you say such a thing?" asked a soldier positioned nearby. "Those poor kids are innocent and have just lost their mother."

The heartless soldier replied, "They'll be gone in a day or two themselves. No food around here. Wolves or bears will have 'em eat up 'fore long."

The distraught children remained by the side of their mother as the last remnants of the Cherokee entourage passed from sight. There were no efforts made in relation to securing the children or to bury the deceased mother.

As the rear of the group reached a distance of one and a half miles from the location of the death of the mother and her infant daughter, the primary conversations that existed exposed the recent tragedy more fully. The talk among the Cherokee explained that the children's father had passed away while held captive at Red Clay. As a result, the father had never seen the infant born weeks after the patriarch's passing.

When word circulated into the ranks of the soldiers, a trio of horsemen took it upon themselves to return and rescue the orphaned children. The thoughts of the youngsters being left alone and desperately struggling to stay alive proved too much for the men to accept. The soldiers discussed the fact that the children's efforts to survive would ultimately be a losing effort. Zane Johnson, Tom Bryant, and Robert Franklin broke ranks and began their fast return to the site of the tragedy, but not before notifying one of their own that they were doing so.

Zane Johnson took a moment to appeal to a fellow soldier, "Savage, won't you come with us? We're going to go save those two kids. I saw you getting upset at their situation, and I know you wanted to help. Let's make a break for it. What can they possibly do to us?"

"I want to, but I have a feeling I'm already a marked man. They think I'm a traitor and that'll get me killed, just like they killed Cook. God bless you fellows." Corporal Savage kicked the sides of his horse and galloped from the trio.

The three men atop their horses sped from the Bell Group. As they neared the rear of the train, Cherokee were cheering them on to success. The tears that had been shed for the loss of lives were now replaced with a sense of preservation and reunion. Although a sergeant ordered the cheering to cease and that shots be fired at the three fleeing would-be rescuers, neither order was obeyed.

Within a short period of time, the three soldiers were close enough to the site of the death of the mother and her child that they could see the mother's body lying in the middle of the trail. Even before reaching her body, it became evident that the other two children were gone.

"Children! We're here to help you. Where are you?" The calls and pleas of the soldiers failed to result in coaxing out the lost children.

Distraught, one of the three asked, "Are they hiding or do you think something got 'em?"

A reply came from a second soldier, "They may think we're here to kill them. I don't blame them with all that's gone on. Try again."

The third soldier, who had stepped from his saddle, tried to make a more accurate investigation. He said, "I see footprints in the snow, but it's impossible to tell which ones are from her kids or the others who were walking behind them. This set goes to those bushes, but there's a lot of others that walked along the side of this little road. I can't tell; what do I do?"

Ironically, two of the sets of footprints that the soldier had discovered did, in fact, belong to the two missing children. The duo had stepped from the trail and made their way into the very set of bushes which the soldier noted. They successfully sought a safe hiding place at that location, and the spot proved to meet their demands. With a limited understanding of English, the two lacked the capacity to comprehend what was taking place.

As the soldiers, with their heads hung low, began their slow return to the train, the children slipped from their hiding place. The entire time they had been no more than twenty feet from the soldiers, but they were able to remain there without being detected.

As dark quickly approached, the bereaved children began digging a grave for their mother and younger sister. After doing so and with the night and the related life-threatening cold upon them, the children slipped into the tree line to sleep.

The next morning's sunrise found the two children huddled together and not far from the burial spot of two of their family members. With no source of heat and lacking proper clothing and bedding, the two toddlers had become victims of the elements and froze to death.

The exact outcome of the two children could only be prophesized among the members of the Bell Group. Without any visible signs of the children, the conjecture ran wild. With more deaths to come, the memory and mystery surrounding the children speedily faded into a mesh with the others who had also died on the trail.

Chapter 22

White Crow understandably found the recent loss of the two orphaned children depressing, and she relayed the mystery of their situation to Dancing Flower. The conversation was largely one-sided, as the deeply-depressed Dancing Flower refused to make any comments or contributions. Dancing Flower had a longtime reputation for maintaining a strong fondness of children, so her lack of making any reaction to the story certainly puzzled White Crow.

The setting for the discussion between the two Cherokee ladies was below a wagon. No less than eight women and three teens sought respite from the cold at that same location. Children were in the wagon above them, and the laughs from the young mouths offered a stark contrast to the emotional conference that was taking place on the thin bedding beneath the wagon.

"It is sad to think about what will happen to Hornbeak's children. I hope they are able to make it through the night. Do you think they will follow our tracks and reach us in the morning? That is my thought and prayer."

The question seemed to fall upon a hardened soul rather than the one that belonged to the usually carefree and loving Dancing Flower. After all, her name indicated the manner in which she regularly conducted herself. The loss of her beloved Corporal Stephen Cook had managed to change her entire persona in a matter of only a few days.

Throughout the lengthy conversation that lasted well into the chilly night air, Dancing Flower made only one comment, "I will be with them tomorrow."

"What are you saying? Are you running away, Dancing Flower? The night is cold and you may not find them. Jake Savage had told me that bears and wolves are very bad in this land where we rest tonight. You do not need to run away. Tell me that you will stay with me tonight. Maybe we can go look for them when the sun rises."

Dancing Flower managed a smile, but said nothing in reply to White Crow's request. The two ladies embraced as Dancing Flower began to weep loudly. The ladies and children who were huddled with the two ladies all managed to slip under the safety and protection of the wagon, while a light rain began to fall. As the temperatures dipped below freezing, the rain began to freeze, making the miserable night seem much colder than it was.

"Are you okay?" White Crow inquired of Dancing Flower. "Let me know if you need to talk. You know I will be here for you."

As Dancing Flower's tears subsided, she managed to utter, "Thank you" to White Crow.

White Crow replied, "I will be here for you tonight and in the morning. Will you still be here in the morning?" The question yielded no visible answer.

The answer to White Crow's inquisition would come in the morning, but not in the manner she desired.

After a restless night's sleep in which she dreamed about the probable deaths of the two missing children and the possibility of Dancing Flower running away, White Crow awakened at the sound of the bugle resonating throughout the camp. She rubbed her eyes and looked upward, seeing the bottom of the wagon under which she had been sleeping. Icicles hung from the edges of the wagon, and the ground was covered in a sheet of ice that crunched below the feet of the Cherokee stirring around the campsite.

The children in the wagon began their morning ritual of waking their friends whose sound sleep refuted the bugler's request. The laughter brought a smile to White Crow as she realized the situation of the night before.

"Dancing Flower, it is time to wake up. Don't you hear the bugle?" Upon asking her question, White Crow turned over in order to shake Dancing Flower. Another Cherokee lady, Snow Lady, had been sleeping on the other side of Dancing Flower. However, Snow Lady was propped on her left elbow staring blankly into Dancing Flower's face.

Snow Lady said, "White Crow, I think Dancing Flower is dead." The fate of her friend struck White Crow just as she was becoming fully aware of the fact that day had dawned.

White Crow's eyes moved suddenly toward those of Dancing Flower. The appearance of Dancing Flower's facial features was unusually ashen, with a minor smile upon her lips and both eyes opened slightly. Although Dancing Flower appeared peaceful, the situation invoked panic among those who were in here vicinity.

"Dancing Flower. Dancing Flower. Wake up! Dancing Flower. Oh, no!" White Crow began to cry loudly. As those around her fully awakened and became aware of the state of affairs, many of them did the same.

White Crow, lamenting the loss of another friend and loved one, summed up the feelings of many Cherokee. "When is this going to end? There have been so many tears shed on this trail. The heartbreak is complete and we are near the end of our strength. Please help us, dear God."

The bugles again sounded, summoning the Cherokee to hasten their gathering for roll call. The bugler was unaware of the death of Dancing Flower, yet he was also likely to have been indifferent to the situation that transpired on a frequent basis.

Seventeen less souls were present for the roll call that took place on the morning of Dancing Flower's death. A gloomy facet of that number rested in the fact that none of the seventeen had run away; all of the missing individuals had passed away during the frigid night. Just as had unknowingly taken place with the two children, the punishing cold temperatures of the night had robbed the individuals of their time on earth.

The large number of deaths would have proven costly from a time perspective if the bodies were permitted to be buried, so no funerals took place that morning. The heavy loss of life was the most the Bell Group had experienced in any single day aside from those on which large numbers of escapes were calculated. Grief was the dominant emotion of the day; practically every Cherokee family had endured the forfeiture of a friend or family member in the few hours of sleep on that miserably cold night.

Chapter 23

The careworn caravan consisting of Cherokee and military personnel made little progress in the days immediately following the night that needlessly cost the group so many lives. As a result of the extreme cold, it was recorded that daily marches covered no more than two to three miles on any single day.

Estimates from participants bore credit to the sluggish situation the Bell Group had encountered. A member of the detachment wrote, "We have only traveled sixty-five miles in the last month."

The low level of foodstuffs did little to add peace of mind to the crowd. Deaths mounted on a daily basis over the next week and a half, with no less than a dozen people succumbing to the horrid conditions on any given day.

Jake Savage, determined to do more in order to quell the epidemic of death, met with Colonel Tetleton and laid out a bold plan. While questionable from a moral standpoint, it did provide a means by which the survival rate of soldiers and Cherokee alike would be improved.

"There are almost always farms and towns near the road we're traveling. We've got enough soldiers and guns with us to fight off an enemy with great numbers. Does it not seem reasonable that we should be able to raid some of the houses we pass and not suffer repercussions from the people who live on the farms? Without stealing from the folks who have plenty, a lot more of us are going to die."

Colonel Tetleton seemed interested in the plan and remarked, "Go on, Corporal Savage. How do you plan to go about organizing and implementing such an operation?"

"Most of the townspeople in these areas know that the Cherokee are near, but they don't see them. I could take nine men with a couple of wagons, and strike a small town or farm here and there. We're far enough off the main roads that by the time the townspeople begin to think we're part of the group, we'll be long gone. That's especially true if we don't wear our uniforms; just borrow some regular civilian clothing from some of the Cherokee men."

Tetleton seemed genuinely interested in the prospects of acquiring supplies, regardless of the exact means. "Corporal Savage, it just may work. This would have to be done without my permission. In that way, I can report that we didn't endorse the operations, should they somehow become known to my superiors."

Jake Savage added, "The extra food will give these folks and us more strength, and it should keep so many people from getting sick. We're never going to make it out of this area unless we get some food in our bellies. Children are sick in many of the families, and there is a lot of talk of escape and revolts. Something has to be done and soon."

Colonel Tetleton lamented, "Even our boys are feeling the effects of the shortage of food. Am I correct? I don't seem to have any rapport with the men any longer. The incident with Corporal Cook seems to have messed up a lot of things. Then there was Brantley."

The conclusion of the comment about Lieutenant Brantley resulted in Tetleton placing his head into his hands and shaking his head.

"Some of the men are thinking about leaving their posts, sir. The morale is low and between the cold and no food, they've had about all they can take." Jake Savage was the sort of man who avoided stating anything other than the facts. Therefore, his proposal to steal from area residents clearly showed Colonel Tetleton how desperate the situation had actually become.

Colonel Tetleton concluded the bulk of the conversation. "Very well, Corporal Savage. If you feel that you can do it, it will be a good thing for our group. Just keep in mind that I don't want to know when you're leaving, at what time you plan to return, and where you are going. Is that fully understood? An undertaking of this nature is completely against our protocol."

Jake Savage answered, "Thank you, sir. I will do as you ask."

Corporal Jake Savage walked from Colonel Tetleton's tent and nodded in the direction of over half a dozen soldiers standing nearby. Knowing that the time to begin the covert mission was then at hand, he stepped toward the soldiers and gave the directions for the upcoming event. Most of the groundwork for the shenanigans had already been discussed.

Savage asked, "Do you all have a change of clothes?"

Answering in the affirmative, the soldiers hurriedly donned their new attire, most of which had come from the baggage the few fortunate Cherokee men had managed to lag with them for the early months of the journey. In all, ten men were dressed and ready to accompany Jake Savage as the ten o'clock hour approached.

At the designated time, the military men turned thieves made their way toward where they understood the nearest town was located. The rumor was that the town had sprung up in reaction to the discovery of gold and that the businesses in the community were known to harbor rather unseemly behavior and similarly characterized customers.

Barroom music could be heard as the horses and duo of wagons rolled into the streets. The appearance of the strangers drew little attention, as the area was known for the transients who would make any number of visits to the town before moving on to another similar location.

One of the soldiers with Savage commented, "Been a long time since I seen somethin' like this. Don't really miss it, but I can't say I wouldn't mind havin' a steak from there."

The soldier pointed to a café that staked its reputation upon its thirty-ounce steaks. The smell of the cooking meat, frying eggs, and baking bread almost deterred the group from their mission at hand. The intense hunger that raked their weakened bodies seemed to know that the ability to conquer the growling stomachs was only feet away.

"Okay, boys, let's keep movin'." Jake Savage was as hungry as any member of the ill-intended group, and he took a deep breath and licked his lips at the smells that filled the air.

Near the edge of town, the party spotted a general store. Their eyes met and smiles appeared across their faces. The unanimity of the soldiers was apparent.

"Pull one of those wagons around back. We'll get what we can and get out of here before morning. They'll never know what happened." A usually quiet soldier named Sandy Taylor made the strong suggestion.

The first wagon was positioned perfectly at the rear of the business and the group set about in fulfilling Taylor's directive. Within a matter of thirty minutes, everything the soldiers deemed as consumable had been loaded into the two wagons, with a few items requiring the placement of the second vessel. A vast array of pickled and smoked foods, as well as blankets and a few items of clothing, completed the cache.

Heading out of town in the identical undetected manner with which they entered, the soldiers traveled in the direction that was opposite of their camp. The hope was to reach a small farm or some other source of food. Within a mile, they found a farmhouse that had a barn on the side farther from town.

"Do ya'll hear what I hear? Sounds like cattle to me." Jake Savage's mind was set on obtaining fresh meat to complement the preserved items he and his comrades had illegally obtained minutes earlier at the general store.

The soldiers made the most of the time at the farm, gathering a few eggs and a dozen chickens, as well as six sheep. The three milk cows the group spotted would enable some of the children in the group to gain a portion of their much-needed nourishment. Therefore, the bovines became property of the caravan as well. It seemed that the night had been somewhat profitable, yielding enough food to easily feed a couple of hundred adults.

The jackpot of the trip was obtained when the soldiers had completed half of their return trip. The milking cows evidently stirred a herd of deer, as the animals ran across the road and fell victim to the marksmanship of the soldiers.

Eight deer were shot and gutted on the spot, providing more meat for the members of the hungry caravan that was located only a short distance from the kill zone. The process of gutting and preparing the deer took little time, as all of the soldiers on the hunt had performed the bloody task numerous times before.

North of the camp, the group spotted a small herd of beef cattle, with no apparent home or owner nearby. The well-fed animals were initially bypassed due to a shortage of manpower. When the Bell Group made their way from the camp early the next morning, the fifteen head of cattle were also rounded up to become provisions for the hungry members.

The midnight foray had proven highly beneficial to the men, women, and children who comprised the Bell Group. The smiles and overall level of approval created a better morale than had existed in almost two weeks. Fifteen miles were traversed in the two days after the raid, and the bivouac of the following night became almost carnival-like in its passage.

Jake Savage became something of a hero to his fellow soldiers, as well as to the Cherokee mothers. The number of deaths among infants and toddlers decreased in the two weeks after the initial raid. Unfortunately, the success of the first incursion led to the expectation that additional similar acts should and would take place.

In order to lessen the effects of illnesses and deaths, Jake Savage and his group made ten other raids over a three week period. None reaped the amount and quality of profits that the first swoop did, but all were able to be carried out without detection from the storeowners and farmers whose property became food items for the Bell Group. The continued safety of the members offered some degree of compensation for the mounting guilt many of them felt for taking advantage of the people who they were supposed to be serving and protecting.

While Corporal Jake Savage's actions gained positive comments from Colonel Tetleton and Lieutenant Deas, the same incidents garnered even deeper admiration from White Crow. With each return to camp and the subsequent distributions of foodstuffs, Jake Savage and White Crow seized the opportunity and struck up a series of conversations, sharing with each other the rationale of conduct of their respective peoples. There were also incidents in which the content of the meetings moved toward the mutual admiration the two held for one another.

Chapter 24

Facts and points of view that White Crow shared with Jake Savage literally gnawed at the young soldier's conscience and served as the primary content of his contemplation during his waking hours. The compassion White Crow held for the preservation of her culture was far deeper than what Jake readily held for his own. Although the contact between Corporal Savage and White Crow was illegal, or at the least inconsistent with the process of the relocation, White Crow and Jake made it a point to converse with one another on a frequent basis.

Jake Savage began to hold a completely different stance about the removal than what he had initially thought. Corporal Savage decided that rather than fulfilling his mission of moving the Cherokee to a reservation westward from their Red Clay, Tennessee base, he should help White Crow find a viable means of restitution or escape.

Escaping, or at least the attempt at doing so, would be the simpler of the two choices. Corporal Jake Savage could turn his back during guard duty and allow White Crow to run from the camp, an idea he had pondered weeks earlier. As for restitution, Jake believed that an appeal from a legal standpoint might allow White Crow to return to her Tennessee home, if she did so under the guardianship of someone. That someone, at least in Jake Savage's mind, would be him, especially if he married the young lady.

As before, Jake Savage determined it would be the safer option to continue to visit with White Crow on a regular basis along the trail and hope that the completion of the relocation process would enable the two of them to pursue their relationship in a far safer location. However, the multiple interactions with White Crow soon made his recently reaffirmed mindset far more difficult to maintain. The facts related to the relocation that Jake was privileged to hear quickly shed a great level of understanding and insight upon the situation at hand.

During one of the visits, White Crow shared details about the deaths of a number of her family members. With each facet from the myriad of stories, Jake Savage became more determined to seek justice or freedom for the intelligent, beautiful, and considerate White Crow. The Cherokee maiden exhibited her increasingly trusting attitude regarding Corporal Savage as she divulged details surrounding a myriad of her most personal tragedies.

White Crow explained how her mother had died during a measles outbreak when White Crow was only a child. As she had done at various times during the march along the trail, White Crow shed tears at the thoughts and discussion centered upon her mother.

Her mother, the product of a white man's liaison with a teenaged Cherokee, had provided White Crow with her name, one that reminded her of the birds that seemed to fly into her village during the season when the corn was ripe, leaving as soon as suitable amounts of the grain was gathered. White Crow added that the exact nature of the bond that had existed between her maternal grandparents was a taboo subject. Therefore, she knew nothing as to the type or duration of the circumstances immediately preceding her birth.

This freedom of movement which the crows possessed seemed to present a foretelling of White Crow's adult actions as the young lady longed to go where she wanted and to do what her mind desired. Even from her early years, White Crow was known throughout her village as an individual who would seemingly go on an adventure without consulting those around her. Doing so tended to cause an obvious level of concern and, at times, disgust among those who looked out for her well-being and safety.

White Crow also took time to tell Jake Savage about how her older brother had died. He was killed while offering resistance to the initial move of the Cherokee. White Crow stated that her brother had been shot when he appeared firm in his refusal to leave the only home he and his younger siblings had ever known.

"The way the soldier shot him was like how your people would kill a sick dog. The soldier was on his horse and rode up to my brother and pointed his gun at the back of his head. My brother was standing with five other men who also refused to leave our village. After the soldier shot my brother, other soldiers fired at my brother's friends who were resisting. All of them moved around on the ground before the same man who shot my brother stood over them, loaded his gun and aimed at each of them. He shot each my brother's friends in their heads and kicked their bodies to make sure they were dead."

White Crow also detailed how her younger brother, as well as her sister, had joined a warrior named Tsali and had made their escape early on the day when she and her fellow Cherokee were being rounded up for the move to Red Clay, Tennessee. As far as White Crow knew, her sister and younger brother had managed to accompany Tsali and dozens of others and traveled toward the safety of the mountains in western North Carolina.

White Crow emphasized that she was no militant, but she had wished that she was able to have attempted to leave with the remaining members of her family. Their common ancestry and the love they shared were the only thoughts that had kept her alive and strong during the time she lived in the holding pens at Red Clay, Tennessee.

Corporal Savage's curiosity soon got the best of him and he found himself asking a rather personal question. He inquired, "Why didn't you leave with your sister and brother? You are a strong lady in spirit and body; you have proven you can survive when the situation is tough. It just doesn't seem like your sister and your brothers were more independent that you."

White Crow explained to Jake Savage that she had been assisting her aunt in childbirth. Her aunt was the younger sister of her deceased mother, and White Crow felt that she should help her family member through the difficult situation. Her siblings were less apt to assist in such a process, so White Crow remained with her aunt.

As a sign of conciliation for her efforts in assisting with her aunt's labor, the infant was named for White Crow's mother. That facet of the event greatly pleased White Crow, and made the birth more fulfilling for her. However, with the fact that she was engaged in assisting her aunt in childbirth, White Crow was unable, or temporarily unwilling, to make any attempt to avoid the captivity that had cost the lives of many of her people.

White Crow grew highly emotional, "Then, they took away my mother's sister. She and her baby died about two weeks before you arrived, Jake. The hot sun and no good water took the lives of two more of my family's number." The tears again flowed freely as White Crow tried to finish relaying the impact of the personal tragedy.

"I want it all to stop. Why are they doing this to my people?"

Jake Savage had no answer that he felt would possibly explain the situation. He simply bowed his head and nodded from side to side. Jake's upper teeth bit into his bottom lip in an effort to avoid weeping in front of White Crow.

As if the recent revelations of her personal life had not been enough to provide an intensely emotional perspective to the day, White Crow began to provide information about the effects the loss of her father had upon her. She briefly managed to regain her composure and revealed the story to Jake Savage.

"It has been longer since my father left us. I still miss him and I get very sad at times, but it is easier for me to talk about him. I still hope that he is alive. I know the others chose to run away or died, but my father went to find food for us. He did that many, many times and always came back. That was, until that day he left and said he would return in two days."

White Crow discussed the incident concerning her father, a well-respected warrior in what the white men called "her tribe." She told Jake how her family patriarch had gone on a hunting trip with four other Cherokee men some three years earlier. The incident had taken place before the roundup, and he had, unfortunately, failed to return. Speculation of his outcome was the only sense of direction White Crow had. However, as she had said, she held hope that her father, as well as those who left with him, would return to her people one day.

Briefly leaving the topic of the calamities and mysteries that had affected her family, White Crow delved into a discussion about another aspect of her past: an alternate name. Her father had been a deeply religious man. He had taken White Crow as well as her siblings to a series of church meetings that had been held near her childhood home.

"At one of the meetings, the man who was called Preacher baptized me. After that, he and my father spoke of a need for another name. Preacher said that White Crow or any other Cherokee name might be used against me some day if cruel people moved to our area. I think he knew that we would be taken away one day, don't you?"

"I don't know. I knew very little about what was going on with the Cherokee or the other Indians until I joined the army. Things have changed so much, White Crow."

"Please, if you like, you may call me Naomi. That is the name that Preacher gave me. It sounds like a name a woman of your people would have. Don't you think so?"

Jake Savage smiled and said he would consider the request. He seemed puzzled at the appeal and ducked his head as he had earlier in the conversation. Corporal Savage seemed really reluctant to agree to use the name Naomi rather than calling White Crow the name to which she was more fully accustomed.

The discussion then ventured toward the Cherokee peoples' past. Jake became engrossed in the knowledge and insight White Crow had for her people's history. Jake made a mental note that the history of his people was written, and that he had never taken the time to read all of it.

Corporal Savage began to spill a portion of the contents of his heart to White Crow. "And you have all of yours in your head. The things I've heard about your people isn't true. You are really smart. Many of your people are so intelligent. In the army we're taught to stay away from your people, and that all you are good for is to be in our way or to take what we have. I now think that's what we've done to your people. "

Jake Savage appeared to be fully transformed from the young soldier who fought, chastised, or attempted to kill any Native American he encountered in his early days of military service. The future visits Jake would have with White Crow added to his level of affection for the beautiful maiden and likewise hardened his heart toward the actions of the nation he had earlier pledged to serve.

Chapter 25

In more deeply exploring the history of the Cherokee, Jake Savage listened intently to White Crow's disclosure of the word Aniyunwiya. The meaning of this new venture into the exploration of the Cherokee language was "the principal people." White Crow had learned that it referred to the name the Cherokee people originally called themselves. Jake conversed intently with White Crow to assure himself of the superlative level of the title the Cherokee held for themselves and how it could not legitimately apply to the people with whom he grew up.

Jake Savage looked at White Crow, and he felt strongly compelled to ask, "Do you know what ironic means?"

"I do not understand that word. Please tell me about it, Jake Savage." White Crow's reply indicated a strong interest in learning what Corporal Savage could share with her.

"If you can't help somebody get well, and you're a doctor or a medicine man, that's irony. My people sometimes get haircuts from men who don't have hair. That's irony. It's a lot like your people being the main people and my government comin' in here and driving you away from your homeland. Somebody wants to take what belongs to your people and make it theirs. The principle people are begin forced away and someone else is taking over. I think that's ironic like some of those other things."

"I understand. It's like you." White Crow's words puzzled Jake. "You are supposed to force me to leave, but you are thinking you are not right. I am supposed to hate you, and I should not trust you; and I think I did when we left our home. Now, I don't hate you; I trust you. You are a nice man. You are confused about what your people are doing to my people. That, Jake Savage, is irony. Am I right?"

"I think you've got it. Let's talk about something else. I think you need to keep only one name. I feel like the name you use should be White Crow. If we are ever able to meet in another situation, you may have to use your name of Naomi. Someone may want to hurt you because of your Cherokee name. For now, let me call you White Crow. Keeping in touch with your past, the past of your parents, may be the only thing that gets you through this situation."

White Crow's reply was full of implications. "I will let you keep calling me White Crow. Keeping in touch with my past keeps me happy, but thinking about what may be in the future makes me happier, Jake Savage. God will get me and you through this and help me forget about the pain my people are living on the trail. My future will hopefully include you."

"I will try to find a way to make that happen, White Crow. For now, let's get you, me, and as many other people as we can through this situation. Traveling on the trail has to come to an end soon. I hear talk that we're headed to the Indian Territory. That's where I understand some of those other groups, like the Creek and Choctaw, were moved. I've never been there, so I can't say, but that's what a lot of the boys are saying that they're hearing."

Among the many revelations Corporal Savage provided to White Crow were the confirmations of other Native Americans being moved westward prior to the Cherokee relocation. White Crow explained that the wise and older members of her village had talked to her people about the rumors surrounding the disappearance of their enemy, the Creek. The superstitious members had attempted to quell the realism of the facts surrounding the eradication of the Creek from the area.

Those who were less prone to listen to logical explanations saw the disappearance of the Creek as some type of intervention from a plague or a natural disaster. The Creek, in the eyes of the more superstitious, were too powerful to be moved from the area through the intervention of any other group of people. Interestingly enough, many of those who saw the Creek as invincible were the Cherokee people who were most likely to make escape attempts when faced with their own captivity. As Jake and White Crow had discussed, the situation was filled with irony.

Corporal Savage also told White Crow that the Chickasaw had been moved westward in 1837, with the Choctaw falling victim to a similar manner in 1831. The year after the Choctaw, the Seminole had been targeted. The Creek had followed in 1834. Those facts provided pieces of the puzzle to White Crow, and she began to fully realize what had happened to those with whom she was familiar and some of which she had merely heard.

The duo also found time to discuss the designation of the term Five Civilized Tribes, and how the Cherokee, reportedly the most civilized of the five, were unfairly treated. Jake Savage and White Crow pondered the rebellious reaction of the Seminole and wondered how such a response from the Cherokee would have changed the movement to the Indian Territory.

Jake discussed how the Seminole had waged war against those who tried to force them from their homeland. White Crow listened intently to how the Seminole had engaged in an earlier war against the United States and were hiding in the swamps of Florida as Jake, White Crow, and the massive group of Cherokee and soldiers were moving westward.

White Crow stalwartly stated, "They are fighting the soldiers like my people should be. I wish we had prepared for a fight before being caged like animals. That would have kept so many of my people from dying like they have on the trail. But, if we had gone to war, I would not have been able to be with you like I have. Please, tell me we will be okay, Jake Savage."

"I don't want to tell you something if I don't know it will happen. I want us to be okay. I want this journey to end. We have to hope and pray that that will happen soon."

White Crow changed the direction of the conversation when she informed Jake Savage that almost all of her people, including her, felt that they could not trust the government of the United States. She then talked about a half-dozen treaties the white man has made and broken with the Cherokee and other Native American nations. The older men of her village had talked about the broken promises and how the white men who ruled the United States were full of lies and deceit that often lead to death and destruction.

This set of circumstances, White Crow noted, had led to her disgust with the entire white race and her initial reluctance to trust Jake Savage. White Crow stated that she was finding it fulfilling that Jake Savage was providing her with hope that the nation contained citizens who were capable of caring for the Cherokee.

"You are a soldier, like those who have killed many of my people. You have even killed some men from other nations, like the Creek. You are different from those men, like Andrew Jackson, the man who my people say is the reason for our time on the trail."

"I once had a great deal of respect for Andrew Jackson. He was an acquaintance to my father. My daddy also served under him. Many of the people in my state think he is a great man, but most who know about what is taking place don't agree with what is being done to your people."

Corporal Savage shared with White Crow that he once met the general and future president Andrew Jackson. Jake also told White Crow that Jake's father had served with Jackson during the War of 1812. Savage noted that the former general, the reason why his father had chosen to make a career as a member of the military, was well-respected among most members of the Savage family.

"He is a man who stands for what he believes in. He will not let people run over him. I understand there are some men whose wives were cruel to his wife. After she died, he blamed those men and did everything in his power to make certain that those men paid. You have to admire him for that."

"Then, you think it is fine for someone to get revenge? Hurt them or take their life? Would it be wrong for my people to rise against the soldiers? There has been talk about that, Jake." White Crow's words were growing more forceful.

Jake Savage attempted to diffuse the situation. "I hope it doesn't come to that. There will be blood spilt and many of us, soldiers and Cherokee, will die. Those who survive will probably keep moving westward on the trail. What would be proven if they have a fight with us?"

"Jake, who is us? You don't know where your heart belongs. Would you strike against my people?" White Crow was growing agitated.

"I think we're taking about something that won't happen. If it does, I will try to take you from here. We will have to be fast."

When Andrew Jackson had defeated the group called Red Stick Creek at Horseshoe Bend, Alabama, Jake Savage's uncle had been with Jackson and shared in killing an estimated eight hundred Creek warriors. In turn, Savage had been prompted from his childhood to believe that killing an enemy, British or Indian, was the way to obtain freedom or land. The push of the Cherokee people from their homeland, Corporal Jake Savage admitted, was a gross act of negligence and utter lust for land that had rightfully belonged to the "principle people."

"My government will have to answer for the events on the trail for generations to come. It may not happen while you or I are alive, but people will talk about what has happened here, even when my grandchildren are dead."

"I hope that the children of your children will also be the children of my children. We have to make that happen, Jake. You are a special man."

At that point, Jake realized that the time had come for him to serve his time on guard duty. With all the emphasis being placed on following the rules, he felt it best to be where he was supposed to be when scheduled. The young couple concluded their extensive and insightful discussion with an innocent hug.

Chapter 26

The tension that had been evolving between the Cherokee and soldier factions during the trip on the trail to that point had begun to take a massive toll upon the morale of the once-proud soldiers. The strain had led to increased violence between the soldiers and the Cherokee, with both groups regularly taking the initiative of directing some form of animosity toward the other "side." Although the incidents of visual animosity had been minimal in recent days, the situation was doomed to change.

It had become a regular practice throughout the month of January for Corporal Jake Savage and his comrades to be the recipients of various unfriendly acts. The severity of the Cherokee actions grew as the days passed, and only the counterattacks toward the Native Americans tended to lessen the frequency of those directed toward the soldiers.

An occasional snowball or rock thrown against a soldier's horse provided the catalyst for the onset of the debacle. The early attacks drew little attention and no acts of retaliation, but one particular incident initiated immediate and strong consequences.

An anonymous Cherokee cast a four-inch diameter rock into the right rear leg of the horse upon which Corporal Abner McIlwain rode. The horse began bucking strongly, and McIlwain struggled to maintain his place in the saddle. A second rock was thrown against the steed's left side and agitated the animal's anger to an even higher degree.

Corporal McIlwain fell from his horse and slammed the ground with a resounding roar. The bone in McIlwain's right leg snapped in two places, and his neck appeared to have been twisted. The horse miraculously managed to regain its footing and hurriedly ran from the scene. McIlwain never uttered a word as he exhaled and passed away.

Little time passed, maybe no more than a minute, before an act of retaliation took place. The method in which it was carried out, as well as the targeted individuals, made the event heart-wrenching for the hundreds of souls who chose to avoid taking part in its commission.

A group of seven soldiers fired an identical number of shots in the direction from which the first rock was cast. Four young Cherokee, three boys and a girl, were struck when the projectiles entered a nearby wagon. Blood from those struck spattered against the opposite side of the wagon, and the unwounded children inside the wagon feared for their lives and simultaneously mourned for their friends.

As five Cherokee men hurriedly approached the wagon in order to investigate the scene and rescue the remaining children, a second round of gunfire erupted. Four soldiers on horseback galloped toward the scene, while the seven soldiers who had initiated the killing spree stepped into formation and lifted their reloaded weapons.

"Fire!" was the order that one of the soldiers on horseback yelled to his cohorts. The five Cherokee men fell, victims to the round of shots, as screams from their loved ones filled the air. For a brief period the two groups stood facing one another. The number of members on either side of the confrontation grew to include several dozen people.

The standoff was finally dispersed without additional bloodshed. For the time being the serious issue seemed to have subsided. However, two and a half hours later another incident signified the onset of another round of violence.

In the meantime, a detachment of four soldiers were ordered to bury McIlwain's body. Little emotion was shown during the process, but one of the soldiers, Stanley Moss, a man who had maintained a friendship with McIlwain since childhood and enlisted in the army with the recently-deceased soldier, uttered a strong proclamation.

"I'll get those folks for what they did to McIlwain. He saved my life last year when I almost drowned. We joined this group the same day and were buddies for years. Those people will pay." Moss was clear at the direction in which he intended to move.

Apparently feeling deepening and sudden anger over the tragedy of Corporal McIlwain, Moss tugged at his horse, guiding it toward a wagon.

Moss grabbed a whip from its stand near the seat of the wagon. The act caught the driver by surprise, but the young soldier's look of determination garnered a quick response from the teamster. "Moss, you okay? What are you doing?"

The loudly uttered inquisitive statements from the driver drew the attention of people nearby who had also failed to observe the procurement of the lash.

Kicking the sides of his horse Stanley Moss rode into a group of elderly Cherokee ladies who were struggling, but managing, to make acceptable levels of progress on the trail. None of the members of the group had participated in the earlier acts of obstruction, as their physical conditions necessitated their full focuses to be placed upon the act of keeping up with those around them as they marched.

The enraged Moss, apparently indifferent to the innocence and fragility of the aged individuals, held the whip in his right hand and extended it above his head. As hastily as the act became apparent to those around him, the soldier began brutally beating one of the helpless elderly Cherokee women.

Moss seemed to search for rationale for inducing the tirade, and he began shouting the justification in order for those around him to understand his reasoning. For the first six seconds he continued shouting that the elderly woman was not getting into one of the wagons quickly enough. Moss then added that he would make certain that she sped up.

No one seemed to realize exactly what Stanley Moss was using as his point of elaboration, but the shocked witnesses failed to stop the senseless act. The elderly women who had attended to the beating victim lifted their hands in defense and moved from the scene as rapidly as the walking conditions and the gathering crowd of dumbfounded people allowed.

The screeches of the elderly women and those people surrounding the location of the beating were beginning to attract dozens of witnesses. The progression of the train of weary individuals ceased when people to the rear of the incident as well as for some near its front struggled to gain some understanding of what was taking place.

Shouts for support or intercession on behalf of the victim arose throughout the captivated crowd, yet the vast majority of the bystanders barely managed to perform any additional perspective or action regarding the murderous deed directed toward one of the senior members of the burdened caravan.

Jake Savage managed to force his way through the onlookers and grew determined to halt the apparent disposal of an innocent Cherokee female. "Moss! Stop what you're doing this instant." The strength of Corporal Savage's words was apparent.

Moss offered a quick glimpse and disgusted grunt in Savage's direction, but Savage's plea did nothing to cease the debacle. Jake Savage stepped closer to the blood-soaked area and began to stoop over in order to shield the prostrate form.

Stanley Moss grew livid at the seemingly misleading act on Jake Savage's part. "You want me to stop what I'm doing? Then I'll give it to you, you Indian-lovin' traitor."

The whip was then redirected toward Jake Savage, and the deadly device immediately found its mark. The improvised weapon's first strike in Savage's direction slapped Jake on his right cheek and opened a distinct and deep gash. The impact of the whip caused Corporal Savage to stand and briefly stagger as he caressed the fresh wound with his trembling left hand.

A second blow from the whip slammed Jake Savage's left shoulder. Corporal Savage grimaced at the strike as a third quickly headed his way. Utilizing the strong flow of adrenaline that had entered his system, Jake managed to raise his right hand and grab the tip of the whip as it cracked on his shoulder. Corporal Savage used his left hand to grasp the whip some three feet from the end that had struck his shoulder. He pulled the weapon from the grasp of Moss and hurled it to the ground.

An element of salvation appeared from someone inside the wagon and located a few feet from where the vicious incident had been transpiring. A hatchet was tossed from the rear of the wagon and landed at Jake Savage's feet. The arm that projected the weapon toward Savage belonged to a child, but it also returned to the safety of the vessel within a second of the hatchet hitting the ground. Taking the sharped device in his right hand, Jake stepped toward Moss.

"You've messed up, Moss." An element of anger rarely observed in Jake Savage drew petrified reactions from those who were close enough to hear the comment and see Jake's face.

Corporal Savage bounced the sharpened weapon in his hand and added, "This is meant for revenge. It's revenge for all the people you and the other folks have killed. Those ladies you just butchered needed someone; they needed me, and I let them down. I won't let your action stand unpunished." He then stepped toward Moss.

In what appeared to be a fraction of a second, Corporal Savage used the hammer-like side of the hatchet head to strike Moss on his head. The hit rendered the murdering Moss unconscious, cracking his skull. Moss fell to the ground as blood seeped from his head.

"Savage, you killed him," stated the first soldier to reach Moss.

The situation would have likely been met with a strong level of punishment, but the circumstances of the moment made that unlikely. Recent increases in illness among soldiers, as well as the growing tensions among the people traversing the trail made arresting Corporal Savage for his participation in a fight seem like a waste of time.

With the set of circumstances in mind, prosecution of Jake Savage would have to wait until the conclusion of the relocation process. However, with the passage of time, the incident was eventually forgotten, and no criminal charges were ever brought against Savage for the incident involving Moss. Additionally, the fact that Moss did not receive a mortal wound eliminated any form of a military trial. The mindset of many members of the military who witnessed the event felt that Corporal Savage was justified in his act against Moss. That viewpoint in itself likely eliminated any major push toward indicting Jake Savage.

Chapter 27

The comment Moss had made to Corporal Savage ate at Jake's thought process the night after the violent event occurred. If Moss believed Savage held strong feelings for White Crow, then other soldiers were expressing their opinion about the situation as well. Corporal Savage's lack of complete compliance with the rules regarding inappropriate contact between members of the military and Cherokee citizens, as well as the recent issue with Moss would result in a severe level of punishment being carried out toward Savage, at least in his mind.

As the march along the trail continued on the morning after Corporal Savage severely injured Moss, Savage looked to his right and noticed White Crow looking in his direction. Jake Savage took advantage of the opportunity and held an important discussion with White Crow. The night after the incident with Moss, Jake had no assigned duties. He took a walk around the campsite just as the sun began to set.

"You have had a bad time in the last days, Jake Savage. I know that you did all you could to stop that man yesterday. My people like you for that. Is there anything you need to talk about? Can I help you?" White Crow asked.

"We have to talk, White Crow. You know that I hit a man yesterday. He will be okay, but I hit a fellow soldier. There was a weapon involved. When we get to where we're going, I think I will be placed on trial. If that happens…" Jake's fast delivery of his words revealed his state of panic. Corporal Savage's statements elapsed so quickly that several sentences had been expelled prior to White Crow's interruption.

"Jake, I know about the soldier, the one they call Moss. I hear he is going to be okay. One of the men who is on the wagon with him has said so. My people like you because of what you did. You must also know that the wise lady the soldier was hitting will probably be okay. You may have saved her life, Jake."

Noticing that a grin appeared on Jake Savage's face, White Crow also smiled, though her expression of the emotion was made more timidly than was that of Corporal Savage. White Crow then caused Jake to cry when she uttered, "You have saved my life as well, Jake Savage."

In contrast to the growing love White Crow and Jake Savage shared, the overall tension level that existed among many of the Cherokee and soldiers at the time steadily increased. One of the most noticeable soldiers who had transformed from a peaceful man into one who held animosity toward the Cherokee soon became a victim of one of the acts of revenge.

The train's trek along the Arkansas portion of the trail continued to be hampered with a severe lack of food. Area residents had regularly managed to serve as black marketers and padded their pockets with profits from the sales of a wide range of products. One of the most easily prepared and quickly bartered items was jerky. While initially sounding nutritious, the jerky sold or traded to the soldiers during that phase of the trial came from a variety of sources such as deer, cattle, and even horses.

The young soldier who was to become the next casualty of the Cherokee exhibition of revolt and protest was Willis, the man who had who had earlier opened his saddlebags and given pieces of jerky to nearby children. The kind act had endeared the soldier to the youngsters, many of whom had lost male role models in days prior to the onset of the relocation process.

However, his rude comments on a later date had caused many of the Cherokee children to flee from the soldier's proximity. The soldier had bellowed harsh words and threats toward the youngsters and promised to kill them if they bothered him again. The time for that promise to be fulfilled was at hand, and the soldier appeared determined to be renowned as a man of his word.

Hunger, as well as hearts filled with forgiveness, led a group of five children to approach Willis, the same soldier three days after the incident between Stanley Moss and Corporal Jake Savage. While Moss, the Cherokee woman he attacked, and Jake Savage all appeared to be on their way to surviving the effects of the altercation, the same would not be said for all people involved in an incident centered on procuring jerky.

As the train progressed along the trail on an unseasonably warm day, a contingency of some fifteen Cherokee children approached Willis. From atop his horse, the soldier clearly saw the children making their way in his direction. The corresponding level of anger he had struggled with on the previous encounter seemed miniscule to that that was about to take place.

"You need to stop right there. I've told you little animals that I ain't gonna share my stuff with ya'll." The soldier had a great deal of difficulty in making his words comprehensible, as he was eating a piece of jerky while the children gathered around him. Ironically, he threw the remnants at the gathering group. Two of the Cherokee children struggled to gather the fragments that had fallen on the melting snow and ice.

One Cherokee girl, no more than eight years of age, appealed strongly to the soldier's emotions. "We will share a couple of pieces if you will give them to us. Please, soldier man, we are so hungry. Can you give us a couple of pieces of your food?"

The apparently heartless soldier began his ranting toward the innocent children. "I told you before that I don't care if you little beasts starve to death. You're no better than the mules my daddy used to use to pull logs out of the woods. With spring starting up, the grass will be coming on good and tender. Eat it like the animals you are."

Willis reached toward an oak branch hanging low above the trail and broke it from the tree. He then used the tree branch to slap his horse and veered the animal into the crowd of Cherokee children. Several of the Cherokee children were knocked to the ground, and the young girl whose heartfelt appeal failed to warrant a positive reaction from the soldier fell underneath the horse. The child's left leg was broken, as a loud snap made that clear to all in the area.

"With a broken leg, you might as well be shot. That's what we do with animals. Take an arrow and shoot her. Shoot her in the head and in the heart. That way you'll be sure she's dead, if she's got a brain or a heart."

As the youngster lay screaming in pain, the soldier galloped away. He managed one last look in the direction of the child, appeared to laugh, and shook his head from side to side.

The child was quickly placed into a wagon for care to be administered to her leg. In her left hand, she grasped the stick that that soldier had used to hit his horse. Holding it like a mixed symbol of hope and defiance, the child had managed to retrieve the stick when the soldier dropped it as his horse had tromped the small girl against the ground.

As with many days spent traveling on the trail, little was said for the remainder of the sunlit day. The tension was at a level that was among the highest of the entire trip, and it was a day in which even Jake Savage and White Crow failed to engage in any type of verbal communication. The only event that seemed to lessen the strain of the day was the arrival of sunset and the establishment of camp for the night.

The peacefulness and quiet of the night managed to hide the execution of a grievous and vengeful act. The young soldier who had managed to mistreat the Cherokee children and offend almost every compassionate soul who was taking part in the relocation process was to fall victim to the retaliation for his deplorable conduct.

The end of the Willis's shift for guard detail was scheduled to come at 4:00 in the morning. He had failed to report to Deas after his 3:00 a.m. rounds, but Deas credited this to the fact that the soldier had experienced a day that was overwrought and nerve-racking. When the soldier had not returned to his assigned post by 4:30 a.m., the apprehension and speculation about his whereabouts became widespread among those soldiers who had completed their stints as well as those who were only minutes into the service of their current shifts.

Just before 5 a.m. the answer to their questions regarding the whereabouts of the soldier became clear. The incident regarding his recent treatment of the Cherokee girl had apparently invoked the violent nature of an individual or a group of people. His corpse was found hidden behind an outcropping of rocks, across the campsite from where he had last been seen.

The young soldier had been killed in a ruthless and violent manner, puzzling people as to how screams for help or intervention had not been duly detected. Closer examination of his body easily made this more apparent as no less than four lanterns, as well as the rising sun, provided more light for the situation.

An arrow had been fired into the soldier's head. The determination was made that the shot had come from close range as the tip of the arrow passed from the front of the soldier's head and actually penetrated the rear of his skull. The tenacity of the killer or killers was clearly shown in that the deadly shot had come from the soldier's front.

Another arrow had been shot from the same angle and had cut deeply into the soldier's heart. The shaft of the arrow that pierced the man's heart appeared to have been made from an oak branch, much like the stick he had earlier used to whip his horse. Comments from the soldiers made accusations of the same, but there was no pursuit in attempting to resolve the issues related to this aspect of the killing.

Lastly, tufts of dried winter grass, mixed with fragments of snow that were tainted with the victim's blood, had been shoved deeply into the mouth of the dead soldier. That was clearly done in an effort to show the disgust of his statement that the Cherokee children were no more than animals. Some of the witnesses noted that the soldier had also stated that the animalistic children should eat grass in order to maintain life. There were no signs of hand ties or any other method of restraint. The deceased soldier was simply lying face up, the highly visible signs of the causes of death apparent to everyone.

Within an hour from the time the sun rose, the soldier was hurriedly buried and the Bell Group resumed its westward journey. No further comments about the death of the soldier were made in a public forum, but the incident did provide fodder for an undetermined number of private conversations over the ensuing days. Even within the ranks of the soldiers, the death was viewed as the epitome of poetic justice.

Chapter 28

Chief John Ross had written a series of letters during the course of recent events, managing to have some of his letters delivered by procuring the services of couriers in towns through which the Bell Group passed. The strongly worded messages had voiced requests for additional supplies to aid the group be sent as soon as possible. Without the immediate intervention, Chief Ross stated, the number of deaths among the Cherokee and the soldiers were assuredly destined to continue but likely escalate.

One of the letters from Chief Ross managed to make it to the proper place and, in doing so, reaped results that would temporarily provide relief from the ongoing food and supply shortage. The arrival of the items was announced during one of the group's mandatory early morning roll calls. The response of the crowd as they learned of the letter's contents was largely composed of cheers, clapping, and an overwhelming shedding of tears of joy.

The train of wagons had been sent eastward from Little Rock, Arkansas and had arrived at the Bell Group's location a few miles outside Marion, Arkansas. The wagons' contents were comprised of hams, eggs, preserves, and a large number of blankets and clothing.

The vast majority of the soldiers were originally unaware of a particular situation until several hours after the wagons arrived. A meeting of the officers was held and made them conscious of the tragedy. Corporal Jake Savage and the other enlisted men heard of the events as time warranted.

It seems that a wagon filled with pickled and preserved items was also lost in an unfortunate incident. In an apparent act of sabotage, the wheel on one wagon fell off just as the vessel pulled away from where it had been parked during the previous night. The event occurred on the day before the massive amount of supplies arrived, and it seemed to have been an indiscriminant act. The amount of food that was lost proved tremendous.

As the damaged wheel fell from the wagon, the vessel shifted toward its left side, and a number of preserves and other items fell from their positions. Broken glass from the jars sprayed throughout the wagon and punctured a stack of hams that rested on the opposite side of the carriage. The total sum of food that was ruined was estimated to be equivalent to three days' worth of forage for the group of Cherokee and soldiers traversing the trail.

The loss of the food failed to foil the hearty consumption of foodstuffs as many of the Bell Group's members were on the brink of participating in an around-the-clock feast. It became a common practice for small groups of people, Cherokee and military personnel alike, to walk or ride up to one of the supply wagons and ask for food items from the particular craft's attendant. Within two days, the lack of self-control and absent attempts at moderation had depleted the ten-day supply by a substantial and alarming amount.

The decision was made that the group would once again deploy a cluster of its members to act as a hunting party. The game that would hopefully be procured in the effort would offset the lost wagon-load of goods as well as what had been devoured in the day and a half of overindulgence.

The plan was well-conceived in that the hunting party would move ahead of the large group in order to minimize the fear on the part of the animals invoked with the sounds emitted from the hundreds of members and their draw teams. Compromising the group were four well-armed soldiers and six trusted Cherokee men. The hope was that each of these men who possessed hunting skills would rise to the occasion and provide a sufficient amount of meat that would be used to sustain the group until the next round of food arrived from the town of Little Rock, Arkansas.

Colonel Mark Tetleton failed to fully take into account the composition of the hunting party he detailed, an error in judgement which proved to have devastating effects. More specifically, the lack of proper planning was related to the fact that only one of the six Cherokee had any family members who remained in the wagon train. As a result, the five other Cherokee members of the hunting party fired arrows into the backs of three of the soldiers and placed three arrows into the stomach and chest area of the fourth.

During the assassination, the sixth Cherokee hunter appeared spellbound at the violence erupting in front of him. Offered the chance to escape with the five culprits, the sixth Cherokee balked at the suggestion. The remaining Cherokee debated as to what should be his fate, but they determined that killing him would make them equal to their counterparts in their lack of concern for the Cherokee people.

The sixth Cherokee was then sent running toward the approaching wagon train, and he was informed to tell the leaders of the Bell Group that the hunting party had ridden into an ambush. He was to state that the soldiers had been killed and their bodies left grouped in a field, a statement that, while slightly misleading, was not totally accurate.

Another aspect of the ruse was that the returning Cherokee hunter was to express that the five Cherokee men who were with him had been captured. Their whereabouts were to be detailed as unknown. The latter portion of the tale was truthful in that the exact location of the escaped murderers was a fact only they knew.

Bruises that were inflicted upon the shocked survivor's face in order to add credibility to this story worked well, and no one in the crowd appeared to doubt the fabricated account. The members of his family swore vengeance upon the people who had harmed him and captured the five Cherokee. In turn, the organization of a search party constituted a great deal of conversation among soldiers who deeply desired revenge upon the fabricated kidnappers.

By the next day the loss of the five Cherokee hunters had sadly become old news. Evidently hardened through the exposure to months of similar deaths and tragedies, the hearts of those who survived found the recent loss to be a similar to the untold numbers who had met their demise on the trail. Therefore, the five Cherokee who made their escape were never heard from or seen again. Their fate was left to conjecture.

The Bell Group eventually crossed the White River near the location of modern-day Forrest City, Arkansas. There, a lack of game and access to suitable water caused more malnutrition. Sadly, scores of Cherokee succumbed to the hardships. More deaths and sadness lay ahead for the group.

For example, when the group neared Little Rock, Arkansas in February 1839, Quati Ross, the beloved and faithful wife of Chief John Ross, yielded to an illness that was originally thought to have been minor and that would affect her for only a short time. The Cherokee chief's wife had given her blanket to a sick child a few days earlier in an effort to provide additional warmth to the youngster. Quati Ross then joined hundreds of other displaced Cherokee in walking through a driving snow storm that proved to be the last such winter weather event of the season.

While her status as the wife of John Ross would have easily enabled Quati to ride in the comfort of a wagon, the kindhearted mistress had chosen to walk with those whom her husband and she gladly represented and served. The trek was endured with Quati lacking the benefit of any type material to serve as a blanket. The once-strong and healthy lady suffered through the final miles of her journey while wearing only a suit of well-worn clothing that did little to lessen the effects of the wind and frozen precipitation.

Accentuating the bleakness of the situation was the fact that Quati Ross had struggled with various lung problems throughout most of her adult life. This had apparently escalated with living in the close quarters in which her people had earlier been confined. Quati's voice became noticeably hoarse, and she had begun to cough deeply. Mrs. Ross quickly developed pneumonia and suffered at the brink of death for an entire week.

The weather quickly turned warmer, and the snows began to rapidly melt. Despite the hope of life that sprang from the dirt that surrounded the confines of the trail, Quati Ross's health continued to decline. On the third day of the escalation of her illness, Quati began coughing up blood. A diagnosis from her attendant, and one which was confirmed upon the physician's examination, was that her throat was highly irritated from hours of almost incessant coughing.

The latter aspect had caused her throat to bleed, although the doctor shared with John Ross that there was likely a tumor growing inside his wife's right lung. The pneumonia only served as an added issue that aggravated what appeared to be a host of health matters.

With her illness necessitating that Quati Ross be transported inside a wagon, the months of physical tribulations she had endured along the trail proved too much for her weakened and weary body. Quati Ross had grown even weaker throughout the week, and by the fifth day she was unable to eat or drink a sufficient amount required for proper health. The seventh night of her illness, Quati asked to be taken from the wagon and to sleep under the stars.

John Ross approved such a move and actually entered into a brief argument with Quati's doctor regarding the issue. Chief Ross noted that both his wife and he knew that her time on earth was limited and that fulfilling such a request would likely be the last granted to her.

The starry night completed a day that had signaled the beginning of spring-like weather. The Cherokee queen was known for her love of viewing the sky on a clear and cool night. While resting her head on the saddle of a soldier and having managed to obtain at least three saddle blankets for cover, Quati Ross passed away during the night. Her beloved husband rested at her side and held her hand as she took her last breath.

For those who had managed to survive the trail the time of grief and sorrow had arrived again. Unfortunately, more of the same lay ahead for them as many of the fortunate survivors would find soon their loved ones, or themselves, falling victim to a variety of hardships.

Chapter 29

White Crow, being the equivalent of a goddaughter to the Chief John Ross family, was deeply saddened at the death of Quati Ross. White Crow primarily displayed her emotions when in private or with her close friends she had known for lengthy periods of time.

One person who was a major exception to the long-term acquaintances, and one who was allowed to experience White Crow's mourning first-hand, was Jake Savage. The young corporal had not recently been able to regularly speak with her due to the fact that White Crow had been attending Quati Ross during the final days which the chief's wife had spent on earth. When Corporal Savage and White Crow were finally able to move within speaking distance, her apparent distress and sadness hastily gathered Jake Savage's maximum attention.

Despite her initial attempts to avoid the topic of Quati's death, the emotions connected with the tragic event proved exceedingly strong for White Crow to suppress. White Crow tried to maintain exchanges that focused on the weather, the condition and quantity of food in recent days, and the offensive smell of Jake Savage's horse.

"The sun begins to shine much brighter and longer than it has in the past," White Crow uttered. It was an obvious attempt that fell short of its goal.

"Is that why you are sad? It seems to me that that should be cause for celebration and happiness. I am worried about you, White Crow." Corporal Savage stepped from his saddle and firmly held the reins of his horse as the group settled into its camp for the night.

White Crow began an attempted second phase of the conversation in noting, "I think the food we have been eating has made me tired. I need to sleep more than I have been able to."

"White Crow, you are making no sense. The food isn't making you lazy, unless it's a lack of food. You're worn out from all of the work you have been doing lately in trying to keep Quati from…" Jake Savage's hurried words were interrupted with White Crow's final attempt to deflect the discussion.

"Your horse stinks. It makes my eyes water and my throat itch." As she completed her sentence, White Crow was overwhelmed with emotion. "This bothers me a lot, Jake."

As the sentiments of the situation became too strong for White Crow to contain, the young beautiful Native American maiden eventually sought comfort in Jake Savage's arms.

"I have lost so many people who were close to me. Have I done something wrong, Jake? When we first met I told you to stop all this death; will it ever stop?" White Crow's words were filled with deep anguish and indicated a strong sense of helplessness.

"I am going to do my best to see that it stops for you. I keep working on a way for us to run from this group and make a new life for ourselves. Are you willing to go with me, White Crow? If we try to make a run for it, are you willing to leave the rest of you people behind?" Jake's inquisition was urgent and indicated that he had developed a suitable plan by which the two could effectively escape the likelihood of death that played such a prevalent role on the trail.

White Crow showed her affirmation of Jake Savage's statement by nodding her head. Her outburst of tears began to lessen when she came to the realization that Jake Savage was willing to sacrifice his safety and his career for her. It fully donned on White Crow that the corporal was also willing to risk his life for her.

"When you decide you're ready, and when the chance presents itself, we will run away. I love you White Crow, and I want to make you happy." Jake also began to show a strong sign of emotion as his eyes glistened and his voice briefly broke.

White Crow started to tell Jake a story that her people had developed while traveling from their sacred ground. Jake knew the story, although there was a fact of which he was unaware.

The topic of the talk between White Crow and Jake Savage made a sudden change and veered into a more general topic nature. White Crow's concerns about the past and how those facets related to the Cherokee people.

She shared information related to a term Savage had heard several times while riding his horse in the ranks of the Cherokee. The words had almost always been uttered following the death of a Cherokee, yet Jake had been unable to correctly connect the two.

White Crow said, "My people have a name for this walk. We call it Nunna dual Tsuny." As soon as White Crow uttered the phrase, Jake commented that he had heard the words before and wondered about the meaning.

White Crow's explanation of the phrase was lengthy in its presentation, but the major catalyst for its duration was the renewed tears and sadness that controlled the tone and exhibition of her thoughts. The objective of White Crow's disclosure came evident when she explained that the Cherokee phrase for the forced westward movement was Nunna dual Tsuny.

Jake smiled and said, "Nunna dual Tsuny. I have heard that so many times during the last months. Your people said it when they seemed to think I could not hear it. They were close to right 'cause I never could catch it all. What does Nunna dual Tsuny mean, White Crow?"

White Crow translated the term to Savage, "The Trail Where They Cried."

With that said, White Crow began to sob into Jake's right shoulder. The soldier also became moved to tears as he had not been at any previous point along the trail. He too felt some of the immense pain the Cherokee had endured. He felt a comparable level of agony from the deaths of soldiers who had become victims of various calamities during the relocation.

Corporal Jake Savage reluctantly released his emotions that had largely been held in check to that point. He, like the Cherokee, cried for the situation and the lost lives along the trail.

As the sun set that day, the Bell Group began its routine of making the final preparations for the night. Corporal Savage bid White Crow goodbye and promised to seek her out the following morning. He made his way toward the outer perimeter of the troupe in order to spend the night on his scheduled intermittent guard duty.

"How was the day for you?" were the words that greeted Corporal Savage when he neared a group of soldiers with whom he would spend a majority of the night. Jake spoke with the soldiers and shared the major point of the chat he had had with White Crow. At the same he was careful to avoid mentioning her name.

"One of the Cherokee women told me that the name they are using for this relocation effort shows how saddened they are about the loss of life they have experienced. They were taken from their homes and penned like animals. Men, they aren't as bad as we've been led to believe." Corporal Jake Savage stated these words without any regard to the possible negative impression they made upon his fellow soldiers.

"Corporal Savage, I really think you're getting soft on them. If I didn't know better, I'd think what some folks are saying is true. You've got feelings for these people. I've already heard that the Choctaw had a similar name for their move out here. Don't seem like the Cherokee are too smart, copying a Choctaw name." The comments from one soldier cut Jake Savage to the bone and made him feel the need to avoid additional conversation.

Another soldier in the group spoke, "Hold on now; let Jake speak. I tend to agree with him that what is going on here is wrong. These folks ain't done nothin' to me or mine. What do they call it, Savage? What did you learn from that Cherokee woman?"

Jake Savage informed the five men who were nearby of his conversation with White Crow, again avoiding mentioning her name. He also took time to provide a looser interpretation of the phrase, calling it "The Trail of Tears." At least for the American people, and the books that would record the series of events involving the soldiers and the Cherokee, the name held.

Chapter 30

The Bell Group proceeded across the remaining terrain of Arkansas and passed a host of locations bearing names such as Norristown and Ozark. At Norristown, known today as Russellville, a small uprising resulted in a soldier firing into a group of Cherokee.

Fed up with the increasing deaths that the dust of the drier conditions created in recent days, a group of some fifteen Cherokee refused to begin the march at the designated time. The sentiment of protest increased; no less than two dozen additional Cherokee, equally represented by other men, women, and children, sat in a tightly joined circle with arms interlocked.

Four soldiers rode into the midst of the growing group and fired their rifles into the crowd. "Don't want to move? Then you can sit there forever." The insensitive words were accompanied with at least eight total shots from the soldiers' rifles.

Screams and shouts of pain filled the air as the wounded Cherokee, as well as those in the immediate area, reacted to the carnage. Soldiers in the vicinity took exception to the treatment the horsemen evoked, and the riders became the targets of the more compassionate soldiers.

"Cease your firing, you insane and heartless demons. What do you think you're doing?" The order to end the deluge of lead failed to be followed, either through noncompliance or the inability of the two soldiers to hear their commander's words.

"Take them down" were the words from Colonel Tetleton's mouth. "This has to end immediately." The anger and animosity seemed to overtake all other emotions in the officer.

"The Indians or Russell and Johnson?"

"Shoot the soldiers and do it now." The clarity and insistence of the order from Colonel Tetleton left nothing to the imagination.

Shots rang from approximately a dozen rifles and killed two of the soldiers, Russell and Johnson. The two remaining members of the violent team of troopers were severely wounded. The act had the success of ending the harm the military members had inflicted upon the protesting Cherokee. While not the first incident in which the soldiers had perpetrated harm upon their own, the episode did indicate the most violent act of its kind on the trail thus far.

In addition to the death of the two soldiers, four Cherokee were killed. Three children and a widow, who appeared to be in her early thirties, lay dead. Two other Cherokee were wounded; one of them, an elderly woman, passed away the next day.

Following the incident of that day, the previously closely-adhered-to rule of not allowing the Native Americans to bury their dead was broken. Lieutenant Deas made it possible for the Cherokee to be buried, an act that gained him temporary favor in the eyes of the Cherokee.

Although other Native Americans would pass away from disease and other effects in the days to come, the vast majority of them would be buried in brief ceremonies held on the side of the trail. At least in this respect, something positive clearly arose from a negative event. Unfortunately, other incidents lay ahead.

Despite the measureable success that had resulted from the order from Lieutenant Deas, the exodus of a small group of Cherokee took place near Ozark, Arkansas. In response, five soldiers were rapidly sent as a posse for the Indians who were quickly labeled as renegades. The assignment for the group was to locate and return those who escaped. In turn, any resistance from the escapees was to be met with deadly force. The process was an age-old technique that had proven minutely successful during the foray along the trail.

However, the recruitment of the soldiers to serve as manhunters was met with a great deal of resistance. The knowledge of the difficulties encountered when a previous group pursued the escaping Cherokee added to the general increasing amount of appreciation for the displaced people and resulted in a half-hearted chase of the escapees.

Meanwhile, in an area which the group passed much earlier, Jason Turner, the farmer who had killed a significant number of Cherokee, began his spring plowing. The process was beginning later than he usually did, and Turner managed to incorrectly blame this fact on some type of curse the Cherokee had maliciously placed on his farm.

"The ground was too wet, and now it's dried to dust. Gotta be some of that Injun junk; a spell or something," Turner muttered to himself. His wife Jennifer, a short, homely, obese woman, yelled at him from his cabin and informed him that she had prepared a meal for him.

"You gonna eat today? Food's been ready for an hour and I ain't gonna keep it warm no longer." Mrs. Turner had married Jason ten years earlier, but the relationship had been a rocky one to say the least.

"Ten years I've lived with that hag. It would be fine with me if I never saw her again." Jason Turner had no idea how prophetic and ironic his words would soon become.

As Turner led his mule in breaking the ground for his crops, a small group of Cherokee closely observed the farmer. Those who viewed Jason Turner were the Cherokee who had earlier benefitted from one of his murderous escapades by escaping into the nearby woods. When Turner approached the opposite end of the field from where he had placed his gun against a tree, his wife called to him one last time.

"Jason Turner, it's time to eat! Come get your food." Jennifer Turner stood at the door of the couple's cabin, awaiting a reply. One of her eyes was almost swollen closed, the apparent victim of her husband's violent and abusive temper.

Turner responded to his wife that he would be in the cabin as soon as he made another pass through the field and came closer to the house. The temperamental farmer also mumbled about his improved financial condition due to the funds acquired from burying the Cherokee he had killed months before. While he did so, he glanced toward the edge of the field and witnessed his dog digging in a mound where he had buried some of his most recent victims in a mass grave.

As he paused his plowing and prepared to return to the cabin to eat, Turner looked in the direction of his cabin and unhooked his mule. He then began making his way toward the gun that was propped against a nearby tree. The troubling sounds that he heard caused him to move away from the gun in order to get a clearer view of his cabin.

"Jason! I said it's…" With those words, Jennifer's words were ended and a scream came from inside the cabin. The yell was one of utter terror and, despite the fact Turner was an abusive husband, he wanted no one else to attempt to take advantage of his spouse.

Suddenly, a group of ten Cherokee ran from the woods and ambushed Jason Turner. The members of the attacking party were determined to gain revenge for Turner's aforementioned actions and comments against them. The Cherokee who had earlier escaped the relocation group and somehow managed to survive the winter were resolute in showing no mercy toward Turner. The stout farmer initially managed to fight off the first two men who held him, and he reached for his gun. Soon the sheer number of opponents rendered him helpless.

"What'd ya'll do to my Jenny? I'll get e'er one of ya'll when I git to my gun. You bunch of animals!" Turner's words ceased when he heard the continued screams of his wife escaping the confines of the cabin. As he neared the point of passing out, he viewed an approaching Cherokee who held the decapitated head of Mrs. Turner.

"No! No. I've got to help…" Jason's Turner's fading vocalizations were replaced with groans as knives sank deeply into his upper torso. He made an attempt to yell for help either from Jennifer or someone who may have been passing by; the effort was fruitless.

Jason Turner's faint screams for help were permanently silenced as the muscular Cherokee men used rocks and the butt of Turner's gun to kill the farmer. The body of Jason Turner was dragged to the cabin and placed beside the headless corpse of his wife. As Turner had wished, he never again saw his wife. Ironically, Jennifer's screams were among the last sounds he heard before becoming the victim of people for whom he held high contempt.

Jennifer Turner's head was pushed onto a fencepost where it awaited the arrival of any friends or neighbors of the couple. Although there were no real friends, there were acquaintances the couple had made during their infrequent visits to a local church. As for neighbors, the vile and offensive Turner and his similarly-offensive spouse had managed to ruin any sincere relationships with those who were unfortunate enough to reside within several miles of the Jason and Jennifer Turner household.

In relation to the Cherokee who had exited the scene in relative silence, they had also carried away any weapons or food they found inside the cabin. After doing so, they proceeded to set the cabin on fire, creating a large plume of smoke that filled the air. Disgruntled neighbors paid little attention to the smoke, or chose to ignore it completely, crediting it to one of Turner's random field burnings. As such, it would be almost two weeks before the destruction of the Turner home was discovered. Only the dried head of Mrs. Turner gave evidence of the murder of her, and possibly her husband. No steadfast attempt was made in order to discover who the guilty party or parties of the incident were. The deaths of the Turner couple were soon forgotten.

Chapter 31

Despite the existing government policies and regulations regarding voluntary cordial contact between any soldier and a member of the Cherokee Nation, White Crow and Corporal Jake Savage began to more publically exhibit their strong feelings for one another. What had been, or appeared to be, chance meetings of short durations gave way to prearranged conferences. Jake Savage even managed to establish the guard detail he was assigned every other night to be at the location closet to where White Crow would be sleeping.

The tendency to hold their conversations while the wagon train was moving or to hold a brief summit as the sun was setting was replaced with discussions that transpired throughout the day and well into the night hours. White Crow and Jake held the utmost respect for their separate friends and cohorts, but the increasing love they possessed for one another blinded them to the cautionary advice of those who thought highly of them and held high regard for their well-being.

Warnings about the dangers involved in exhibiting their feelings were issued from those close to White Crow. Likewise, the group of friends Corporal Jake Savage maintained uttered words of caution toward him. Savage, like White Crow, chose not to yield to the admonitions, although the corporal's military career could be placed in jeopardy. There was also the fact that Corporal Savage faced the strong possibility of being jailed or executed. However, due to the military protocol of the period and with the depleted number of soldiers present at the time, the latter negative aspect of the courtship would not likely be able to be implemented until the group's arrival at their destination of the Indian Territory.

One of Jake Savage's comrades, Clayton Morgan, said to him, "Jake, I know you've got feelings for that Cherokee they call White Crow. She's a beautiful lady, and I know anybody, man or woman, would agree with that claim. But you've got to be careful, my friend. There's more talk than ever about you and her being a couple. I don't think all of those Indians are too wild about it, and I know the officers will have you arrested when we get where we're going. It's military justice. You're a nice guy, a great soldier. Watch out for them."

Jake Savage replied in a seemingly defiant tone, "They are, are they? I sort of figured it was coming to that. I kinda hope it does, and I'll tell my side about how cruelly they have treated these people and left many of 'em to die on the side of the trail. There were dead children who were left unburied, food for the coyotes and other animals to eat. How is that for justice?"

Morgan saw he was of one accord with Jake Savage's mindset, "Jake, I agree with what you're saying, but you know, just like I do, that that don't matter. There's gonna be trouble brought down on you and a lot of these men will testify against you. Some of the boys hold it against you for what you did to Moss. Others think you should be promoted. The fact of the matter is that you may be in big trouble. The military court don't care nothing about how the Indians are treated. You might as well end this charade or become one of them. You'd be better off running away with that girl if you really love her. I can't speak for the others, but I'd let you go. There's some here who would shoot you if you tried to take her and make a run for it though. I can keep a watch out for your back a little longer, but not too long."

"Do you think that's what we should do? Make a run for it? Not seek out justice and let this whole incident have its day in court? Do I look like a coward to you?"

"Jake, anyone and everyone knows you're anything but a coward. I think there's a lot of difference between being brave and being stupid. What you're trying to do is not right, at least not in the eyes of the government and many of the people on the trail, soldier and Indian alike. I'm telling you, as a friend, that you need to think of yourself, and, if nothing else, that Cherokee girl you love. Something bad is going to happen, Jake, and I don't want to see you in prison or dead. Think about it, okay?" Morgan continued to offer pleas to his friend.

"I'll tell you that I will do anything I can to take care of her. White Crow may be a Cherokee, but she is also an intelligent and caring person. She has been able to survive a great deal of tragedy, and I want to be a part of her life from now on."

Striving to sway Jake Savage toward more rational thinking, Morgan made a host of new points. "Do you want to become another tragedy in her life? Come on, Jake. Be realistic. Slow down this relationship until we get to where we're going, and then you can take her away. There has to be somewhere you can take her and be safe and happy for the rest of your life. Work out the details before we get there; I hear that's gonna be just a few days."

"Where are we going?" Jake asked. The question may have come from his curiosity, or it may have stemmed from an attempt to change the topic and mood of the conversation.

Morgan offered, "I've heard we're going to Indian Territory. Don't know how the talk got started, but that is what some of the men were saying earlier today."

"How appropriate," Jake replied, "we'll end up taking them to a place where they'll supposedly be safe, but they were safe and happy where they were. I'll end up in a cell or at the end of a rope. Does any of this make sense to you? I've heard about the Indian Territory before. I've told people that may be where we're going. It's all mixed up."

"Jake, it's a mixed up world. The people of the past didn't have all the stuff to worry about like we do. There's more trains back east than folks ever thought would be there, gotta be a few million people in our country now. Looks like the only real problem is the conflict between us and the Indians; that should go away once we get them to Indian Territory. Won't nothing else keep our country from growing, both in size and people coming together. They'll get the Indians on that land, and all will be fine; I promise. I don't see no other issues facing us or our kids."

"What if, just to say, White Crow and I do end up together? What if we have kids? What will happen to our kids? How will they be treated?" Jake concluded the conversation in saying, "It just makes no sense to me."

With that, Jake tossed a clod of dirt to the side of where he was sitting, half-heartedly waved to his compatriot, and walked away. Both Jake Savage and Morgan knew that, although their exchange of words had ceased, the thoughts that began with the onset of the recent conversation would continue for some time to come.

Chapter 32

The stress related to the decision Jake Savage faced was not all that bothered the young corporal at this juncture of the journey. Like many of his friends, he was concerned with the high numbers of sick and dying, an aspect that lessened little with the onset of warm weather. Although the death rate of the soldiers was a small fraction of the number among the Cherokee, there had been some deaths that took place, while a significant number of the troops were sick.

A sizeable sum of severe cases of starvation had also plagued the group a majority of time since the trip began. A host of diseases continued to run rampant among the soldiers and Cherokee. A recent onset of dysentery not only slowed the progress of the group, but also proved deadly to dozens of Cherokee and no less than eight soldiers. Cholera also appeared due to the unsanitary sources of water the members of both groups were often forced to drink in attempts to simply seek pure preservation of life.

The maladies tended to initially disturb those who were of larger statures due to their being more prone to ingest greater amounts of water. None of the people making the difficult journey suspected that a single drink of water, much less handfuls from a seemingly reliable body of water, would lead to such debilitating physical problems.

The ingestion of polluted water triggered severe vomiting and diarrhea that produced dehydration and an even stronger desire for water. Stomach cramps would usually subside, but the thirst brought on through the growing combination of illnesses tended to remain until the afflicted person recovered or, in more unfortunate instances, died.

As if the tragedies already noted were not enough, more disorders reared their ugly heads and harmed additional soldiers and Cherokee. Typhus and whooping cough were leaders among the other diseases that swept the ranks of white and red skinned people alike.

Rivers, streams, ponds, and basically any body of water along the route were used to fill canteens or other containers. The difficulties of attempting to push a massive body of people along the trail created a logistical nightmare when the participants were healthy and lacked outside interference from raiders and the like who hampered the party. With the diseases that affected the guards and guarded alike, the transition from one location to another became almost impossible.

The number of miles traveled often slowed to less than ten per day during the early spring. With the warmer weather came increased consumption of water, and then, often in a short period of time, the symptoms of one or more the ailments appeared again. Guards were far less demanding in regard to the pace of the march when they themselves were forced to climb from their mounts and make sudden trips into roadside bushes.

In turn, the soldiers were becoming more understanding of the health issues that faced the Native Americans. The holding pens at Red Clay, Tennessee had negatively impacted the health of the Cherokee while the soldiers who were there had generally been able to eat and drink more suitable and substantial provisions.

The soldiers regularly held conversations about how they had mistreated the Cherokee as well as various other Native Americans who had been relocated prior to the Cherokee. A man who had earlier participated in a similar event made comments to other soldiers as the group sat at their campfire on a cool spring night.

The soldier who went by the surname Stewart recalled, "This ain't the first time I've helped move these folks out west. I think we're headed to Indian Territory 'cause that's where we took the Choctaw. Tettleton told me to keep quiet about that trip. Now I feel like I gotta talk. Things didn't go right on that jaunt, either. There was a lot of death, sick folks were everywhere, Choctaw and us alike. Not as bad as this one, though.

Don't think I'll join in another one of these; if I live through this one. They can't make me do this again. I don't know if I can explain to my kids why I did this. It just don't seem right."

Another soldier inquired, "Are you gonna refuse an order? You can't just tell 'em you're not going to do something; even I know that and I've only been in this army a few months."

The veteran Stewart remarked, "It's like a curse. These Cherokee, some of 'em anyway, got old ties to strange gods. They say they worship and pray like we do, but I know that ain't so. They can't speak another language and expect other folks to listen to them. I wonder if they're casting some kind of spell on us. It's like witchcraft or something. Them that do believe like we believe are asking God to help 'em. We can't win going against God."

A third soldier, James Mason, had been a member of the military for three years. Standing nearby, Mason said, "Now hold on. There's no such thing as spells or witchcraft. Things happening now are judgment, judgment from God. He knows what we're doing is wrong, and it's time we paid for what we're a part of. I don't know about you boys, but I'm a feared."

Stewart recanted his own statement, as well as that of Mason, in saying, "If God's doing this, why are the Cherokee dying too? They are the ones who are dying faster. There were so many of them and they've been dropping dead, don't seem fair to me to assume they are in the wrong or that they're being judged."

At that moment, Corporal Jake Savage walked up. His turn at guard duty had come to an end, and he was ready for some much needed rest. "You boys ready for your turn at watching out for our prisoners?"

The veteran Stewart, agitated by this point of the conversation, blurted, "The only thing that's your captive is that red-skinned woman's heart! Seems to me what you'd be watching out for is that no one else tries to take what's yours. I've seen boys do what you're getting yourself into before and it never seems to…" Stewart's words were broken with Jake Savage's anger.

"Enough!" Corporal Savage was thrown into a rage in response to the veteran's words. "I've had enough of people telling me what is right or wrong with my life. If someone else tries to tell me something or accuses me, I hate to think what will happen."

Jake Savage threw down his rifle and saddle bags that he was carrying, and made three steps in the direction of where his antagonist was located. Corporal Savage appeared ready to fight Stewart. Savage had clinched both fists, and his face was snarled in anger.

Corporal Savage reached for the collars of the surprised soldier's shirt and lifted the middle-aged man from his resting spot. At the moment in which Savage removed his right hand's grip from the shirt, Jake also pulled his fist back, in an apparent move to strike the soldier. Savage's action was prevented when two of the soldiers who had been sitting near the shocked veteran grabbed Savage and restrained him.

One of the men managed to pull Jake Savage from the target of his anger, while the second used both hands to inhibit Savage's swing. The actions of the two soldiers likely prevented Savage from facing the possibility of being incarcerated for the remainder of the trip, as no one was able to throw or land a punch.

"They should beat you, just like the other man. I got no problem with you chasing that Cherokee, but if you're turning against your own, you need to be whipped. One more time toward me and you may get it." The aggressive words of Stewart filled the night air.

"Corporal Savage, calm down!" The words from one of the peacemakers were shouted to Jake Savage. "You need to breathe, my friend; we're not against you."

Jake Savage's emotions began to overwhelm him as he pulled away from the grips of the two soldiers. Shaking his head, he calmly and softly stated, "I don't know what's wrong. Everything is crazy."

As Corporal Savage walked from the scene he avoided responding to the array of beseeching calls sent in his direction. Even the soldier who had served as the object of his sudden rage pleaded with him to return. The men who had been peacefully conversing at the fire a few minutes earlier were bewildered at the recent occurrence.

"He's gone fellas. I've seen that look in other men's eyes before. He's not a soldier anymore."

Chapter 33

During the third week of March, as the unseasonably warm weather continued to combine with the onset of a host of diseases, relief for the Bell Group arrived in an unexpected manner. The entourage was thirty minutes into the daily process of marching when members at the front of the procession observed a distinct dust cloud moving in their direction. Based upon the misfortunes of the past, thoughts and rumors of approaching hostile Native Americans or area residents determined to harass the sickly and suffering train began to circulate.

A skirmish line was established as quickly as possible, with twenty-three well-armed soldiers setting up an obstacle. The remaining soldiers, including Corporal Jake Savage, were given the assignments of guarding and protecting the Cherokee and unhealthy soldiers. By that point, some two dozen soldiers were confined to respective wagons, with another forty, reportedly unfit to walk, being given extra arms in the case of an attack.

For the first time during the journey, weapons were also passed out to a large number of the Cherokee men. No thought was given to whether or not the recipients were prone to rebel against the procedures or policies of the procession. The goal was simply one of protecting the various members of the Bell Group from harm.

The dust cloud approaching from the west began to give way when it soon reached a distance of approximately three-quarters of a mile from the Bell Group's skirmish line. A set of cavalry flags and blue uniformed soldiers were distinguishable in the midst of the powdery and stifling air that hung over the oncoming crowd.

One of the soldiers in the Bell Group exclaimed, "They're some of us! There are soldiers coming our way. We'll be safe now. They're here to help!"

Comments began to readily spread throughout the weary crowd, with the reaction seemingly less positive among the Cherokee than with the soldiers who were witnessing the event. Almost immediately the recently-issued weapons were being taken from the Cherokee, and the manner in which they were retrieved was far more humane than most interactions among the members of the crowd to that point of the journey.

Jake Savage heard the talk that created calm throughout the ranks of the Bell Group. He anxiously attempted to locate White Crow within the ranks of the group, but his initial effort was unsuccessful. After discovering the true identity of the approaching entourage, he began to make his way toward the skirmish line.

"Jake! Jake Savage!" White Crow's voice resounded over the noise of those who were reacting to the arrival of more soldiers and wagons.

"White Crow!" Jake made no attempt to hide his feelings for the Cherokee maiden nor did he give any indication of thoughts related to his personal safety.

Recollections about the tensions that had existed among his fellow soldiers and him were sent to the most extreme corners of his mind, and Jake Savage found himself hugging White Crow in an embrace like they had never experienced. The episode went completely unnoticed due to the conversations and noise that erupted with the arrival of the contingency of soldiers.

Migrating members from the Bell Group began to encircle the arriving soldiers and wagons as the visitors entered what had served as a hurriedly established skirmish line only a few minutes earlier. The wagons propelled from the westward fort were filled with supplies not limited to food, water, medicine, bandages, shoes, bedding, and clothing. If ever such an offering of relief were needed, that point in history, at least from the perspective of the Bell Group, had arrived. As had occurred before, the reception of the goods lifted the group's spirits.

The recently-arrived soldiers attending the wagons also brought news that some of the Cherokee who escaped before and during the early stages of the movement had reached privately owned land in the mountains of eastern Tennessee and in North Carolina. The landowner, a white man named William Holland Thomas, was allowing some four hundred members of the Oconaluftee Cherokee to reside on his land prior to the Trail of Tears beginning. Thomas saw it as his duty to allow the escaped Cherokee to seek refuge in the area, one that was rich in sources of vegetation, game, and fresh water.

Similarly, statements regarding less-successful escapes of the part of the Cherokee circulated. An estimated two hundred Cherokee had assisted in the capture of Tsali, the Cherokee brave who had escaped and led a small group of followers into the mountains of North Carolina. These individuals who served as a posse for Tsali, in return, were allowed to remain on parcels of land without having to move westward.

Tsali had been taken to Red Clay; there, he was placed on trial for the charges brought against him. Among the list of crimes Tsali faced was that of inciting a riot. The rationale behind this lay in the fact that Tsali's abandonment of the post at Red Clay had resulted in large scale mourning among those Cherokee left behind.

A hurriedly-raised and racially-biased jury of white males quickly found Tsali guilty of inciting a riot as well as of having murdered soldiers and white citizens of the area. Tsali stood no chance of receiving a fair trial, and the jury was quick and decisive in their recourse.

Tsali was placed in front of a firing squad the day after his sentence was announced. The members of the group who would serve as his executioners consisted of Cherokee men who, although initially a part of his band, had eventually turned against him. While some participants and witnesses may have regarded the latter acts of the appointed gunmen as treasonous, others saw the turncoats' action as life-preserving. Additional witnesses viewed the same as an indication of the willingness of the Cherokee to become more compliant with the customs and wishes of the United States government.

The members of the firing squad, in an act of appreciation for their service, were also provided with small land parcels in North Carolina. The United States officials who oversaw the dispersal of the land made it known that the Cherokee who were recipients of the land grants were to be allowed to live on the plots of land for all time.

In addition, the vast majority of the remaining Cherokee rebels from Tsali's group were also captured. While most of the members of Tsali's band were processed for removal to Oklahoma, three of his followers were executed. Against their will, random Cherokee men were selected as members of firing squads and, in turn, were used to administer the deadly volleys.

No less than fifteen men were hurriedly gathered to be used as unwilling marksmen. Three of the Cherokee males were sadistically struck with gun barrels and stocks when the men refused to become members of the firing squads. A fourth Native American, also defiant in his stance against becoming a marksman against the accused, was subjected to six strong strikes from a whip were delivered against his naked back.

Another point of the tragedy was that other members of the coerced Cherokee failed to make their shots deadly. This detail was not perceived to be the results of acts of protest against the soldiers who were forcing the deed. In fact, many of the Cherokee men recruited to deliver the shots into the three human targets were untrained or relatively unaccustomed to the style of weapons they were issued to use in the controversial affair. It was also ruled out that missing the intended target on the chests of the quickly-convicted Cherokee was an indication of insensitivity toward those being executed

The first Cherokee prisoner who was placed in front of the firing squad was not immediately killed, but he was mortally wounded. Having been forced to stand in front of a brushy outcropping, the man dropped his head in prayer and refused to look at those assigned to the deadly task of firing toward his heart. Although he appeared to possess a strong indifference to the situation, the accused had tears dropping from his cheeks and splattering onto the ground at his feet. The teardrops were clearly discernable to a close observer of the situation.

When ordered to discharge their weapons toward the accused, the members of the speedily assembled firing squad pressed the triggers of their guns. The weapons appeared to fire in unison and sent the projectiles toward the accused individual. The indicted individual reeled in pain as the metallic objects entered various locations of his body. Staggering forward with a single stride, the man fell to the ground during his unsuccessful struggle to make a second step.

The five shots that struck the targeted Cherokee landed primarily in his upper body. Three of the shots struck his shoulders, one hit his left collar bone, and a fifth bullet smashed into his right arm. Despite the wounds, the Cherokee man somehow managed to live four days before he passed away. Unhappily, the agony the shooting victim endured resulted in his screams and moans that terrorized those within hearing distance.

Sadly, the Cherokee man's wounds, similar to ones other parties had earlier received, would have likely not been as troubling had he been allowed to obtain proper medical care. Instead, the critically wounded individual was denied the simple courtesy of access to a blanket. As the warm temperatures of the day gave way to the chilling nights that were common on the trail, the suffering soul shivered as his energy and will to survive slowly seeped from his body.

The otherwise healthy Cherokee male, approximately twenty-five years old, was intentionally and insensitively left alone on the barren ground where he had fallen from the inflicted wounds. For the ensuing days and nights following his receipt of his injuries, the young man merely lay alone, unable to receive a drink of water or more substantial care from willing and available compassionate souls.

By the time the chastised Cherokee succumbed to his wounds, he had ended his pleas for help as well as the seemingly incessant moaning. Those gave way to hampered breathing and the absence of movement. It was common for the series of men assigned to offer protection for the dying warrior to use a bayonet attached to a gun to prod the suffering shooting victim as a means of determining the presence or absence of life in the prostrate form.

Subsequent Cherokee chosen to serve on firing squads began to protest as a means of avoiding firing into the bodies of the members of Tsali's group. In fact, one of the five men assigned to help execute the second Cherokee man chose to end his own life rather than serve as what he apparently believed would classify him as a murderer.

When the third Cherokee man was placed in front of the last group of firing squad members, his death arrived more quickly. Four of the shots hit his upper body, one on either side of his heart and two in his left shoulder. The inflicting of the painful wounds caused the forty-year-old male target to scream in agony.

The fifth and fatal shot for the third victim came from a Cherokee who was initially reluctant to use his weapon. The timidity of the final firing squad member was ended only after he was kicked in his hindquarters.

"Shoot him!" shouted one of the soldiers assigned to oversee the execution. No sooner had the words left the soldier's mouth than a second soldier lifted his right foot and kicked the hesitant warrior just below the small of his back.

The Cherokee firing squad member tightly held his loaded weapon. He somehow regained his balance and took note of a pair of soldiers. The blue-clad duo had their guns pointed toward him and one of them threatened to shoot him if the Cherokee failed to quickly and accurately fire his gun at the severely wounded prisoner. The Cherokee reluctantly steadied himself and began raising his weapon.

Appearing to know his time was near, the screaming and wounded Cherokee firing squad victim propped himself up with his right arm. He held his mouth open in a strong effort to ingest every available particle of air. Seconds later, the once unenthusiastic firing squad member aimed his weapon at the convicted Cherokee. As the third victim looked into the eyes of the man who was about to send a fifth bullet in his direction, the slug entered his open mouth and exited through the back of his head.

Witnessing his undesirable task as complete, the individual who fired the fatal shot threw his gun to the ground and ran from the scene. The lack of compassion from the four soldiers who had coerced his action was obvious as each of them took an opportunity to hurl insults toward the fleeing man.

One of the four was heard to proclaim, "He's no better than the dog he shot. I was gonna get him to bury the body; guess we'll let it rot now."

Such were the continual conditions the captive Cherokee faced as they moved along the trail.

Chapter 34

The journey of the Bell Group somehow managed to continue to progress miles from the site where Tsali's followers were being executed. The Cherokee's continued communication with the soldiers who had joined the group two days earlier had confirmed that Indian Territory was the Bell Group's destination.

Fortunately, the following days included fewer deaths than had taken place than in recent weeks. The rates of dysentery and other health issues drastically decreased as well. As a direct result, the number of miles traversed turned into the upper teens and lower twenties for the next eight days. Such progression had only been a dream in the majority of past months, but now it quickly became the expected norm.

The Bell Group eventually managed to reach an Arkansas location known as the Vineyard Post Office. The settlement was located on the eastern edge of the Indian Territory, and the assemblage arrived there in late March of 1839. In an effort to establish a sense of a more permanent dwelling, the Cherokee were assigned temporary living quarter sites.

Wooden huts, complete with small porches, a semblance of flooring, and fireplaces, provided the soldiers with longed-for housing. A pair of bunk beds enabled four of the uniformed men to comfortably occupy the structures. The homes seemed even more spacious when assigned duties typically took at least one of the four soldiers from a shelter at any given time.

Used Army tents were initially used for converted Cherokee accommodations. Substandard by most peoples' judgment, at least for long-term lodging, the tents were far better than the blankets or shade trees that had provided the typical type of shelter for the displaced people in recent months. The tents were not absent of drawbacks. While the soldiers were regularly able to find shelter and gain rest in far more spacious quarters, the tents were hardly large enough for the number of Cherokee who were expected to occupy each of them.

After all of the huts for the soldiers were completed and occupied, the announcement was made that a similar type building would be used to house the Cherokee. Until then, the tents were to suffice for the emigrant people.

The structures that were designated to serve as temporary Cherokee homes in the reservation had to be built first. One facet of the production process that would save a great deal of time was that full walls would be eliminated from the initial process. With a basically unlimited labor force on the part of the Cherokee, the construction of the houses progressed swiftly. Within two weeks all of the Cherokee, as well as the soldiers who had served as their captors for months, were able to sleep in roofed structures.

The process of building the homes preceded planting crops, also a vital undertaking for the sick and fatigued group of Cherokee. Although the vast majority of the Native Americans were aware of the fact the site would only serve as a provisional station for the Bell Group, the motivation to plant, tend, and eventually gather fresh vegetables proved too strong to suppress.

Contact between Jake Savage and White Crow was largely non-existent for the first three weeks in which the Bell Group used the Vineyard Post Office as its base. The tasks of building the housing units and then planting vegetable plots also heavily occupied the minds of those in command of the soldiers.

The construction of the aforementioned structures, along with exhibiting the necessary care of crops, took the preponderance of the schedules in the lives of Jake Savage and White Crow. By the time one of the duo completed the days' needed or assigned duties, the other was engaged in fulfilling obligations or seeking a setting to gain much needed rest and relaxation.

As a consolation for the couple's inability to visit, there were no additional talks regarding Corporal Jake Savage's potential trial or incarceration. Jake dared not ask anyone about the situation, and he knew that a simple statement made and overheard would likely reinvigorate the prospect of his jailing. Jake Savage and White Crow found resolve in the belief that the time would come when they would find acceptance and a related sense of forgiveness for the incidents they had knowingly or unwillingly committed.

One major exception to the hiatus of the suspended White Crown and Jake Savage relationship took place three weeks and one day after their arrival at Vineyard Post Office, Arkansas. Although the meeting was brief, it had major ramifications for their maturing love.

During an unusually warm morning, Corporal Jake Savage had awakened in his cabin to find that he was alone. As he placed his cap on his head and prepared to leave the structure, he heard voices outside.

"Thank you for the fresh food." The soldier's words which Jake heard sounded genuinely appreciative, so Corporal Savage concluded they must have been directed toward another white soldier. As he pushed aside the large canvas flap that served as the cabin's door, he saw White Crow and three other Cherokee maidens holding baskets bursting with fresh radishes.

Corporal Savage's apparent shock at seeing her paled in comparison to White Crow realizing that she was then standing outside the home where the object of her adoration dwelled. Throughout that point of their association, White Crow had only known Jake Savage's more nomadic lifestyle. The sedentary aspect of his normal existence resulted in a look of disbelief.

"This is your home?" White Crow asked.

"Yes; yes, it is. Would you and your friends like to see the inside?" Such a question would have been unheard of weeks earlier, but the comradery many of the soldiers and the Cherokee had loosely come to exhibit was becoming more commonplace and acceptable in the confines of Vineyard Post Office.

White Crow stepped inside as Corporal Jake Savage held back the canvas. White Crow's three associates entered in the same manner while

Jake continued to remove heavy fabric from the entryway. This was the first, but far from the last, time on which White Crow would enter the home and resting place of her cherished Jake Savage.

The four Cherokee females acted as if they had entered a type of dwelling they had either never come across or had largely failed to recall. Jake Savage and two other soldiers, one of whom continued to eat from the handful of recently-harvested and unwashed radishes he held, watched the unfolding scene in utter amazement.

"This is much like where we once lived." Her statement dispelled the perception of the structure having no common place in White Crow's memory. "The fireplace reminds me of my childhood home." Before White Crow could continue, she grew speechless when she saw a drawing hanging from the wall beside one of the bunk beds.

"That! That picture! It is me!" White Crow exclaimed.

"He drew this," Corporal Jake Savage noted as he pointed to the soldier eating radishes. "He knows how I feel about you, and he felt this would help me when I couldn't see you. It's a beautiful drawing, but it is not as beautiful as you."

White Crow stepped toward Jake and the two kissed. This marked the first time they had intentionally and openly exhibited their affection with no regard for who saw it or what type of consequences resulted. The two soldiers standing nearby grinned. One did so with pieces of a chewed radish shining through his teeth.

"Might as well let 'em be," the soldier said as he turned from his recently acquired job as the canvas holder, and he walked from the cabin. The second soldier followed nearby; the three Cherokee moved just outside the door.

Realizing the full effect the situation could yield, Corporal Jake Savage held White Crow at arm's length and told her he loved her. Savage quickly led her to the door in order to avoid undue attention being directed toward them. They then exited the cabin without drawing notice from anyone, aside from the three ladies who had walked to the hut with White Crow.

No nearby soldiers were posted outside their cabins, so the incident was carried out without future ramifications. White Crow walked from

Jake Savage's cabin but continued to look back at him with affection and a smile. Savage countered White Crow's actions with a silent wave and mouthed, "I love you" toward White Crow as she disappeared behind a series of cabins located approximately thirty feet from where he stood.

The four Cherokee women continued their movement throughout the camp, offering radishes to soldiers who were outside their dwellings. The ladies dared not go inside any of the cabins or knock on a door of the same for fear of their safety.

The mental focus of a large number of the Cherokee and soldiers who had survived the months of danger and hardships on the trail now shifted toward the memories of what they had endured, as well as those people who were lost in its navigation. The emotional toll inflicted upon so many of the survivors would affect their health and well-being for years.

Some one thousand two hundred of the members of the Bell Group, under Chief Ross's leadership, had fallen victim to some type of peril while traversing the trail. That number could have easily been accurately tabulated through the daily count of the Cherokee, but the magnitude of it became more realistic or precise as the parties settled into the routine lifestyle that Vineyard Post Office, Arkansas and its amenities provided.

Unhappily, the death toll would not reach its climax until the bulk of the contingency reached its eventual geographical goal, a location that lay fifty miles to the west. That site would not be approached for another month.

Chapter 35

A mid-May announcement stated that the members of the Bell Group would soon be moved from Vineyard Post Office, Arkansas. Given one day's notice, the participants suffered a deep reversal of the recent morale boost they had enjoyed. Their responsive decline in optimism was largely due to the complete comprehension that their gardens, fully indicating the likelihood of a bountiful yield, were to be left behind to potentially to serve as fodder for the soldiers who would remain. Equally disturbing was the fact that the relative safety of their temporary quarters was abandoned for what many perceived as the renewal of the hardships and tribulations they had previously suffered along the trail.

Sundry soldiers who were to take part in supervising the exodus from Vineyard Post Office took it upon themselves to sleep during their last comfortable hours before embarking on another phase of the trip. Several others caused a verbal distraction to the on-duty guards, and the rowdy group held a makeshift drinking binge. The attention paid to the reveling combatants enabled the planning and implementation of an impromptu grievance session for the Cherokee.

The declaration concerning the group's movement from Vineyard Post Office quickly resulted in the Cherokee tribal elders notifying dozens of heads of families that a council meeting would be held later that night. Those men who attended were asked to express their genuine concerns. These feelings were to be stated in low volumes, so as to avoid directing any more attention to the gathering than was already being shown.

One of the tribal leaders sat quietly when those around him asked what he felt should be done. Their questions often centered upon points such as whether or not a revolt should be commenced, if there would be enough ammunition to carry out such a movement, and how long it would take for word of the rebellion to reach a fort from which reinforcements of soldiers and additional weapons would come.

The silent Cherokee elder leader closed his eyes and told those around him that he was allowing his mind to take him back to the conclusion of President Jefferson's January 1806 speech. The tribal chieftain had been among the crowd who witnessed Jefferson that day, and he heard the third President's declaration of unity among the Cherokee and those who governed the United States. The now-aged Cherokee began saying, "My children, I thank you for your visit and pray to the Great Sprit who made all of us and planted us in this land to live together like brothers. I ask that He will conduct you safely to your homes, and grant you to find your families and your friends in good health."

With his conclusion of the utterance of that statement, the Cherokee elder recalled the rotting Cherokee corpses at numerous locations along the trail. These lost souls included the individuals who were victims of natural acts, the innocent and escaping people shot on and beside the trail, and those who were left behind for their bodies to be scavenged. He also noted the Cherokee who successfully escaped but possibly passed away after encountering various situations that may have cost them their lives.

Exhibiting the composure of a Cherokee man who had heard and spoken English for the majority of his adult years, the tribal elder proclaimed, "The tragedy of recent months will forever burn deeply into the hearts of those fortunate enough to survive the ordeal."

The mixed emotions that resulted from his statement were reminiscent of those expressed during the months of hardships along the trail. Men were witnessed sitting in introspection, some quietly used trembling hands to dab tears from their eyes, and still others wept openly. Although it was fully understood that the request may not successfully be followed, the men were asked to show strength and leadership to their respective families during the journey that was to be undertaken in a matter of a few short hours.

Grief and tears unfortunately became as commonplace during the ensuing westward migration as they had been in the earlier stages of the trek. The Cherokee elders prayed for some type of sign that would lead the mothers of the sick, dying, and dead to continue the movement despite all hope appearing to be gone. The elders passed along the content of their prayers to the people who attended the final meeting at Vineyard Post Office, and those individuals were to institute a time of prayer among their respective families.

The morning after the clandestine council of the Cherokee elders was held, a seemingly miraculous and unusual event occurred. Roses regularly began appearing at various locations where tears of mourning mothers had fallen during the previous afternoon and night. The flowers also sprang from the ground along the trail, as each morning short bursts of vegetation somehow grew from the very spots where heartbroken Cherokee had expelled heartbroken tears.

The type of flower that grew in the locations came to be called the Cherokee Rose. The living reminder of the trail's hardships was white in color, a fact that legend holds simply represents the tears of grieving mothers who lost children during the westward journey. A gold center appeared on the roses, a mark that supposedly signified the gold the white men had ruthlessly and selfishly seized from the confiscated Cherokee lands. Interestingly, there were seven leaves on each stem of the rose; that number was identical to the sum of clans that comprised the Cherokee nation at the time of their forced removal.

To this day the roses still grow along the trail, some two hundred years after the event. The plants have not only survived the effects of time, but also of civilization and additional encroachment of vegetation and animals.

No one outside of the tribal leaders had prayed harder for a sign than had White Crow. Although she had determined it best to avoid sharing the prayer with Corporal Jake Savage, White Crow finally felt compelled to do so when she witnessed Jake pluck a group of the flowers some six days after the group had begun the final leg of their journey.

White Crow took it upon herself to voice to Jake Savage some details about the roses he had innocently picked. She began to explain the significance of the seven leaves, and Jake was enthralled. One of the leaves stood for a group who was known as the Aniwodi or Red Clan, a symbol of death. The group had made red paint and was also known as the Corn People. A second leaf represented the Wild Potato Clan; they were called the Anigatogewi. The Anigilohi were known as the Twister or Long Hair Clan and represented day and night.

Additionally, as White Crow expounded, the Wolf or Panther Clan represented war, and the Cherokee called them the Aniwahya. Symbolizing peace, the Anikawi were known in the English language as the Deer or Bison Clan. The Blue or Blue Holly Clan were called the Ansahoni in Cherokee and represented the sky. Lastly, the idea of spirit was represented with the Small Bird or Eagle Clan, known as the Ani Tsiskwa among the Cherokee.

Jake Savage thoroughly enjoyed the conversation White Crow and he held in relation to the roses. The insight he persisted to gain in relation to the Cherokee culture made him appreciate the people more and more. In turn, Corporal Savage apologized for removing the flowers from their positions. He also explained that he had only done so in order to give the roses to White Crow as a symbol of his continued love for her.

"Sometime, in the near future, we will be together, and there will be no need for more tears. If we have the flowers in the yard of our home, they will have to be carried from here." White Crow's feelings for Jake Savage were clearly expressed as she made no effort to hide her love for him. In two weeks the remaining members of the Bell Group, along with White Crow and Jake Savage, would be at the site toward which they had been moving since the initial sudden and violent expulsion from their homes.

Chapter 36

The Bell Group finally managed to reach Indian Territory, the location that was widely assumed to serve as their final destination. The time they had spent moving from Vineyard Post Office to Indian Territory had resulted in far less illnesses and deaths than the previous phases of the journey. However, those who participated in the final phase of the hike were no less aware of the possibilities of the situation being altered at any moment.

White Crow and Jake Savage were able to converse more in the most recent two-week segment of their migration than they had in the previous months of their trip. The overwhelming content of their conversations was carried out with short exchanges of statements and was often accompanied with gestures in which one or both of them pointed toward some natural landmark.

Corporal Jake Savage kept a set of folded sheets of paper in the pocket of his military jacket, but on one occasion they fell from the location of safekeeping. A soldier named Aubrey Loder became a curious bystander when retrieved it from the ground, but the fellow soldier was unable to decipher its markings and words. Seeming to think that Jake had fallen victim to the increasing heat and effects of the excursion, the Loder shrugged off the contents and returned the papers to Jake.

"Hey, Corporal Savage! This set of papers fell out of your pocket. What all have you been trying to write on there anyhow?" the inquisitive Loder asked.

"You read them?" Jake nervously inquired. "These are my private recollections of the last few weeks. I didn't want anyone to see them."

Loder appeared to be aware of the seriousness of his meddling into Jake's affairs, and he made an honest appeal to Corporal Savage. The intrusive soldier's desire to become mindful of the contents of Corporal Savage's papers soon gave way to a sense of guilt. Loder expressed his honesty and declared to Jake, "I looked at 'em but didn't get any sense out of 'em. They wuz just full of a lot of scribbles and poor spelling. You can't draw neither, Corporal Savage."

Blinking quickly, Jake Savage tucked the sheets into their previous spot of seclusion and replied, "Not a problem, Loder. You know how it is; you just dream up stuff and make strange marks. I never have been too much on my clear marks. Teachers never bragged on my artwork either."

Loder appeared to initially agree with Jake Savage's declaration, but he then remembered a pass which Jake had written him a few nights earlier and that had gone unused. Retrieving it from his right saddlebag, the soldier read it aloud to himself.

In neatly written words, the pass stated, "This pass allows Aubrey Loder to progress from Vineyard Post Office to the next town northward for one night. He is to return to duty by…" The remaining phrases were illegible as Loder had spilled coffee on the sheet the same night Jake Savage had given the pass to him.

"Guess I should have gone there instead of joining them boys and drinking. I can't win money at cards anyhow," the soldier contemplated. With that said, Loder grasped the pass in his right hand, wadded it up, and cast it to the ground. Within minutes the passing feet, wagons, and horses had rendered it into shreds.

The Bell Group's arrival in Indian Territory evidently allowed incidents from recent months to be more freely discussed. Among those was Jake Savage's previous incident with a soldier, specifically the episode which had involved a strong altercation with Moss. There were also references to the possibility of Corporal Savage's court martial. Jake was summoned into a large wooden structure which served as the headquarters for a number of officers who were to administer the Cherokee affairs for individuals stationed at or confined to the Indian Territory.

A major read the charges that were related to Jake Savage's incident with Moss, and he assured Jake of the severity of those allegations. Expulsion from the military, as well as a likely prison term, comprised the list of possible actions to be taken against Corporal Savage. Jake explained that he was under the impression that the episode had been forgotten and forgiven.

"Actions toward a fellow soldier cannot truly be forgotten. As for forgiveness, that will be between you and a much higher authority than I. Have you a good prayer life, Corporal Savage? If not, I would think this would be an appropriate time to begin the practice." The officer's words struck Jake Savage as few others had ever done.

"I do, sir. Thank you for the advice. Will there be anything else?"

The major continued the seriousness of his conversation and replied, "Will there be anything from you?"

In order to avoid any possibility of prosecution from the United States government, Jake Savage attempted to talk to his commanding officer about his desires to leave the military and become a married civilian, but the conversation yielded no positive results.

Despite revealing his strong love for White Crow, although her name was not mentioned, Corporal Jake Savage verbally offered his resignation from the United States Army. The reply from the major was short and stern, "That will be all, Savage. This is not the time at which an attempt to leave the service of your country would be in the best interest of you or the young lady who is apparently the object of your affection. I understand from the soldier who is accusing you of violence toward him that you are also seeing one of the Cherokee women. That is something I would also advise you against additionally pursuing at this time."

Corporal Jake Savage stood silently, appearing discouraged, as the major completed his statements, "That, and I emphasize that, will be all, Savage."

As Jake Savage left the building he noticed White Crow standing with a group of five Cherokee ladies. She had evidently been warned of the young corporal's summons to the structure, and her speculations as to why were correct. Regrettably, White Crow's intuition regarding the effects of the meeting upon Jake's demeanor was also affirmed.

As the group of Cherokee women strolled toward Corporal Savage, he lifted his right hand and held it in a manner that indicated a desire that they cease their progress. The members of the group simultaneously complied and ended their movement in his direction. The initial pace of their steps had been brisk, so they were within ten feet of him by the time that occurred.

Jake Savage looked deeply into White Crow's eyes and firmly said, "We need to meet tonight. You know what we must do. Have your things with you. It is time."

All but one of the ladies was puzzled at Jake's statement. White Crow was fully aware of what had to be done. The muffled conversations and gesturing that had occurred in the final two weeks of the movement along the trail were then within a few short hours of being implemented. However, White Crow and Corporal Jake Savage, the two organizers of a particular event that was soon to transpire, were the only ones privy to the initiation of the same.

Just as White Crow and Jake Savage had spent hours in recent days whispering between themselves, the ladies who had been within hearing range of Jake's recent comment to White Crow did the same. Their inquisitions of White Crow yielded nothing in respect to the meaning of Jake Savage's imperative statement.

White Crow appeared to be involved in deep thought the remainder of the day. She said little toward the other women and regularly looked toward the ground as if profoundly contemplating her future. Her actions were reminiscent of those in which she partook when she stood in the holding pen in which her friends and family suffered greatly at the old Cherokee capital in Red Clay, Tennessee.

White Crow's moments of concentration and contemplation seemed to yield their control of her mind to those that allowed her to focus upon the daily sunset. White Crow looked toward the setting sun for a few moments as she strove to regain her awareness of what was transpiring around her. She also realized she had been largely abandoned, as all but one of the women she stood near and walked with earlier that day had gone to their respective families for the evening.

"Darkness arrives," stated White Crow's sole attendant. "I will wait with you to make certain the soldier you like does not hurt you. I know he will not hit you like some soldiers hit our people. He may choose to leave this place without you."

Another soldier, one who had not made the trip along the trail, had walked by them immediately prior to the comments, but both the attendant and White Crow conversed in Cherokee, resulting in little more than a glance from the passing guard.

"I am fine. There is nothing to be afraid of. I need to get my things. We both know I need to go with him. I love him." White Crow was determined to return to the location where she was designated to spend the night. Her tenacity in achieving that goal was calmly carried out, and she gathered a collection of seemingly worthless items and prepared to leave the young attendant.

"Please do not follow me. I am going to tell you goodbye now. Do not ask me where I am going or what I am doing. There is no good that will come from you knowing, and I promise you they will ask you. Rest. We will hopefully meet another day when we are old and our children have children the age we are now." White Crow wiped small tears from her dusty cheeks and hugged her attendant. White Crow then began walking away from her friend and the lifestyle that had been hers her entire life.

Both ladies seemed acutely concerned for the other. White Crow glanced backward at her friend several times. The young lady waved at White Crow, but she sensed a full effort to do so would likely result in unwanted attention. White Crow's final words had pierced the attendant's heart and made her conscious of the danger which White Crow was soon to face.

White Crow slowly strolled through the multitude of men, women and children as many of the final evening conversations were yielding to individuals preparing for a night's sleep. The temperatures had become rather brisk and resulted in White Crow using her blanket, previously folded in her arms, as a makeshift coat.

White Crow had no doubt of where she was headed as she witnessed Corporal Jake Savage sitting atop a horse near the spot where she had last spoken to him. The building that housed the officer who had earlier berated Jake Savage was a short distance away, but the dimly lit room in the center of the structure clearly indicated that the major's day had drawn to a close.

Jake Savage saw White Crow within seconds of her spotting him, and he placed a finger toward his lips in an effort to indicate that she needed to remain as silent as possible. The only sound White Crow detected arose from the mouth of a second horse, one that was originally undetectable. Corporal Savage pulled the reins of the extra horse and led the animal to a position between White Crow and himself.

The content of the discussions White Crow and Jake Savage had held in whispers and mumbled words now became clearly evident. The couple whose love stood against the entire purpose of the trail now planned to make an escape.

Luck and fortune, as they had been in the past, would have to continue to be on their side in order for the attempt to be successful.

Chapter 37

The pounding of the horses' feet on the ground surrounding the command cabin combined with the seemingly uncontrollable neighing of the recently-mounted second horse to apparently alert a nearby sentry.

"Savage, stop! I'll shoot you if you keep going." With his musket already raised and pointed in the direction of the couple, the soldier fired into the growing darkness. White Crow was riding her horse immediately in front of Corporal Savage, a setup that provided her with a safety net, but one that also subjected Jake to receive the brunt of any intended harm.

The sound of the guard yelling immediately prior to the gunshot had caused Jake to move his legs in order to kick the horse's sides in a desperate attempt to solicit an increase in speed. Jake Savage was unable to completely carry out his attempt to boost his horse. Instead, the movement of his leg, initiated at almost the same second the guard had discharged his weapon, resulted in Jake's right leg moving into the target zone of the shot and suffering an agonizing, but not severe, wound.

The shouts and the sound of the gunshot alerted numerous soldiers positioned nearby. Cherokee resting in the vicinity were also brought to a sense of alarm with the agitated voices and the gunfire from no less than three additional soldiers' guns. Uncertain of what direction either White Crow or Jake had been headed toward, those soldiers arriving at the side of the warrior who initially fired at the bolting couple inquired as to what had taken place.

Jake Savage felt his right leg increasingly throbbing with each successive gallop of his speeding horse. By the time White Crow and he had ridden a safe distance from the camp, Jake urged his accomplice to slow the pace of their escape. Corporal Savage managed to move his foot from the stirrup and used his left leg to step from the horse.

White Crow sobbed as she saw Jake Savage limp briefly and then fall to the ground. There was a substantial loss of blood, but the wound Jake suffered was far from life-threatening. His boot had evidently served as the recipient of the force of the shot, the effect of which had also been lessened with the distance that existed between the shooter and Corporal Savage.

Taking a few minutes to examine the severity of his injury, Jake Savage attempted to regain his composure before mounting his steed. He was confident that any attempt at utilizing a search party would not be initiated before daybreak, a fact that gave White Crow and him a few hours' head start. In addition, the number of creeks that flowed through their area of escape would assist them in partially obstructing the tracks of their horses, a venture now slowed from the tremendous level of discomfort Jake Savage was experiencing.

The escaping pair of young lovers was somehow able to progress several miles during the first night. Shortly after sunrise they were frightened at the appearance of a small band of Cherokee who had armed themselves with stolen and handmade weapons.

The Cherokee men who originally came into sight had clearly detected the arrival of the young Cherokee maiden and a soldier who was clearly in pain. Reeling in his saddle from the loss of blood and a lack of sleep, Jake Savage initially shook his head in an effort to clear his mind and hoped the men were simply figments of his imagination. He pointed toward the warriors at the same moment in which White Crow began to address the men.

White Crow recognized the Cherokee attire and informed them that Jake Savage and she were approaching the area in peace. One of the young men called White Crow by name, having realized her identity during her short proclamation. Though Corporal Savage was clad in his uniform, his reputation as a peaceful man and one who held a great deal of affection for White Crow assured him of a place of safety with this group of escapees.

One of the men took hold of the reins of Jake Savage's horse, an act that allowed Jake to simply focus on staying in the saddle. White Crow stepped from her horse as one of the Cherokee took control of her ride. In turn, White Crow sat behind Jake and endeavored to assist the injured corporal in his feeble efforts to stay atop his horse.

The group of escaped Cherokee took White Crow and Jake Savage, also considered renegades for their flight from the camp, into hiding. A hidden oasis located miles from the trail served as the group's lodging location and provided Corporal Jake Savage with a safe area in which he could completely recuperate from his wound. One of the Cherokee men appeared to have some knowledge of anatomy and informed the corporal that if the projectile struck another inch to the left, the results could have been more serious, likely breaking Savage's shin bone. Such a wound would have likely negated the successful escape.

As it were, Jake Savage was able to fully recover from the pain of his wound in less than a week. Well rested and with his skin speedily healing over the spot of the injury, Corporal Savage warned White Crow that the time had arrived for them to resume their movement eastward. Thanking the group of Cherokee for harboring them and enabling Jake to convalesce, White Crow and Savage abandoned their horses and made their way from the sanctuary on foot.

In an effort to completely erase any detectable presence of the horses or knowledge of the couple, the Cherokee shot the animals and used them for food.

Chapter 38

Jake Savage and White Crow seemed to literally disappear from the face of the earth. Neither military personnel nor members of the Cherokee nation were made aware of their journey or struggles. No reported sightings of the couple surfaced, so their escape from the so-called Indian Territory was largely uneventful.

The primary incident surrounding White Crow and Jake Savage was their reveling in marriage which took place in the days following them resuming their eastward movement. The situation surrounding that occasion was interesting and provided the few clues that ever arose as to the whereabouts of the couple. They were able to maintain the secrecy of their movements while also celebrating their recent unity.

During one phase of their journey toward White Crow's childhood home, White Crow and Corporal Savage encountered a particularly vicious rainstorm. Fearful of the tempest's accompanying lightning, the couple had sought shelter in a barn that was situated a short distance from a petite farmhouse. Jake searched the outbuilding and found it absent of any livestock aside from a horse. The presence of an attached smokehouse also provided White Crow and Jake Savage with the ability to fill their stomachs through their consumption of a portion of the salted ham that hung from one of the barn's rafters.

Sunrise brought the stillness and silence associated with peaceful weather, so Jake Savage and White Crow determined it would be safe for them to move from the confines of the barn. As Jake hesitantly opened the door, he witnessed an armed man and a girl walking toward the structure. White Crow quickly backed up with Jake's warning of the same. The creaking of the door, a sound seemingly hidden with the noise of the previous night's thunderstorm, provided the farmer and his child a warning that someone was inside the structure.

The muscular and determined farmer lowered his weapon and pointed it toward the barn door. He then whispered to his daughter, resulting in the young girl running toward the family's cottage. Jake Savage looked through a crack in the barn boards and watched while the man eyeballed the area for any strange or misplaced items.

"I know you're in there. I advise you to show yourself peaceful and unarmed. In about one minute I'll have more guns pointed at you; you can't get away. There ain't no back door. Been meaning to put one there, but didn't take the time to do it." The farmer's warning was stern, but Corporal Jake Savage also sensed a tendency of hesitation.

Jake Savage looked toward the other end of the barn and visually verified the farmer's claim. Jake whispered to White Crow that there was no way to escape without bloodshed. Fearful that his earlier leg wound would inhibit their safe and speedy escape from the outbuilding, Jake proposed to White Crow that he should step through the door and explain the situation. She thought briefly before agreeing with guarded optimism.

As Jake Savage opened the door, it struck him that his discussion of the situation with White Crow had taken more time and concentration than he thought, as the farmer's wife and two older sons had returned in the meantime with the little girl who had earlier run for help. The weapons the farmer's wife and sons held made the quartet of armed homeowners the holders of superior numbers and firepower.

As Jake Savage moved outside the barn, the farmer asked, "Are you alone? What are you doing in a soldier's uniform? Gone runaway? Keep them hands up and explain yourself. I was in the army once, and I know you can't go moving 'round like you are and hiding in a barn unless you're on the run." The farmer's words appeared far more excited and apprehensive than at first.

Jake Savage rapidly explained that he was a soldier and that he had left the military without permission. Corporal Savage also added that he had fallen in love with a Cherokee girl and simply wanted to get married and make his way home in order to begin life as a civilian.

"She speak English?" the farmer pointed his gun toward the barn where White Crow was hiding and made the inquiry toward Jake Savage.

"Yes sir, she does right well."

"Call her out. If she's alone and there ain't no weapons, I'll look out for you." The farmer's voice was sincere, and Jake witnessed a peaceful tone in the farmer's changed nature.

"I'm gonna keep one on you." With that declaration, the farmer moved his weapon toward Jake Savage's head and asked his family members to lower their weapons.

White Crow had seen the entire situation evolve and felt that she should step through the door. Jake asked her to do so, and she gently emerged from the confines of the barn.

"She's a beautiful girl." were the first words from the farmer's wife. Although she appeared somewhat reluctant in regard to the runaways, the wife's own Native American heritage was visible to White Crow and Jake Savage.

The farmer's spouse stated, "You boys check out the barn and let your daddy know if this soldier's tellin' us straight. If he ain't, I imagine we'll have to take care of the soldier and this woman."

The farmer cautiously seemed to exhibit a sense of trust toward Jake Savage and held sympathy for the corporal's situation. At the same time he was ready to defend his family and farm by killing White Crow, Jake Savage, and any other person or people who had come to the location uninvited.

The farmer's sons examined the structure and affirmed Jake Savage's words. With that completed, the farmer revealed a significant fact to the couple. "I guess now is as good a time as any to tell you." He looked at his wife who seemed to know what he wanted to say. "I'm not only a farmer; I'm a man of God. Over that hill's a church. I'm the preacher in this part of the county. My wife's mother was a Cherokee. I understand what you're doing. You'll be safe here."

The preacher took that afternoon to perform the wedding ceremony for White Crow and Jake Savage. The lady of the house also cut White Crow's hair, lessening the ability of her appearance of a runaway. A gun, a new set of clothes, and an extra outfit for both White Crow and Jake Savage served as the wedding presents from the preacher and his family.

"It ain't much, but we got a small house next to the church. We use it sometimes for visitors, just like they do in the big cities. We thought it would be a nice place for the two of you to spend your first married night together. You can call it a honeymoon home if you'd like."

"We don't have any money to pay you and your family for your gifts and kindness. I would like to stay here and work for you until I pay off these debts." Jake Savage's request was granted, and his bride and he remained in the farmer's extra house for almost one month.

One month and a day after their wedding, White Crow and Jake Savage resumed the longest leg of their eastward journey. Weeks of living off the land and attempting to avoid detection took a toll upon the newlyweds' physical and emotional condition. The couple eventually made their way across some of the same areas where their love had earlier been forged on the Trail of Tears. While their first trip had been filled with despair and lamentation, the second trip signaled the birth of hope for the couple and fashioned their plans for a happy and long-lived future together.

Over the next three years White Crow and Jake Savage had two children. Jake worked a number of odd jobs as means of providing for his family. The eventual arrival of cruel remarks and harsh treatment led White Crow and her husband to seek more peaceful locations to establish their home. The reluctance of people to accept their marriage, as well as to question the origin of their relationship most frequently led to their regular relocation practice.

A small number of trusted individuals told White Crow and Jake about rumors that had circulated in the months which immediately followed the Cherokee movement from the South. Folks in the hills of East Tennessee were said to have regularly seen Cherokee men, women, and children escaping from the forced removal and making their way to the mountains where they sought safety. Initially dispelling the talk as myths, White Crow and Jake Savage felt that it would be best for them to conduct a first-hand investigation of the situation before their ages and physical condition limited such a trip.

Chapter 39

White Crow, Jake Savage, and their two children arrived in the mountains of western North Carolina in the fall of 1843. There, they were able to locate White Crow's siblings who had managed to successfully escape the forced military movement in the initial phases of the Trail of Tears. Although the separation from her family had taken place several years earlier, White Crow was able to reestablish a firm relationship with her kindred.

With the inevitable tendency of the world to forget the so-called crimes of the past, Jake Savage and White Crow found it more acceptable to visit and take part in the society that had once turned its nose at their marriage. Growing tension between the North and South had diverted a lot of the racial animosity from the Cherokee and other Native Americans and was focused more on the issue of slavery and its exploitation of people of African descent.

Jake Savage ultimately managed to establish himself as an efficient tobacco farmer and utilized the equestrian skills gained from his military experience to begin a lucrative farrier business. As his children grew in number and eventually included three boys and two girls, Jake's reputation as a fair and honest businessman increased proportionally. The tobacco business and Jake Savage's proper care of area horses soon provided the financial means for the Savages to open a much-needed local store, the most fully-stocked in the area.

The three small businesses continued to grow into prosperous ventures that demanded a great deal of time and labor. The positive side of this was the fact that, not only did Jake Savage and White Crow become wealthy, but the need for additional employees also enabled White Crow's family to leave the confines of the mountains and settle into a more populated part of the South.

Having invested heavily in areas other than the production of cotton, as many of their Southern counterparts had done, the Savage family and its employees were able to avoid the widespread financial devastation frequently associated with the American Civil War.

However, the loss of one of their children, a captain in the Confederate Army, took a serious emotional toll upon White Crow. The oldest of their sons, Wyatt Lynch Savage, had joined the military after Fort Sumter's surrender and vowed to serve the newly-established Confederate government until it confirmed itself as a free and independent nation. Wyatt's decision had weighed heavily upon Jake Savage and White Crow, as both had endured and witnessed the effects of racially-motivated incidents as well as the brutality of combat.

The death of the young Confederate officer took place at Fredericksburg, Virginia in late 1862. Bitter fighting near the stone wall at Marye's Heights resulted in hundreds of deaths and an untold number of wounds. Among those who lost their lives at the bloodied battlefield was Wyatt Savage. News of his death and his burial in a battlefield mass grave reached the Savage home in February 1863 and resulted in a heavy state of mourning on the part of White Crow.

White Crow's deep distress, increasing age, and a subsequent bout with pneumonia robbed her of the majority of the strength, resilience, and physical beauty she had longed possessed. The few years that followed the American Civil War left her a literal shell of the physical and emotional pillar she had once been. Jake Savage's age, long hours of work, and stress level, which only increased after the death of their son, did little to lengthen his years on earth.

Chapter 40

Fall 1870—

As the wind blew autumn leaves from surrounding trees, a young lady, bearing the mixed-blood characteristics of a Native American and a Scot, arose and walked from a hand-carved headstone where she had been kneeling. She strongly resembled how White Crow appeared in her younger years. Interestingly, she was, nonetheless, a strong possessor of Jake Savage's appearance as well.

The youthful woman wiped tears from her eyes as she walked from the dual gravesite, and she held hands with a five year-old girl who walked and skipped beside her. The aforementioned lady's husband strolled nearby and carried a newborn in his arms. Additional people, most of them white, also made their way from the recently turned dirt that rested atop a grave. The scene was reminiscent of the 1806 meeting President Thomas Jefferson had overseen when proclaiming that the Cherokee and the United States would work together for the good of both groups of people.

In the midst of the gathering's demise, a rather odd sight appeared. An albino crow flew from a tree near the new grave and peacefully flew over the young mother and her daughter. The child pointed to the bird and asked her mother what type of bird it was.

The mother wiped tears from her cheeks and replied, "That is a white crow; it is rare, majestic, and beautiful. It stands out from the others and causes people to look wherever it appears. That which makes it different is the main thing that makes it beautiful. That was like your grandmother. That is why she was named White Crow."

The child smiled and looked up at her tearful mother. In an attempt to cheer her saddened matriarch, the child said, "Tell me about the trail again, Mommy. I want to hear about Maw and Pops and how they fell in love even though they wasn't supposed to."

So, the story of White Crow and Jake Savage was to be told again and again, never to pass from the lineage of the family that lived then and was yet to come. As the weeping mom continued her movement from the gravesites, she began to tell her daughter of the time when Jake and White Crow met. Simultaneously, the albino crow flew from their presence unnoticed, and the rare bird perched atop one of the headstones in the community graveyard.

As if keeping watch, the crow balanced upon a pair of headstones that marked two burial sites outside the North Carolina settlement White Crow and Jake Savage had called home. The dates and names on one side of the first headstone revealed that a middle-aged man by the name of Jacob David Savage occupied the grave. The opposite stone denoted the burial location of the former soldier's wife, White Crow Savage.

The couple had completed their trail together and had reached a heavenly home in which they would be at full peace with one another and in their surroundings. The story of The Trail, at least from the perspective of the two young people who overcame its hatred and dissolution to fall deeply in love and marry one another, had reached its conclusion.

Printed in the United States
By Bookmasters